At the academy, funn

MW00835094

Reckless, brilliant and incredibly resourceful, Liam can handle any crisis with a devilish grin—but his razor-sharp sense of humor hides a desperate truth. In an elite society where magic is the most coveted commodity, he's been judged as second-rate, a castoff. Weak.

Liam hasn't let his lack of inner magic slow him down, of course. He's mapped all the secret passageways beneath Wellington Academy, he's stolen the most arcane lore, and he's managed to siphon energy out of the very air. When he touches me, we light up the room, and when we kiss...it's pure fire.

We need that fire, too. A new threat has stormed into Wellington Academy, an illusionist magician who threatens to destroy our team of monster hunters and take down the whole academy once and for all.

Even worse, the only way Liam can access his full magic is if he and I fully bond...but he's determined not to take advantage of me. So if I want to get this party started, I'm going to have to take control.

...Not a problem.

THE HUNTER'S SNARE

MONSTER HUNTER ACADEMY, BOOK 3

D.D. CHANCE

LIAM

What's a girl want?

I scowled at the rough stone wall six feet from my face, the blood rushing to my head. Strung up like this two stories below ground, locked in a spike-ridden snare that Houdini wouldn't have dared attempt even at the height of his fame, I'd already worked out a half dozen impossible equations in my mind to pass the time. But I always ended up back here.

The life-or-death question I couldn't ignore. The riddle buried in the puzzle locked within the enigma that was Nina Cross.

Harbinger. Monster bait. Cipher.

The answer to all my deepest desires and biggest fears wrapped up into one completely unexpected package. She'd run into our lives not two weeks ago with a monster on her tail and an entire lifetime of mystery surrounding her very existence. A mother who'd lied to her. A father who'd left her to rot, so far as we could tell. A power so incredible, she would lose her ever-loving mind if she had any idea of who and what she really was.

I

But I knew.

I'd read the ancient texts, found the forbidden knowledge. I knew everything there was to know about the harbinger...everything Nina had yet to learn.

And oh, what I could teach her, if I could find a way to tempt her into letting me. Lure her into being willing to reach her full potential. But how?

What's a girl want?

I blew out a long breath, glancing at the gleaming LED stopwatch on the floor. Four minutes past the official record set by my late Great-Uncle Spencer Graham, the family's most prolific and blindingly rich magician in five generations. He hadn't been able to endure the suspended magical tourniquet for longer than two minutes and forty-four seconds. I'd blown him away nearly three times over today. He was no longer the boss of me.

Not that anyone would ever know that.

My family had written me off a long time ago—too weak to be a spell caster, too mercurial to be an enforcer, too talkative to be a ward for the family secrets, too much of an ass to be a negotiator or diplomat. They'd done everything to improve my chances, to help me live up to the powerful magic that was my birthright. They'd even buried tuning rods beneath my skin to pick up any errant supernatural currents that might be floating around in the atmosphere, but nothing had taken.

I'd remained stunted, muted. My magic a shrunken husk.

So I'd studied. I'd learned. I'd fashioned tools to pull power out of the air, created concoctions, devices, and weapons of intricate and stunning beauty. And I had suffered. Oh, yeah, I'd suffered.

Then a harbinger had hit Wellington Academy and set my world on fire.

I twisted in my vicious tourniquet, feeling the blades cut deep, swinging in a lazy arc as the blood traced familiar trails down my skin.

What's a girl want?

As I turned slowly, the trove of glorious arcanum slid into view, soaking in its pool of oil. It was time, I knew. I'd studied the pages I'd stolen from the Apocrypha long enough. I had memorized every inscrutable prognostication, dire warning, and taboo ritual specifically proscribed...yet still included in that friggin' book as if the old wizards couldn't help themselves. I knew everything there was to know, now.

A little knowledge might be a dangerous thing. But too much?

Magic.

I rotated another quarter turn. With a flick of my fingers, I tripped the nearly invisible metal trigger trapped in the crease of my palm, causing a spark to flare, then drop to the trail of oil. The fire caught immediately, throwing shadows against the wall that made me look like a slowly swinging slab of meat. Not a bad analogy, really, considering how I'd been carved up over the years.

But this wasn't about me. It was about the tongues of fire that now lanced greedily into the carefully oiled maze. Racing along the snaking lines I'd traced, a complete replica of the Wellington campus map of subterranean byways. I watched with eager eyes to see if this, finally, would reveal the path I needed to take, if this, finally—

But no.

The fire guttered out, dead-ending far short of catching the forbidden pages on fire.

The secrets of the academy would live another day, it seemed. I hadn't solved the riddle. I hadn't earned the right. I would need Nina Cross to walk those dire pathways with me blindly, foolishly, if she was willing. If she dared. If she agreed to finally break me free of the trap of my own life.

I contracted my muscles, straining my joints to the max, and breathed out a long, shuddering breath.

So, what's a girl want?

I didn't know...but I'd do anything to find out.

1

NINA

It's the monster you don't expect that you have to watch out for.

"Hold up," Zachariah Williams murmured beside me, his whispered words brushing past my ear and filling my mind. I slowed, sensing more than seeing what had alarmed him. Because there *was* something out there, pacing us. Tracking us.

Being followed by a person or persons unknown would cause alarm for most college students, no matter who they were. For monster hunting minors facing their school's first major monster outbreak in a hundred years? Tack on a whole new layer of crazy.

I scanned the path ahead of us as casually as possible, but the cobblestone streets and neatly manicured sidewalks weren't quite ready to give up their secrets. The night was dark and warm, streetlights cheerily providing cones of safety at regular intervals. Up until a few seconds ago, Zach and I had been holding hands as we made our way across the campus of Wellington Academy. Despite our PDA being accessorized by legitimate prep school attire—Zach in dark pants and a dress shirt, me in a blouse, plaid miniskirt, and knee-high black boots—the display of intimacy was way more than I would ordinarily go for, no matter how close Zach and I had become over the past couple of weeks.

But the romantic gesture was deliberate, designed to make us seem more normal to the other students—or really, to anyone who happened to be watching who *wasn't* a member of the academy's deeply mistrusted and increasingly reviled monster hunter minor. Wellington might have gotten its start as a monster hunting institution, but that aspect of its past definitely was not aging well.

Otherwise, the academy was holding its own. Honestly, if it weren't for the fact that Zach and I were heading toward a haunted campus chapel recently incinerated by demons, Wellington Academy could have been any exclusive, upscale private college in Back Bay, Boston. Perfectly trimmed trees lined every quad and street corner, while square, staid buildings in dusky stone formed dark angles against the starlit sky. The residence halls looked as haughty as the classroom buildings, but at least they were cheerily lit at this hour, and laughter flowed across the open spaces and darted through the trees.

It was any college, anywhere, with an extra dose of things that went bump in the night.

"You have any idea...?" I murmured, but Zach shook his head as I slanted him a glance. A bloom of quiet reassurance flowed out from him, comforting despite his evident wariness, and I couldn't help my smile. He was only *slightly* capable of psychic mind pushing, though he for sure could read my thoughts, since I didn't have my warding bracelet on.

But Zach's gift of reassurance was more innate than any sort of magical ability—it was what a preacher's son did.

Especially a preacher's son who moonlighted as a demon hunter in the only remaining monster hunting collective at Wellington...regardless of the fact that, once upon a long-ago century, the academy had been founded with the express purpose of graduating scores of monster hunters a year.

Not so much anymore. Worse, even the ones the academy had managed to graduate over the past fifty years had gone distressingly MIA.

But if we *were* down to our last few monster hunters, at least Zachariah Williams carried the banner proudly. Silhouetted by the competing beams of streetlights, he looked like he'd been born to the night. His dark hair tumbled around his ears, offsetting his fair skin and deep blue, almost purple-hued eyes. He'd struck me as vampire-hot when I'd first met him a couple of weeks ago, on the run from the latest monster trying to turn me into a midnight snack, and since then, he'd become even more supernaturally beautiful. Now his gothic-angel face had hardened, and his intense blue eyes scanned the quad with more than passing worry.

"No clue," he finally answered. "It's not a demon or a blood-sport monster. Doesn't smell right for that."

I made a face. "Monster smelling is a thing for you now?"

His laughter huffed in the semi-darkness. "It's always been a thing. I just didn't talk about it. That skill never played well with the ladies."

"Uh-huh. But is it sharper now, do you think? More well honed?"

He shot me a quick glance, but didn't deny it. "It's sharper now. Something else I have you to thank for, yeah?" He scowled. "I've lost them again. Let's keep moving."

I nodded, and we turned forward, my mind ranging ahead to what awaited us at Bellamy Chapel. Not exactly a monster, but not a bouquet of roses either. I mean, what kind of psychopath commissions a headstone for a woman who wasn't dead?

"It's not necessarily a real headstone, you know," Zach said, reading my thoughts as he gave my hand a squeeze. "There could be some completely normal explanation for it."

The flow of his comforting warmth allowed me to take in a short breath—but only a short one. I exhaled quickly, not yet willing to be kicked out of my defensive cocoon.

Still, I offered him a grateful smile. "Thanks for saying that. But there's no way this isn't something seriously screwed up."

"Nina—"

"No," I cut him off. "There's no coincidence that can explain the existence of a headstone with my mother's name on it, sitting in an abandoned crypt that magically opened up for us to explore barely a few days after I show up on campus...a campus I didn't even know existed until, like, two weeks ago. I know that headstone wasn't made for my mom twenty-two years ago, no matter what date's carved on it. More likely some asshole ordered it made after I showed up here. It's not like I've hidden the fact that Mom's dead—or that I'm trying to find her family."

Zach didn't argue with me. In the days after I'd arrived in Boston with a letter from my mother that she'd never sent, addressed to a mailing address that didn't exist, it hadn't occurred to me to be circumspect about my interest in finding her family...the same way it'd also never occurred to me to ask about the possibility of there being other relatives out there while my mom had been alive. Like most kids, I accepted what she'd presented to me about our little two-person household as absolute fact. We were alone, my dad had no clue I existed, and that was that.

I had other things to worry about, anyway. Since I seemed to attract monsters wherever I went, most of my days were filled with trying not to get eaten.

Nevertheless, the arrival of a headstone bearing my late mother's name, even one carved as some sort of sick joke, wasn't exactly reassuring.

"We're going to find out who did this," Zach said quietly, and I shook my head, my stress ratcheting up a notch.

"That doesn't make things any better, you know," I protested. "Someone is trying to mess with me—and with you guys, through me. And I have no idea why."

"Then they're taking on all of us, not just you," Zach said. "You're a part of our collective now. Don't forget that."

I grimaced and turned my attention forward, wishing I still had my mind-warding bracelet on. I'd ripped it off during our last fight, but at the moment, I *really* didn't feel like having Zach crawl around inside my anxiety-ridden—

"Whoa." He stopped short, glancing down at me as he turned my hand over, peering at my empty wrist. "You just cut me off, and you don't have your bracelet. How'd you learn how to do that? Did you, um, level up when we... I mean, because we..."

I pulled my hand free of his, peering at it as well, as if it might spontaneously sprout a new mind-blocking bracelet on its own. "I...guess so," I allowed. "Maybe?"

Leveling up, as Zach had put it—spontaneously increasing one's magical or monster-fighting abilities—was the nifty gift with purchase I'd discovered after joining the collective. Basically, any intimate bond I forged with the other guys on the team resulted in an automatic upgrade to their skills and abilities. I hadn't had any reaction after I'd, ah, bonded with Tyler, but when I'd hooked up with Zach, things had changed for me. I wasn't sure exactly how, but if one of the bonus results was an on-demand cancellation of Zach's mind-reading intrusion, I'd take it.

Because Zach was right, of course, about me being part of the collective. I'd come to Boston to locate my mother's family, but I'd found a different kind of tribe here at Wellington Academy, and I'd embraced it with open arms. Never mind that my mom had warned me specifically to avoid a group exactly like the academy hunters—four guys, uniquely bonded, who hunted in a pack. Check, check, and check. She'd absolutely warned me to run the other way...

I hadn't.

"They're back," Zach said, interrupting my unruly thoughts. He turned his head, his sculpted profile catching the light as he focused on something in the distance. "There's more than one. They're moving fast, tall and thin. Can you see that? Over in the trees. Look now. Act natural."

I coughed a short laugh at his last request as I shifted my gaze toward the far-off tree line. I didn't see anything at first, but I felt them, all right. Feral and cold. Watching us. "So you say they're not bloodsucking creatures, but can you get any more specific than that? Maybe use your mind tricks on them? I kind of doubt they have any protective bracelets against you."

Zach blinked at me, then arched both of his preternaturally perfect brows. "You know, that's not a bad idea."

He turned back toward the tree line, reaching for my hand again, and this time gripping it tight. Zach was nervous, on edge, in a way I'd never seen before. I frowned at him. Was he okay? Given his mental outreach capability, was it painful for Zach to get up close and personal with monsters this way? Was confronting the creatures watching us the right move?

"Okay, here goes nothing." Zach's eyes narrowed. A strange, unsettling light entered them. While I'd watched his eyes go blood red when he fought demons, I'd never really paid attention when he was squaring off against other monsters. So now the silver glow that flared deep in his beautiful deep purple irises took me by surprise. As it gained brightness, I turned toward where he was looking and focused more intently, opening my mind once more to Zach. I needed to be a part of this.

Images flashed in my mind's eye, an overlay that gilded reality and elevated it to the next level. As I stared, the far tree line lit up in full and vivid color, and I could see exactly what Zach saw.

Oh...*crap*.

I knew these guys.

2

There, standing among the trees, were easily a dozen figures—all tall, slender, and impossibly beautiful. Definitely human-esque, yet not exactly right. Like Tolkien's wood elves come to life, complete with the slightly pointed ears.

Were these a real-world incarnation of the Fae? I didn't know, but they seemed way more dangerous than they should. And way too familiar for comfort. Either they or their equally tall, dark, and forbidding cousins had been lurking in the woods beside my off-campus apartment since I'd blown into town a few weeks ago. Never getting any closer, but never fully stepping away.

And now they were here, on Wellington's campus. Something about that struck me as impossibly wrong.

"Because they're not supposed to be on the campus," Zach murmured aloud, taking advantage of our restored connection to read my mind and confirm my unspoken worry. "Wellington Academy is warded against monsters of all types, even pretty elf-like ones. They shouldn't be here. Not within the walls. And definitely not so many of them."

"Maybe Wellington's wards are starting to suck? Your demon buddies seemed to have an all-access pass."

Zach shook his head. "Different kind of monster, different rules. With demonology as a major, we couldn't very well have a campus that didn't allow demons. And we know how to handle them, more or less. I mean yeah, there were more of them than usual, but they weren't barred from campus. These guys are." He slanted me a look. "You keep saying the name 'Fae' in your mind, and—you're not wrong. I don't know that they've read all the same Celtic mythology books we have on campus, but they're no doubt the inspiration for those stories. And they're warded against my touch. I keep trying to reach them, but it's like climbing through vines, thick branches surrounding me, the forest growing closer, tighter. Drawing me to them. It's like they want me to come closer, but I don't...I don't know why."

I narrowed my eyes at him. "Uh...Zach?" I didn't like the odd note that had crept into his voice, even as he drew his fingers away from me, dropping my hand. He took a step forward, and I moved as well, stopping only when he gestured sharply.

"No, can't you hear?" He waved me off. "They want to talk to me. They're here to warn us, not to attack. But they can only talk to one of us. Me."

I bit my lip, looking rapidly from him to the figures in the trees. Zach had dropped my hand, but I could still see what he saw. We'd stepped nearer to the watchers, almost despite ourselves, but I wasn't getting any sense of warmth or helpful vibes from them. They looked as cool and feral as they had every time I'd seen them watching me from a distance, their long lean bodies held tight to the shadows, their eyes slitted and silvery.

Silvery. Just like Zach's eyes currently were.

13

I blinked hard, surprised to see that Zach had moved several strides ahead of me. He was almost at the border of the woods, and far worse, though his mouth was moving, I could no longer hear what he was saying. Something had come between us, despite me opening up my mind wide to him. I couldn't hear his thoughts anymore. I couldn't hear his words.

"*Zach,*" I managed, but his name came out as barely a squeak. Panic rushed through me, and I lurched toward him, trying to make up the ground between us. A flash of silver among the lamplit cobblestones of the street caught my eye, and I blinked at it, momentarily distracted—

The trees exploded.

A dozen projectiles shot toward us—not arrows, exactly, but thick, pointy rods. With shocking speed and force, they struck Zach and knocked him flat, landing in his shoulders, his legs, pinning him to the ground. I raced forward and could see the archers more clearly, a line of warriors standing behind the first line of figures who'd seemed so silent and watchful. The second line of elves notched another round of arrows as Zach struggled upright, blood streaming from wounds that...

I stumbled to a stop as I reached him. The wounds were still there, but there were no arrows, no pointy rods. Nothing stuck in him at all.

"What the hell?" I managed.

"Magic," he gasped, as if that solved everything. It didn't, of course. Magical attack or not, he was still spouting blood. I dropped to my knees, then flinched back as he grabbed my hands.

"*Protection,*" he growled, more harshly this time, and I blinked. Was he asking me for help or throwing some kind of spell?

Zach's best skills weren't in spell casting, but there was a certain capacity for the work in all monster hunters—all of them besides me, anyway—and he was bringing it fully to bear. I offered him whatever energy I could and felt him strip it away from me as he spouted Latin, Akkadian, and other languages I didn't know, an alphabet soup of arcanum I couldn't hope to follow. I hunkered down beside him, covering as much of his body as I could with mine. I could practically *feel* a new wave of arrows notching, notching— then the creatures fell back.

For a moment I was with them, feeling their thoughts, experiencing their surprise. Their *interest*. Their reaction to us wasn't at all dismayed, but more...intrigued. Excited. These were ancient warriors, creatures who had been sent on a mission and were going to see that mission through because it was *required* of them. Because it was their vow.

Their vow? I turned back to Zach, confused, and then jolted as something sharp and hard pierced my right shoulder.

I whipped around as another barrage of sharp pointy things shot out of the tree line. Sharp pointy things that *hurt*. At least this time, they seemed to only be hitting me, not Zach. My shoulder took a couple of hits, and so did my waist. The magical arrows disappeared as soon as they buried themselves in me, but that didn't make them hurt any less.

"Oh, no, you *don't*." Zach roused himself, his sudden anger surprising me even more than the pain lancing me. The fire he'd called upon to fight the demons was back in his eyes, replacing the silvery echo of the Fae-like creatures' gazes. He flung out his hands, and a wave of blistering heat swept across the open courtyard and pummeled into the trees, sending up plumes of smoke, though there was no fire. The creatures in the woods keened in sudden, violent agony.

"*Run.*" Zach turned to me, reaching for my hand. Together, we staggered forward, bleeding from several different places.

Within thirty strides, the pressure lifted, the blood quit gushing, and we stumbled to a stop, gasping. I twisted back around, straining to see our adversaries. But there were no more plumes of smoke, no shadowy figures trapped in the woods. Even our wounds seemed to be closing up. There weren't any students either, thank God. In this hidden pocket of the campus, we were alone in our crazy.

"What's going on?" I hissed as Zach's grip tightened on my hand. "Was that all an illusion? Did it not really happen?"

"Oh, it happened," Zach said. "Look."

He pointed back the way we'd come, and I saw it. Silvery drops of blood that shimmered like moonbeams caught in the water. Our blood, mixed with whatever had been in those bolts from the trees.

"We've been marked," Zach gasped. "We need to get out of here, make it to the chapel. Liam will know what to do."

"He'd freaking *better*."

We lurched forward as a new chill rolled through me. I didn't feel terrible—which had to be a bad thing. If I hadn't been brutally aware of what had just happened to me, I don't think I would notice the strange, otherworldly sensation shimmering along my nerves.

"They didn't expect you to approach," Zach said. "They were sent here to watch. That's what their job was, to watch. When you moved forward aggressively, fighting against their illusion, their defensive line stood up and took action.

They weren't planning on that. They weren't planning on *you*."

I blew out a sharp breath. I hadn't thought I'd been all that aggressive, frankly. I'd just been trying to reach Zach. "So is that a good thing or a bad thing?"

He shrugged. "I don't know. But you can feel it, right? You can feel the drain on us. We're being tracked. They're going to know we're heading for Bellamy Chapel."

"Well, it wouldn't take a genius to figure that out. But why aren't they still attacking us? How did we get away?"

"Because I served them up some personal protection wards, some of Wellington Academy's finest." He slanted a glance to me, giving me a smile that was unabashedly filled with wonder and maybe a little shared pride. "Which I only succeeded in casting so well because you let me use your strength. In other words, it looks like congratulations are officially in order. I don't know how, since it didn't happen with Tyler, but when you hooked up with me...you totally leveled up."

"Yeah?" I turned to look back at the silvery drops of spelled blood that now trailed us across the campus, dread curdling in my stomach. "What's that get us, though? Besides becoming elf meat?"

A thin whistle sounded along the breeze behind us, making me shiver while Zach huffed out a breath. "Let's not wait around to find out."

We turned again toward Bellamy Chapel.

3

———

Moving as quickly as we could without drawing attention to ourselves, we passed through the ancient wall that ringed Wellington Academy. This was the barrier that supposedly protected the centuries-old academy from all the monsters of the world, though I remained unimpressed with its track record on that front.

Worse, as we neared Bellamy Chapel, we started springing more leaks.

"This...sucks," Zach wheezed. He didn't argue when I pulled him close to lean more of his weight on me. He'd been struck far harder than I had.

Fortunately, the faintest light gleamed from a narrow slit amid the charred ruins of the front of the old chapel. The fire that had swept through the tiny chapel had left the church door blackened and warped, but it still stood, and someone had propped it open for us. Liam, had to be.

We crept inside and shoved the door closed, Zach gritting his teeth so hard against the pain, I was surprised he didn't crack something.

"Hey, I was wondering when you—*whoa*." Liam Graham emerged from a section of charred pews, his hands going up as he saw us. "Jesu—sorry, Zach, but, what the hell happened to you guys? Get in here, for fuck's sake."

"Fix this." Zach staggered forward. Liam caught him, turning to me as I moved up to help.

"You got hit too? By what, protesters?"

"Elves," Zach gritted out, practically draping himself over Liam in an attempt to stay upright. "Might as well just call them that until we figure out the truth. In the woods. They'd been watching Nina before, and now they're here."

"On *campus*?" Liam asked with such outrage, it almost made me smile. His dark brown hair now stood on end, and his river-stone hazel eyes gleamed with worry. In the flickering light, his dark tan deepened, making him seem almost swarthy, a whimsical smith interrupted at his forge, crafting arcane weapons and totems of absolute power. Liam wasn't as big as Zach and definitely not as buff as Tyler, but his lean body gave him the air of strength and flexibility that only added to his air of capability. Combine that with his whip-smart intelligence, dark humor, and keen appreciation for puzzles, and the challenge of a new brand of monsters landing on Wellington's doorstep should have been right up his alley.

Instead, he mostly looked put out to learn that the wards had failed. These guys believed wholeheartedly in the academy's protections. Too bad they clearly were screwed on that count.

Liam's attention zeroed in on Zach, his mouth twisting as he scanned his friend's new assortment of wounds. "Okay, okay, here we go, my man," he said as he eased Zach down into a pew, one of the few sections in this area of the chapel that hadn't been damaged by fire. "Nice and slow." Then he stepped away, his hands remaining up as if Zach might keel over at any moment.

"I'll be *right* back. Do not move. You either," he said to me. His gaze went to my shoulder, his eyes narrowing.

"You're hit, but you're not hurt as bad, not by a long shot," he said, then his mouth quirked into a grin. "Pun intended."

"I didn't draw on her strength at first," Zach said, laying his head back on the pew. His wavy black hair was drenched with sweat, and his skin seemed drawn too tightly against his skull. "Once I did, she was left unprotected. She got hit on the second wave. Then we blasted them back and started running."

"Her strength?" Liam's eyes widened at this information, but he shook his head hard, as if forcing himself to stay focused on the situation at hand. "I'll be right back," he said again. He turned on his heel as I moved over to Zach.

"How're you doing?" I sat beside him in the pew, able to assess him more objectively in the dim light. Liam was right, Zach had started bleeding again at all the points that the arrows had struck him. Strangely enough, there were no open wounds there, just bubbles of blood trailing down his body. "This is so weird," I muttered.

Zach chuckled, low and raspy. "It doesn't really hurt that much," he said, though he couldn't quite hide the strain behind the words. "I don't think I want to keep feeling this way, though, I can tell you that."

"Yeah." I reached up to wipe away the trace of my own blood dribbling down my arm, but Zach weakly raised his hand.

"Don't touch it, not with your fingers. There's something in the poison that's...important. It's linking me to them. I can sense their thoughts, their resolve. Like I said, our attack was unexpected."

I shot him a sharp glance. "Attack? You walked four feet in their general direction, and I hustled to catch up with you. I'd hardly call that an attack."

He shook his head wearily. "I don't know…"

Liam rushed back up the stairs, distracting us. "Elves, you said. They shot you with crossbows, didn't they? Like some sort of Fae stepping out of the green forest? That kind of thing?"

"Sure," Zach grunted, shifting uncomfortably in his pew. "You have something for that?"

"You bet your ass I do," Liam said, throwing his pack into the pew in front of us and turning our way. He held a silver vial and what looked like a surgical sponge in his hands, and he waved them both at me.

"You're less injured, but we're gonna need your help when this gets bad. Take your shirt off."

I blinked at him, but he spoke with such focused intensity that I pulled off what was left of my blouse and stripped down to my sports bra, wincing only slightly, and not from the pain. Who wears a sports bra under a dress blouse? Who does that?

Someone who hasn't needed to put on a pretty bra for any reason for way too long, that's who.

I lifted my chin, daring Liam to make any sort of comment. He didn't say a word. A flare of some emotion I couldn't quite identify crossed his face as he advanced on me, but he stared me resolutely in the eyes.

"This is going to sting like a bitch, so suck it up." Without further explanation, he dumped some of the liquid from the vial onto the sponge and pressed it against my shoulder.

I screamed.

The pain was absolute, a white-hot ripping sensation that shot through my body from the point of the injury all the way through my chest and torso and down to my core. As quickly as the arrow of pain had penetrated, it wrenched itself back out, leaving another strip of agony in its wake. I jerked back, and then it was done.

"What the hell was that?" I gasped.

"Consider it a magical form of leech." Liam grinned as I struggled back into my blouse, reeling from the pain a second more before it cleared completely. "No bugs required. But you can see why I might need your help for Mr. Demonslayer here."

We turned to Zach. This was a guy who'd stared down curly horned demons bristling with fire, but he gaped at us with genuine horror. "Are you *serious*?"

Liam stepped forward, his expression brooking no bullshit. "Nina," he ordered, and I instinctively knew what to do.

My connection with the guys was ever evolving, but with Zach, the one thing I could do to keep him out of his own mind long enough to heal was simple and direct. I swung toward him, cupping his face with my hands as Zach bit out a curse. He reached up and shackled my wrist. "Nina, no. You're becoming an *empa*—" he began.

I didn't let him finish. Leaning forward, I covered his lips with mine.

Pain ripped through me.

4

_____

When I'd kissed Zach in the past, we'd managed to leave this current plane of existence and go someplace else, sometimes good places, sometimes bad—but we didn't go anywhere this time. Instead, no sooner had I covered his lips with mine and felt time and space shifting than Liam moved forward and a burst of white-hot pain branded my legs.

Zach had been pierced there by the Fae's arrows, I hadn't. But his fear about my growing empathic nature wasn't entirely off the mark. Our connection was so absolute that I felt his pain as my own, took on his wounds as my own. We were locked in a horrific symbiotic give-and-take of wounding and healing as Liam moved quickly from leg to leg, to Zach's torso, to his shoulders and arms.

It was an endless echo chamber of agony, and at some point, Zach passed out. What seemed like a lifetime later, Liam peeled me off Zach's inert form and held me as I sagged against him.

"It's all right, it's all right," he said. "It's over. He'll be okay."

"You got all the poison out? The tracking stuff?" I gasped, turning toward Liam, not even remotely self-conscious at the fact that I was leaning heavily against him in nothing but my bra.

Well, fine, maybe a little bit self-conscious.

But it felt right. It felt important, and Liam's surprisingly strong arm came around me, hugging me close. He drifted his lips over the top of my head, brushing softly against my hair, the gesture so intimate it made me catch my breath.

"I got the poison out, yeah," he murmured. "Did Zach tell you anything he picked up from them? Specifically about the tracking agent?"

I shook my head woozily. "He said they were surprised when we approached them, that we triggered some of their defenses. That's why they attacked. But why would they need to track us? They didn't seem to have any problem finding us in the first place."

With a soft sigh, Liam set me away from him. "This isn't the kind of tracking that involves a map. They're tracking our thoughts and feelings, our reactions. Remember, these guys are monsters. Whether you think of them as elves or the Fae or tiny winged fairies dancing around on the head of a pin, they're not us. They don't understand human emotions or human reasoning, no matter how human they look. So they have to watch and do what they can to understand us in order to predict what we'll do. But they can't track you anymore, I'm pretty sure."

"But why would they in the first place?" I pressed, pushing farther from Liam to stand on my own two feet. I missed the contact immediately, but he dropped his arms without apparent concern. "Why do they care about us?"

He snorted. "No friggin' clue, though there are plenty of ideas floating around about it. Maybe we're the assholes, and we've somehow knocked them out of their natural habitats and forced them to adapt. Maybe they're guardians of portals to other dimensions, which I personally think would be awesome, and they need to make sure we don't show up on their side of the wall. Or, hell, maybe they really are the Fae, ancient gods come back to hang out among humans, trying to bend us to their will."

He said this last with a brow waggle that made me smile. "But they're here now, in living color," I pressed. "On Wellington's campus. You don't think that's weird?"

"*Au contraire,* I think it's batshit crazy." Liam glanced over toward Zach, eyeing him critically before turning his attention back to me. His bright eyes gleamed with interest. "But it's not the only thing we should be focusing on here. You, my friend, have clearly leveled up, based on your whole empath show back there and Zach being able to siphon off your energy. Which means we need to start figuring out what you're capable of."

"Oh?" I felt uneasy with this assessment, though I already knew it was true. There was so much about the monster hunting collective that made no sense, but if anybody would understand it, Liam would...

Liam, who was practically bouncing on his toes now, waiting for me to connect the dots.

I narrowed my eyes at him. "Wait a minute. Do you know something I don't?"

His return grin was cocky and almost made me laugh out loud. "Without a doubt. But we'll get to that later. While I've got you here, though, and while Zach is down for the count, there's probably something I should show you."

I nodded. "You found that headstone with my mom's name on it. It's gotta be a fake, though, right?"

"Hang on, let me get a babysitter for our little bundle of

joy," he said, pulling out his phone. He keyed in a text and sent it. "Tyler isn't gonna want to miss out on this, especially since Grim has probably already split campus for the night."

"Yeah?" I pictured the largest, grouchiest member of our monster hunting collective, but I suspected Liam was right. "Doesn't he sleep on campus? Why wouldn't he be back at Fowlers Hall?"

"He's got rooms at Fowlers Hall, way over on the far east wing. But I don't know how often he stays there. He doesn't like people all that much."

I snorted. Grim was probably the most aptly named guy I'd ever met, big and stoic and not given to chatter. His bond with the other guys was absolute, and I believed he'd defend us all to the death...but that was more about him always being up for a fight than anything else. "That I can believe."

Liam gestured to Zach, who lay perfectly still in his pew, his chest rising and falling easily. "Tyler will find him. I've warded the chapel against intrusion from anybody but one of us and Commander Frost, and as you saw, it looks abandoned from the outside. Just like a good crime scene should be."

He moved down the aisle, and I followed him, frowning as we reached the nave. A ladder had been extended down into the undercroft through a charred hole in the floor.

"This was where the timbers fell, isn't it?" I said, casting my gaze upward. In the gloom, it was impossible to tell what the ceiling had looked like before the fire had ripped through it during Zach's epic demon confrontation earlier today. "How come the ceiling didn't cave in completely?"

"According to my research, we were lucky it didn't. It should have, but they made these old chapels strong. Back then, fire was a giant problem, like, all the time." He waved my attention back to the room below us. "Check out all those shelves down there. That's not where I found the headstone, but they're still pretty damn interesting."

I waited until he scrambled down the steps of the ladder, then followed. By the time I reached the floor, Liam had flipped on two portable lights, casting a dim glow around the area.

"I figure we only have tonight to get anything out of here that's critical. I've already got Frost on the phone with the cleaners. They're going to make a sweep as soon as we give the all clear. Which I was going to do, when I found..." He looked at me. "While I'm at it, is there anything else you haven't told us about your mom that you can remember? Anything at all? Because, not going to lie, super creepy to run across the woman's headstone. There's no way it's a coincidence."

I sighed. "No, I've told you everything I can remember. We led a very simple life. She was a professor at a small college in North Carolina. We lived more or less off the grid, but not in any sort of strange granola way, and I grew up. Everything was pretty normal, if you don't count the monsters."

He snorted. "Yeah, if you don't count those."

"But you know what I mean? I didn't think anything about a family or a history beyond what we'd created for ourselves until she died and I found her letter to someone in Boston, a someone who was clearly a member of our family that she'd never told me about."

"Frost has that now. The lockbox is safe, and he hasn't tried to open it. He wants you there."

I shrugged. "At this point, I'd welcome anyone making sense of it. As far as I could tell, it was a letter about me and my development, along with a laundry list of the monsters that attacked me and how I fought them off."

He nodded, tilting his head slightly, as if the gesture could trigger a recording mechanism buried in his neck. I frowned. Could it? And why was such an idea *not* ridiculous when it came to Liam?

"All the attacks?" he pressed. "Did you report to her every time?"

"No, not every time. I didn't want her to worry. It was only if I got seriously injured that she seemed to notice. Then she'd help patch me up. She'd ask me a few questions, but it was never a big deal. She told me once that some kids were born to fight monsters, and that I shouldn't tell anybody because they would tell other people, which would be bad. We didn't want anybody in our business."

Liam grimaced. He seemed about to say something when a new sound echoed from farther in the undercroft. He turned sharply.

"There's nobody down here but us."

"Maybe it's the cleaners?" I didn't know much about the shadowy service the guys had first tapped to help get rid of a monster corpse that wasn't decaying fast enough, but they were quiet, thorough, and seemed to have a particular skill for discretion. It wouldn't surprise me to find them already on the grounds of Bellamy Chapel.

But Liam shook his head. "Not yet." He held up a hand and ventured forward, and I smiled as I fell in line behind him. He was so fearless, walking into the shadows, not knowing what would be waiting for him, but more interested in learning what it might be than worrying about it being dangerous.

Had he always been that way? Curious to a fault? Probably. But what had driven him to such a headlong dive into the dark?

I shivered, though not from fear, exactly. Something

about Liam pulled at me in a different way from my attraction to Zach or Tyler—something dark, forbidden, and strangely exciting. He'd always been the jokester of the group, the consummate clown, but now...

We crept forward together out of the range of the portable lights, deeper into the shadows. He didn't reach for my hand—and I strangely wished he had, even though the thought made my cheeks flame with embarrassment. Above us, I still couldn't sense any movement from Zach, his mind blessedly blank.

The strike of a match made Liam and me freeze. Without saying anything, Liam stepped forward almost silently into the far room.

It was now lit by a single flaring torch, and dominated by a white-blonde giant of a guy whose rugged jaw was clenched tight enough to crack marble.

"This is bullshit," Grim announced, scowling down at the slab of stone sitting on the bench. "Someone is trying to fuck with you. With all of us."

5

"But why?" I lifted my hands, palms out, as much to block Grim's words as to slow the world down. "Janet Cross died months ago, nine hundred miles away from here. Why create a gravestone here?"

Grim turned and glowered at me, his normally cold, blank expression shifting through half a dozen emotions so quickly, I couldn't track them. "Your mother died," he agreed after a long hesitation. It felt like he was choosing his words with care—which shouldn't be necessary, since I knew without a doubt that Mom had died. The cancer that'd taken her had been worse than any monster I'd ever fought. And unlike those creatures, it kept coming back no matter how many times we'd thought we'd killed it.

I bit my lip, forcing myself to focus on Grim as he continued. He'd already changed his clothes from our group dinner, I realized dimly, once more wearing heavy pants and a worn T-shirt, scuffed boots encasing his large feet. "But this stone wasn't meant for her. It was meant for you. Someone knows you're sniffing around, and they're trying to tell you something. Poorly."

"How'd you get in here?" Liam demanded. "There's only one way in, down the ladder."

Grim grunted. "There's always more than one way in. You should know that better than anyone." He glanced around. "What is all this junk? And when was it put here? Because this headstone is new."

Liam sighed, already giving up on trying to determine how Grim had entered the undercroft. "You're right on both counts," he conceded, turning to me as I peered around the space. "Most of the crap down here is at least twenty years old. That's the most recent record I could find, and a lot more of it goes back decades earlier. It's mainly junk, as Grim said. Records from the church and other churches in the area, books from classes that went defunct, and a ton of cheap religious artifacts, nothing with any magical mojo to it. The kind of thing you'd find in any small-town chapel."

"But this is a chapel on the campus of a monster hunter academy," I protested, looking everywhere but at the headstone of Janet Cross. "Shouldn't it have more interesting stuff?"

Liam shrugged. "Arguably, yes. Which is why we're having all the potentially valuable artifacts taken out as judiciously as possible, then probably starting another fire."

I blinked at him. "I thought you wanted to avoid attracting attention. Arson would seem like maybe not your best bet."

He waved off my concern. "It's a calculated risk. The likelihood of a burn site catching fire again isn't completely out of the realm of possibility, and again, nobody's going to be looking too closely at this."

"Because the message has already been received," Grim said. He was back to scowling at the headstone, and I finally worked up enough nerve to approach it.

When Mom had died six months ago, she'd been adamant that she didn't want to be buried, didn't want to have any marker indicating that she'd spent time on this world. I'd scattered her ashes in the woods and streams of our small college town and hadn't found the letter she'd written to her family—or the people I assumed were her family—until days later. Her last entry on that letter had been more than four months prior.

But there was no way she could have forgotten it. So why hadn't she told me she'd written it? Why had she left me to find it locked in an iron box, with my birthday as the password? So many questions I didn't have answers to, and now never would.

Her funeral had been quiet, also by her request. A few members of the staff at the university had attended, along with some of my high school classmates, and that was it. My mother hadn't formed relationships within the community outside the school, and even those who'd shown up to pay their respects didn't have much to share about her. None of that had seemed odd at the time. Now it seemed glaringly obvious that my mother had deliberately cut herself off from the rest of the world, content to focus her attention on me, her beautiful garden with all its funky plants and flowers, and not a heck of a lot else.

But she *had* left the letter. Maybe by not acknowledging it, she'd fulfilled some kind of promise to herself, but by leaving it somewhere where I could find it, some tiny part of her hoped that I would find her family...so that someone would at least mark her passing. That had to be what she wanted, right?

My eyes blurred with tears as I stared down at the stone slab, with its carved letters, numbers, and the small, delicate spray of leaves on either side of my mother's name. Grim shifted uneasily beside me. He wasn't a guy who would know how to handle deep emotion, I suspected. Or, really, any emotion. I willed myself to pull it together.

"You said somebody was trying to screw with me," I said, the words only slightly garbled. I cleared my throat. "Who? Who would give a shit?"

He scoffed a short laugh. "You might be surprised."

Liam stepped forward and leaned close to the head-stone, as if it might be willing to whisper its secrets only to him. Once again—I couldn't discount the possibility.

"It's a message, for sure. But to our benefit, there are only so many businesses locally who make headstones. And this one does look new. I don't think it was carved a long time ago and spiffed up for us. I suspect we'll find it was created within the last few days. Headstones get commissioned all the time, usually for legitimate purposes, but sometimes for pranks or jokes. The stonemasons don't know one way or another, and they probably don't care. They just do the job as it comes in."

"But this date," I said, jabbing my finger at it. "It's twenty-four years ago, but it isn't tied to my birthday, though it's the same year. It's eight months before."

"Maybe that's when your mom left the area?" Liam said. "Like if she was pregnant, but before she was showing, which she may not have been at a month?"

I flapped a helpless hand. "Maybe? I don't know."

"But it's possible. Maybe she *was* pregnant. Maybe she felt like she had to leave town. That would explain why you never knew who your father was."

Grim made a disgusted noise I had to agree with. "Dude, this isn't the 1800s," I said. "It's not even the 1950s. People get pregnant all the time, especially professional women. There wouldn't be that much angst over an unexpected pregnancy in Boston, Massachusetts twenty-four years ago. I refuse to believe it."

Grim folded his arms over his chest, while Liam huffed a wry chuckle.

"Ordinarily, I'd agree with you, except for the Boston part. Especially if she was from around here," Liam countered. "If she came from a prominent family who cared about such things, particularly a prominent *magical monster-hunting* family..."

"But she didn't," I protested, turning on him. "She never once fought against any monsters, she just sort of defended me long enough to get us home. She got hurt a couple of times max, and never badly enough to scar."

I shivered a little, thinking about the scars I'd gotten that had disappeared over time, as well as the ones that'd never faded, including a few I couldn't quite remember how I'd gotten. But Mom had carried no scars. Even if I hadn't understood that to begin with, I learned it well enough this past year when I'd taken on the task of helping her bathe. No matter how seek she got, she was beautiful to the end.

I cleared my throat again. "There's gotta be a way for us to figure this out."

Liam nodded. "I've been working on it. Frost too. It's a mystery that doesn't sit well with him, not with you being a harbinger. That's a very rare genetic marker among the magical families, particularly in our neck of the woods. It hasn't happened in so long, we don't even know what it means anymore."

"Yeah, well, up until now, my life has been pretty boring. I mean, yeah, I may have attracted my share of monsters to Asheville, but it's not like I brought any sort of monster apocalypse there. Why wouldn't I have? Why is it just happening now?"

"You hadn't been triggered yet," Grim answered for Liam. "Harbingers are a key, not the entire mechanism. The academy hasn't dealt with a real monster invasion in over a hundred years."

"He's right," Liam said. "Even then, it wasn't an invasion so much as a parley, I guess you'd call it, a meeting of opposing forces where treaties were drawn up and power was split. Basically, the monsters agreed to go back to where they came from, and Wellington agreed not to chase them down."

I snorted. "That sounds kind of one-sided to benefit Wellington."

"Well, not exactly—"

Liam was cut off by a sharp exclamation above us. I looked up, recognizing the voice of Tyler Perkins, the head of our monster hunting collective. But he wasn't alone. Another voice, deeper and older, carried over his. In my mind, I felt Zach stirring awake.

"Tyler and Frost," Liam said. "That means the cleaners aren't far behind. We're going to need to figure out what of this we want to take."

"Not that," Grim said flatly, pointing to the headstone. "It should be destroyed."

"Well, not right away," I said in a rush, surprising myself. "We should investigate it, shouldn't we?"

"You took a picture of it?" Grim asked Liam, who nodded.

"Of course, first thing."

"Good." Grim turned and picked up one of the heavy iron boxes that lined the shelf beyond the headstone. Without any warning, he swiveled back and crashed it down onto the slab of granite.

6

———

The headstone cracked down the middle, but Grim wasn't finished. He hauled off and smashed it four more times, moving so quickly, I barely had time to draw in a breath to protest. And by the time I had, it was far too late.

"What the hell is *wrong* with you?" I demanded, surging forward, then stopping short in front of the pile of rubble. "Why did you do that?"

"For the exact reason you're reacting the way you are," Grim retorted, his words sharp and harsh. "This slab of rock was a trap. A lure. You carry it with you, even if you take it into Fowlers Hall, or Lowell Library, it'll serve as a beacon to whoever put it here. It's garbage, and you should treat it as the trap it is. Any credibility or significance you give to it simply means they win."

"But who are *they*?" I demanded, rounding on him. As always, his face remained flat, impassive, though his pale-gold eyes now seemed to burn with interest, an emotion I'd never before seen in them.

. . .

ANY RESPONSE he was going to give was cut off as Frost's booming voice called down. "Liam, what do we have? How many trucks am I going to need to smuggle this shit out of here?"

Liam scowled, then yelled back, "All of it should go. You know that."

"Well, that's not going to happen." Frost said something quietly to someone near him, and I felt Zach's energy lift. I heard more murmured conversation as the sound of feet on the ladder filled the space.

A few seconds later, three guys entered the space, which suddenly seemed very crowded. Frost was rocking his usual Paul Bunyan look—dark shirt, work pants, and big bushy beard that hid most of his craggy face—while Zach looked far steadier than he had passed out in the pew, and Tyler merely grinned at me, tall, strong, and sexy as usual from his tousled dark brown hair to his whiskey-colored eyes and easy smile. The sheer energy of all of them together was overwhelming. I edged closer to Grim, and immediately regretted it. The power of him pulverizing the stone slab still emanated off him in waves, feral and intense. But there was nowhere else for me to go.

Frost gestured Zach and Tyler forward. "All right, so what do we have here, specifically? Hit me."

The guys looked at him in surprise, but Tyler caught on first. He breathed out something in Latin I couldn't quite catch but that Liam clearly recognized, if the grin on his face was any indication. Tyler and Zach had recently leveled up, with Tyler's skills in spell craft rocketing off the charts, while Zach could now sense any magic or emotional resonance in a room far more deeply. It looked like they were getting the chance to show off what those skill improvements could mean in real time.

Meanwhile, Zach lifted his hands and turned around to view the space, his eyes narrowing. He frowned a second later and glanced at Tyler, but Tyler shook his head.

"I've got nothing," Tyler said. "There are absolutely zero items of interest down here, at least not in this room."

"Junk," Grim agreed.

"But this is interesting," Zach continued, stepping over to the remains of the headstone. "There's energy here, an echo I can't quite pick up anymore. I may not ever have been able to," he amended as Grim scowled.

"Do I want to know what happened to this?" Frost asked, striding across the room.

"It's exactly what you think happened to it," Grim growled with an underlying sense of menace. Frost didn't seem to notice the extra anger and merely nodded.

"Spelled, there's no question," he said. "Better to leave it here and in such a state that nobody else could recognize what it is."

He turned to Liam. "What else do you want us to look at?"

Liam had already shouldered his pack and turned deeper into the undercroft. "This is fantastic. I've never had two bloodhounds to assist me with research. Come on, guys."

He disappeared into the next room with Zach and Tyler, while Frost turned to me.

"Liam texted me the same picture he undoubtedly sent you," he said. "It's not every day that you get to see a head-stone you didn't commission inscribed with your mother's name."

I grimaced. "It would've been easier if it had been inscribed with my dad's name, at least we would've learned something."

"Oh, we learned something," Frost countered as Grim grunted in agreement. "We learned that our enemies are drawing closer. I'll give all of you a fuller briefing when the guys are done, but the cleaners are on the way and I don't want to waste their time. Unfortunately, we've got new and more complicated problems to solve."

My brows went up. "Another monster outbreak?"

"I wish it were that easy." Frost sighed. "Word has gotten out to the families that a number of the academy's monster hunter graduates have been killed—and still others are missing. So that puts Wellington Academy at a distinct disadvantage in the balance of power between human and monster. According to our charter, we can deputize additional fighters, but Dean Robbins has ruled that out. Which means—"

"*Hey.*" The call came from deep in the basement, with enough urgency that Frost broke off. Grim pushed past us, and I was hot on his heels. It was Liam's voice, threaded with excitement, and when we reached the final chamber in the undercroft, which was little more than a closet, it was easy to see why.

"What the hell is that?" I asked, staring at the metal rectangle. It glowed as Zach passed his hand in front of it, looking like a mirror that had been broken out, its interior replaced with static electricity.

"My first thought is it's a portal," Liam said. "But we'd have to test that."

"We are *not* testing that now," Frost countered. "It goes to the cleaners, then the library. Anything else?"

"These," Tyler said, indicating several boxes that glowed with the same faint aura of electricity. "It was definitely worth us coming down here. There's some great stuff down here, magical artifacts, records, and boxes we can't open."

"Can't open *yet*," Liam corrected. "It's not going to take long once I can focus on them."

"This is the mother lode, then," Frost said, looking around the closet. "Not a lot of cleanup required."

"So we don't need a fire?" Liam asked, sounding disappointed.

Frost huffed out a short laugh. "No, Mr. Graham, we do not need a fire. We need to get these items out of here and to the cleaners, and they can reassemble them in Lowell Library when it's safe to do so. We've got eyes on us tonight. Better hope your wards hold."

"Of course my wards are going to hold," Liam scoffed. As he turned away from me, his arms laden with boxes, I noticed that the collar of the shirt had dragged down—revealing a surprising sight. The same static electricity that danced along the boxes and the knocked-out mirror skittered over his shoulders, flickering in the gloom. I opened my mouth to ask him about it, then shut it just as quickly. The other guys doubtless already knew about it, and now wasn't the time.

Given how few boxes there were, the guys mobilized quickly, carrying things up out of the undercroft as Frost and I stood by. Grim positioned himself at the bottom of the ladder and, rather than haul loads to the next level, merely tossed things up through the opening in the floor for Zach and Tyler to catch. He seemed to get angrier with each new box, but then again, that wasn't anything new. The guy made grumpy into an art form.

As they worked, Frost turned to me again. "We're going to have to accelerate the search for your mother's family. Somebody went to some trouble to taunt you with that headstone, possibly trying to incite a reaction. Maybe they're just trying to jerk your chain. The question is, why?"

"I wish I knew," I said as Grim glanced over to me, his pale-gold eyes flat and emotionless, though his manner still managed to be faintly judgey. "There's too much I don't remember."

Frost flattened his lips, considering that, then seemed to come to some decision. "Well, we're not going to figure out anything tonight. Tomorrow morning, I need you all front and center at Lowell Library. Tonight—Nina, I think you should stay at Fowlers Hall. Grim, make sure she gets there safely. I'm going to need the others with me to unload these boxes."

A flare of panic skittered through me. "I can—"

"I'll take care of it," Grim said, cutting me off.

I glanced his way, shivering as a chill slipped along my arms. His face was set in stone. "Sure," I heard myself say as internal warnings slammed against my brain like zombies at the kitchen door, setting off every hardwired alarm in my body. "That sounds great."

7

New voices sounded overhead, and all of us glanced up, despite the fact that they were neither extremely loud nor forceful. But there was something chilling about the conversation, even when Liam's louder, more excited voice cut in to offer directions.

Frost stared at Grim. "How *did* you get in here?" he asked, with the kind of certainty that indicated he knew Grim hadn't come in through the front door.

Surprisingly, Grim didn't evade the question. "Chapels like this cater to the dead as well as the living. There's a passageway from the edge of the cemetery to the undercroft, used when they needed to carry bodies out without anyone noticing activity. It wasn't hard to find."

I kept my face carefully neutral, though in my mind's eye, I imagined Grim surveying the desolate graveyard and using his almost feral sense of direction, maybe even smell, to sort out where the door might be.

Frost nodded. "One of the larger markers?" he asked. Grim merely shrugged.

Apparently satisfied, Frost refocused on me. "Stay in Fowlers Hall until tomorrow. It's safest for everyone."

I made a face. "What's that supposed to mean?"

He waved his hand at the now-empty room around us. "It means I don't know what's going on, I just know that it's centering around you. That makes you a liability to our team and a risk to yourself."

Embarrassment and real hurt surged up within me, but I managed to nod as Frost refocused on Grim. "Get her out of here. You know we're being watched."

Grim pivoted without another word. I didn't need any encouragement to follow him back into the shadows, where, despite his bulk, he seemed to slip easily between the haphazard stacks and overloaded shelves of the undercroft. Moldering fabrics, decrepit tools, and rows of iron boxes leaned out into the space, adding a sense of claustrophobia that only worsened as the light dimmed. Soon we were walking in pitch-darkness, my hands drifting up and out to try to anticipate direction or obstacles.

Grim stopped so abruptly and with such little warning, I crashed into his back. Awareness flared through me, setting off a firestorm of reaction—excitement, danger, power. It was like this every time I touched the guy, part and parcel of the crazy reactions I had to *all* the guys that it almost seemed normal...except nothing with Grim was normal.

Grim drew in a long breath, then exhaled in a slow hiss. "We have about fifty yards where I'll be bent over to get through the narrow passage and you'll need to watch your head. It'll be easiest for you to hold on to the back of my shirt. No talking." As he spoke, I could hear the slide of fabric, and I imagined him loosening the hem of his shirt from the heavily belted waistband of his work pants. A soft aroma of heat and cinnamon surrounded me as he bared his skin, a welcome change from the heavy, loamy scent of the passageway.

Except now I was imagining Grim's naked torso. Which was less than ideal.

"No problem," I blurted, trying to stay focused. "But who's going to hear us down here?"

He glanced back toward me, and though there was no light that would allow me to see him clearly, I could almost feel his feral eyes glittering in the darkness. I rolled my own eyes at his glance.

"Right, right, the walls have ears. Got it."

He huffed a surprised chuckle, then turned back, waiting until I tentatively reached forward and grabbed the hem of his shirt, which I realized he'd already knotted into a ball. Had he led other people through dark passages before? The question assailed me as Grim moved forward, but I couldn't focus on it for long as his swift strides picked up pace almost immediately, and I found myself trotting in short hopping steps to keep up.

The passageway was dark, damp, and seemed to press in on us both—but Grim didn't hesitate, even when, as promised, he was forced to bend over nearly double at one stretch. There was absolutely no sound other than his measured steps and my more frantic ones, and I found my heartbeat slowing, the chaos of my mind easing because of it. For this strange time out of time, I didn't have to think about anything but putting one foot in front of the other, with a single objective of breaking back into the night. I had no choice but to trust Grim instead of my own rioting reactions and panicked resourcefulness. It was...actually kind of restful.

We went on like that for what seemed like far longer than the cemetery warranted until Grim slowed again, reaching back in an apparent attempt to keep me from crashing into him again. Instead, his hand connected with my chest, his fingers setting off a thrill of sensation along my collarbone. He pulled back almost immediately, leaving me rocking back on my heels. We'd come to the end of the road. A faint gloom illuminated the dank passageway, and I could almost pick out the stairway beyond Grim, carved into the earth and reinforced with concrete.

"The dead won't harm us, not here," he said quietly. "But if the Laram have reached the campus walls, they'll know about this passage too. I'm hoping the activity at the chapel will distract them, but there's no guarantee."

I didn't miss the strange word. "Laram? The elves—that's what they're called?" It didn't surprise me that Grim had identified the creatures before Liam could—he'd seen them once or twice with his own eyes and hadn't seemed surprised by their existence.

He pressed his lips together. Was he upset that he'd let the name drop? I didn't know, but he didn't dispute my conclusion. His eyes gleamed in the faint light. "They're here for the same reason all the monsters are. To see the harbinger. To come to where she's called them."

"You know, you guys keep calling me that, but nobody knows what the hell it means."

Grim grunted a harsh laugh. "Liam does. You should ask him."

With that announcement, he turned more fully toward me, his jaw set as hard as the rock steps in front of us.

"I can mask your presence, but I'll need to carry you until we get past the cemetery and to the main wall. Can you let me do that without losing your shit?"

I made a face that I suspected he could see in the darkness. "Of course I can."

"Good. Follow close behind me until we reach the top of the stairs. Then keep your mouth shut."

He spoke with such derision that a low boil of irritation bubbled inside me as he moved down the corridor a final few paces, then shifted up. The stairs were unexpectedly steep, and my fingers dropped from the knot of his shirt hem to the thick leather belt circling his waist. Curling around the belt, the front of my fingers grazed his lower back, and an unexpectedly sharp ridge of scar tissue pressed hard against my skin. I managed not to gasp as awareness flooded through me, but I didn't miss Grim's low grunt, his own shudder. Still, he pressed on, and a few seconds later, he paused. He turned back to me, lifting his arm for me to move forward, against his body.

"Keep your eyes closed, your mouth shut," he warned me again. "It will seem brighter than it should, chaotic."

I nodded, then barely suppressed a squeak as his arm dropped around me, heat and fear rocketing through me in equal measures. Grim hiked me high against his body. "When we get through the door, it'll be faster if you can move to my back. But I need you surrounded for the first few steps. You got it?"

I wanted to ask *surrounded by what*, but I knew the answer soon enough. Surrounded by him. He wrapped both arms around me and pulled me tight, bracing me against him. He opened the door and shouldered through it, then took half a dozen long strides.

I screwed my eyes tight as directed, but then he muttered "Now," and shifted, shoving me behind him and leaving me to clamber higher on his back. My eyes naturally popped open to get my bearings, and I had to bite my own lip hard not to scream.

The graveyard was aglow with light, and a full-on army

of monsters pressed in from all sides. All sizes and types—some I recognized, way too many I didn't. There were minotaurs and winged lizards, not to mention stomping fire bulls with full-on flames crackling along their shoulders and legs, their bulky, horned heads shaking back and forth. A burst of slithering eels shimmied in one corner of the cemetery, while smoke-footed succubi writhed in another. And other animals too—lions, tigers, wolves, all the size of smart cars, their eyes gleaming white. The entire horde of creatures swayed, howled, *roared*, though there was no sound. Their fists pounded the air, their wings flapped, their powerful legs stomped the earth. All of it silent, all of it horrifying. I bent my face forward into Grim's shoulder as he ran, willing it all to go away.

And just like that, it did. I blinked my eyes open and realized we'd breached the more modern, reinforced wall of Wellington Academy. Grim stopped short, allowing me to slide down his body and back to the ground. I stepped away as he turned to me, my nerves on fire, my heart racing as I struggled to breathe.

His face was resolute. "I told you not to look."

"Was that real?" I demanded, my entire body trembling as I wrapped my arms hard around my torso. Grim made no move toward me. "Is that what you see all the time? My God, all those creatures. I don't even know what some of them were."

"The time of reckoning is coming," Grim said. "Frost and Liam know, but they don't want to believe it. That snake Dean Robbins knows, but he doesn't understand it. The administration of Wellington Academy knows too. They just don't want to face the truth."

"And how do you know the truth?" The question seemed natural enough, but Grim stiffened and scowled at me.

"Where I come from, we don't have the luxury of ignoring what we are. We pay the price for it, nothing more."

He gestured deeper into campus. "Can you find your way back to Fowlers Hall? I've got other things to do."

It was implied that those other things did not include babysitting me across campus, and I was happy to agree.

"One problem." I lifted a hand. "I don't have a key card to get in. Should I just hang around at the front door until the guys show up?"

He made a face. "Use mine," he said, fishing a lanyard out of his pocket. "Go in the front door, or if that doesn't feel safe, there's another entryway along the low stone wall thirty feet from the building."

I peered at him. "There are back entryways into Fowlers Hall?" I asked disbelievingly, although at this point, nothing should surprise me about Wellington Academy.

Grim huffed a laugh, the sound easing my tension. "There are secret entryways into everything, if you know where to look. Will you be okay?"

That last question was so surprising that I smiled at him. That seemed to be the wrong thing to do, as he took a sharp step back and scowled. I pushed on anyway. "Yeah, I'll be okay. You don't need to worry about me, promise."

He snorted, but didn't say anything more. He turned on his heel and melted into the shadows, his pace kicking up to a trot—then a flat-out run.

I watched him go for a few seconds, marveling at his surprising grace and near-silent footfalls as he loped through campus. The night swallowed him up quickly, and I turned toward the monster quad of Wellington Academy and Fowlers Hall. Even as I took my first steps toward the residence hall, however, I hesitated.

Frost had said straight up that we had to solve the question of my family, and Grim had destroyed a grave marker that had been created specifically to taunt me about my mother. I needed to bring as much as I could to the table—everything I owned. My mother's letter was triple locked and safely stored in an iron box at Lowell Library, but maybe there was something else in what I'd brought from home that could help. God knew there wasn't much left in my apartment off campus—clothes, shoes, some of my spare knives. I should go and get them now, have them ready for whenever we were summoned in the morning.

My lips twisted. Okay, so I was avoiding going to Fowlers Hall. Sue me.

I changed direction, heading for the gates of Wellington Academy—and the world outside those gates, which was all that passed as freedom for me anymore.

I had to get out.

8

————

My mood lightened dramatically as I made my way across campus. I felt more relaxed, almost hopeful. The best I'd felt in a while, honestly. Maybe I should get away from Wellington more often? Maybe I should leave altogether? I was never one to back down from a fight, but I didn't think the fight was the issue. It was just that I preferred to take out the big bads on my own, versus bringing down an entire campus with me.

I thought about the monsters ringing the chapel cemetery as Grim and I had raced past the tombstones. They'd been so furious—stomping, howling, crying out for...well, for me, I guess.

I scowled. What had I ever done to them? My whole life, monsters had cut me, bitten me, flat-out tried to eat me— me or, if I wasn't paying enough attention to them, taken swipes at my friends and neighbors. It made for some pretty impressive motivation for me to step into the fray and kick some monster ass. But it wasn't like the guys needed my help killing these things on the regular. They'd been doing fine on their own until I'd brought the monster whirlwind to campus.

Chewing over that, I turned the corner. The lights of the food-and-entertainment district came into view. There were students here, milling around, laughing and talking, enjoying the balmy late-May evening in Boston. Most classes had ended for the semester, though it seemed like there were still plenty of students on campus. But the attitude was looser, easier. Exactly what it should be for a university at the start of its summer term.

Maybe Wellington Academy wasn't so different from regular colleges after all. Maybe for the right kind of student, it was like coming home.

I sighed, an unexpected twinge of sadness shimmering through me. Home. I'd thought it would be a homecoming for me as well, traveling to Boston. My mother had always smiled when she'd spoken about Back Bay, talking about the trees, the flowers, the beautiful summers, the horrible winters. The sense of history and mystery simmering in a haze of beer, baked beans, and lobster boils. She hadn't talked a lot about her time here, but it always struck me as being a happy place for her. Or maybe she'd just seemed so wistful talking about it, I'd assumed it was because she loved her time here.

Either way, Grim was right. Liam would know how to decipher my mother's letter and everything else I'd brought up with me. Once he peeked into that hidden world she'd created, which I'd played such an important part in without realizing it, he could tease out the truth once and for all.

Once I passed through the final walls of Wellington Academy—even the buried ones that circled the adjacent bars and cafés and offered a sort of half-assed protection—a weight lifted off my shoulders. To anyone looking my way, I was an ordinary college student walking along the sidewalks of Back Bay, Boston. I headed toward the hopping restaurant, indie store, and coffee shop district of Newbury Street. The stores here were all open late, taking advantage of the nice weather and foot traffic, and I happily stepped into the crowd.

I didn't even mind that my path wasn't taking me directly to my apartment, but to the Crazy Cup. After all, I'd posted up many a morning at the coffee shop after I'd first come to the city, mapping out the day's search for my mom's family. I hadn't been there in several days, so I should probably get coffee now, I decided. Do my part to support the local economy and all that.

I pushed into the coffee shop. The baristas looked up, smiling in welcome. I'd been there often enough that they recognized me, which warmed me more than it should. *See? I'm not a complete menace to society.*

And to be fair, I was also helping the guys at Wellington, in my way. I mean, yes, I'd brought them more monsters to fight, but I'd leveled them up as well. Sure, that had proven to be a far more intimate process than teaching them a new fight move, and I'd only gotten to two of the guys so far, but...

Stop thinking about that. To refocus myself, I blurted out the first question I could think of to the barista. "So school's letting out, looks like—what does that mean for you guys?" I tried, going for casual. "Have you been slammed more than usual?"

The barista serving me grinned back. "Oh, yeah, everybody's been out with this weather, which is really great," she enthused, her dark hair piled high on her head in an intricate sixties-style beehive that somehow managed to look chic, paired with her darkly lashed eyes and ruby-red lips.

Her name was Betty, and despite the fact she'd been on the wrong side of a monster attack about a week earlier, she seemed in exceptional spirits. That was one of the unsung benefits of most monster attacks—if you survived them, you generally forgot they'd even happened pretty quickly.

"They're tipping too, which is unusual," Betty continued, her grin radiating satisfaction. "That means they're tourists more than likely, but we've got no problem with that. It seems like there's all sorts of new people in town these past few weeks."

Something in her words caught me, and I frowned at her. "Yeah? You've gotten a sense there are more strangers around?"

"Oh, sure. I mean it's the summer, right? Everybody wants to visit Boston in the summertime."

"I guess so." Her words made total sense, but I couldn't help turning them over, looking for connections that probably weren't there. "So you have about the same number of tourists every year?"

"I wouldn't know, thank God." She chattered happily as she worked the coffee machine, adding milk to my espresso. "I've only worked here one year, so this is my first summer. Hopefully, I'll be out of here after this summer."

"Hey, hey, hey," a second, older barista protested from the other side of the bar—Joe, I remembered. I'd really been here too often if I knew the baristas' names. That or they worked way too much. "It's not such a bad place, even with the crazy."

"Oh, totally not," Betty agreed. She handed over my insulated cup as Joe kept going.

"To answer your question, there are more tourists than usual, yep. I've been here going on three years, and we usually don't get crowds like this until early fall, when the heat of the summer lets up. Boston can be kind of a mud fest some springs, so it doesn't usually pull in a ton of people until later in June. The weather's been kind of awesome for a few weeks, though, so maybe that's what's bringing them out. Either way, we'll take it."

"We totally will. Enjoy!" Betty danced back behind the countertop to greet the next customer, and I turned with my steaming cup, glancing over the room. There were some students, but also older singletons or couples hunched over their coffees or engaged in lively conversation—maybe a dozen customers in all. Still other people milled around outside the Cup, reveling in the warmer evening weather.

To me, there seemed to be a lot of folks on the sidewalk on a random May night, but maybe Joe was right and this was just a normal uptick of tourists coming in to enjoy the unusually pretty weather. I shoved my left hand into my pocket and felt the smooth edges of Grim's key card, my fingers playing along the frayed edges of his lanyard.

I froze.

The group surrounding me in the coffee shop was no longer a mix of students, locals, and tourists—or at least those weren't the only patrons. Two enormous gray wolves —easily seven feet long, with long, twitching snouts, high peaked ears, and ice-white eyes, had stationed themselves at the high table along one wall, their tails swishing. A man so emaciated he was barely more than a skeleton sat hunched over his coffee, his bony hands gripping his mug as he inhaled the steam rising from it. The steam floated out of his eye sockets and ears as I stared. Three feet away from him, two purple-hued wraiths, barely more than mist, swirled together in rapt conversation. Out of the dozen people in the coffee shop, fully five had transformed into monsters. I didn't like those odds.

As I watched, gape mouthed, I sensed the creatures' attention shifting, alarm slithering through the room. I released Grim's lanyard, whipping my hand out of my pocket. Instantly, everyone returned to normal—the wolves turning back into a couple of rangy-looking biker types, the skeletal man transforming into a squat tweed-wrapped grandpa with white, tufted hair flaring over his ears, and the two wraiths a young, prep-school couple in love, practically wrapped around each other as they sipped their matching lattes.

"Hey, what's wrong?" Betty's question jolted me, fortunately several decibels lower than her usual tone, and I realized I'd stopped short at the edge of the counter, as if afraid to move any deeper into the room. "You okay?"

"I'm totally good," I said, lifting my insulated cup. "Thanks."

She winked. "No worries! You should come back Tuesday night. Hugh over there plays guitar, and he's offered to do a couple of sets to keep people entertained while he's in town. It'll be a full moon, so that's going to be amazing."

She gestured over to the far end of the room, and I didn't need to turn to accept the fact that Hugh was undoubtedly one of the wolves I'd noticed a few seconds ago.

I nodded, still cheerful, but refused to look anywhere but at Betty. "I'd love to see that," I agreed brightly. "Tuesday will be great."

I had a feeling I wasn't going to make it to Tuesday.

9

The moment I walked outside the Crazy Cup and scanned the street, a renewed chill crawled up my spine. I didn't need to stick my hand in my pocket again to know I was surrounded by monsters.

Dammit, I shouldn't even be out here. We were in the middle of a bona fide monster mash, and I was apparently the headline entertainment. It was stupid of me to be wandering around Boston by myself.

I pulled my phone out and sent a text to all four of the guys. It wasn't Grim's fault I hadn't listened to him—he'd told me to get to Fowlers Hall. I wasn't going to throw him under the bus.

Heading to apartment to get what's left of my stuff. Realized I should probably have backup. Can any of you break free?

Liam texted back first. *Where are you?*

Crazy Cup, I confirmed.

All good?

I snorted. Um, no...but there was no way I was going to explain what I'd just seen at the coffee shop over text. Instead, I typed an affirmative, and Liam gave me the location of a shop down the street, some sort of half-price record store. As I walked, he continued texting.

Zach and Tyler are performing mind melds on the stuff from the basement, Grim is MIA. I'll be there in 15. Stay on the line. Tell me your favorite songs.

I laughed, but did as he asked, keeping up a running commentary of my musical preferences as he directed me down the street to the store. I walked in and immediately understood why Liam had chosen this location. There was a different energy about the place, a sense of safety that had been distinctly lacking for me in the Crazy Cup. I looked around with surprise, but couldn't immediately figure out what was so different here. A tattooed, goateed thirty-something was engaged in a heated conversation with somebody about the resurgence of vinyl, and the other patrons in the store seemed happily lost in their own music-focused bubbles. They all seemed incredibly...normal.

One way to tell for sure.

Steeling my nerves, I reached into my pocket and drifted my fingers along Grim's lanyard—and blew out a long, careful breath. Relief washed through me.

Throughout the store, nothing had changed. These were ordinary people bonded together by their love of music, not supernatural beasties rocking out to some arcane monster ritual. Thank. God.

Liam showed up no more than ten minutes later, breathing hard, his backpack slung over both shoulders. I blinked at him, taking in his flushed skin, the sweat darkening his sandy-brown hair.

"Oh, man. I'm sorry," I said automatically. "I didn't mean to scare you."

He shot me a grin. "You didn't scare me. You got me out of watching two other people do bullshit I can't do and gave me a purpose for this evening. I appreciate it way more than you can possibly know."

True enough, he fairly bounced on his toes. "So where to?" he continued. "Your apartment or back to the Crazy Cup? I assume the coffee shop is where you decided you needed backup? Why, are there bad guys there? Because if there are, I'm kind of in the mood to bash some heads, I'm just sayin'. So I'd be down with that."

I laughed. I didn't know that much about Liam, other than his insatiable curiosity and his willingness to dive headfirst into any new adventure. He seemed so much more open to learning more about whatever might be hiding around the corner then either Tyler or Zach, let alone Grim —who didn't care what hid around the corner, he simply knew he was going to kill it.

"My apartment," I decided. "And I'm glad to have you with me. Grim seemed to think you would be the most likely person to be able to decipher Mom's letter from a glance. So you'll be able to tell me if anything else I've left behind there is worthwhile."

Liam blinked at me, genuinely surprised. "Really? He said that?" He sounded so taken aback that I frowned at him.

"Well, yeah. You know more than any of us about the history of this place, let alone all the monster spells."

He considered that, then shrugged. "Okay, fair. It's just kind of cool to hear Grim admit it. I always feel like most of the time he doesn't quite know what to do with me."

"Really? I figured you did a deep dive into his history at some point, and you all hashed things out."

But Liam shook his head. "Oh, don't get me wrong, I tried. Frost put me on it almost immediately, and some of that research led me into some pretty dark places. The old world does *not* fool around when it comes to monster hunting. Best I could find, Grim's family, if you want to call it that, was more of a mercenary guild. He probably never knew his real parents, and he certainly has never expressed any interest in returning home or having anything to do with the people who raised him. Our search yielded a string of dead creatures starting from when he was young, but was super sketchy on the details of his upbringing. There were no photos, no official records of him as a kid, nothing. Real love fest happening over there, basically."

"It sounds like he had to grow up pretty fast."

Liam chuckled. "Didn't we all in our own ways," he agreed, with such an underlying melancholy that I shot him a surprised glance. But as if sensing my shift of attention toward him, he waved his hands at me.

"Enough about that for a minute. What are we walking into at your apartment? Why are you so nervous?"

I blew out a sharp breath and realized I wanted to tell him the truth. I wanted to tell him everything. It wasn't like when I was with Zach and I figured he could read my mind if I'd let him. It definitely wasn't like my reaction to Tyler, who'd made me spill the beans about myself before I was ready with a well-thrown spell.

With Liam, I wanted to offer up the information because, well...he was smart. He could see connections and identify patterns, and he knew how to put things together. The only way that skill was going to work, though, was if I gave him all the pieces to the puzzle I had. At this point, I was tired of questions that had no answers. It was time to understand what was going on here.

"Grim gave me his lanyard and told me how to get into Fowlers Hall. Then he said he had to do something and took off," I began, and Liam nodded.

"That would be classic Grim."

"I decided almost immediately that I didn't want to go to Fowlers Hall. I needed to get everything I'd left at my apartment, just in case it might be relevant."

He cocked me a glance. "Any reason why you didn't want to wait till tomorrow morning to do that?"

I scowled. "Oh, gee, I don't know. Maybe because I just saw a headstone with my mom's name on it? That's some seriously mind-breaking shit. So maybe I'm tired of not knowing what's going on."

Liam hiked his pack higher on his shoulder. "Fair enough," he agreed. "So you decided to head over to the apartment and, what? Stopped off for a cup of joe?"

I smiled, thinking of Joe the barista. That line was one of the Crazy Cup staffers' favorite jokes, and it never seemed to get old.

"Exactly," I said. "It was a gorgeous night, there were a ton of people out, and I was keyed up. Everything was great, I walked in, the place was hopping, no problem. Then I stuck my hands in my pockets and connected with Grim's lanyard, and whammo. Practically half the clientele freaking changed into monsters. They weren't bothering anyone, and I didn't feel like starting a fight before I got my latte, but they were totally there."

"*Really*," Liam said, his eyes lighting up. "I always knew that Grim rocked it as a tracker, but it didn't occur to me that he had a tool to help him."

"I don't know if it was the lanyard itself, or simply that it had Grim's essence all over it." As soon as the words escaped my mouth, I grimaced. "Okay, that sounds completely gross."

"Ha! Agreed," Liam conceded. "Still, it's kind of cool. May I check out ye olde lanyard?"

"Yup. And for the record, it doesn't seem like it's the plastic card, just the cloth strap. But here you go." Obligingly, I pulled the woven loop out of my pocket by the thick plastic card and handed it over. Liam took it eagerly. He gripped it, winding the strip of fabric around his hand, and looked around. He scowled.

"I got nothing. What about you?"

I took the lanyard more carefully back, holding my breath as I gripped the cloth strap. I glanced to the right and froze. "Shit."

Beside me, Liam instantly tensed. "What? What is it? What are you seeing?"

I slowly and carefully turned back to him, and when I spoke, I tried everything I could not to move my mouth. I didn't know if that would make any difference, but I wasn't taking any chances. "Okay. There are four of those tall, beautiful elf-looking people, the Laram or whatever you want to call them, hanging out across the street." I said. "I don't think they saw me. I don't want them to see me, and I definitely don't want them to come over here. Especially if *you* can't figure out which ones are monsters and which aren't."

"Laram?" Liam asked, his eyes narrowing. "Where'd you get that name from? What language is it?"

"I..." I frowned, hesitating. "It was something Grim called them. I don't know where he got it from, but—shit," I muttered. Out of the corner of my eye, I caught movement across the street. Had the Laram figured out that I was on to them? Would they come over and try to shiv us with their pointy arrow-rods?

One of them took a step toward the street, and I flinched, making Liam chuckle.

"I hate to break this to you, but you're sort of a walking billboard for *Don't Look At Me Right Now*. That's not good."

"No kidding it's not good," I bit out, keeping my forced smile intact. "You got any suggestions?"

"Oh, sure," Liam drawled. "I mean, when you get right down to it, monsters are as distractible as the rest of us, eager to drop humans into any of a dozen rough categories. Threat, nonthreat, smart, dumb, fast, slow, you name it."

"They're moving, Liam," I murmured with more urgency. "I can feel them getting closer."

"And I'm sure they're picking up on that," he countered, making my tension wind another notch tighter. "There's only one way to make them drop you into the 'random stupid human' bucket, I'm thinking."

"Which is?" I asked, hysteria spiking as I gripped Grim's lanyard. It was the exact opposite of a security blanket, though—the more tightly I clutched it, the more intensely I could feel the attention of the Laram. I let go, but it didn't seem to help—it didn't help!

Apparently oblivious to my growing panic, Liam leaned forward and lovingly took my face in his hands, staring down at me with his soulful, river-stone eyes.

"Liam..." I began warningly. "What are you—"

Before I could finish the last word, his lips came down on mine.

Danger. Desire. Need.

Power.

So much power sweeping through me. Lifting me up, pulling me around, filling me with—

Liam pulled back as I gasped, sensations swamping me. He glanced over my shoulder. "It's the frat guys, right?" he asked.

I jerked in his arms. "What?"

"The frat guys. Bif, Lou, and Freddo, hanging by the hoagie shop. Those are the guys you'd picked out? Because I can see them now too. They don't look like monsters to me, and they definitely don't look like elves. But they do look like assholes, so I feel like they have to be our guys."

I laughed, managing a swift glance to the right. "Yeah, those are the guys. But they're not looking our way anymore."

"I concur. Apparently, my swashbuckling ways took us off their Persons of Interest list." He looked back at me and waggled his brows. "Shows what they know—but we should probably keep it up."

Without more explanation than that, he swung me around, sliding his arm over my shoulder in a proprietary gesture that somehow felt completely natural. Once again, a curious heat powered through me, completely different with Liam than it had been with Tyler or Zach. When Tyler touched me, trees literally shook. With Zach, it was like time stopped—and the two of us were swept away to somewhere else entirely. But neither of those reactions was the case with Liam. Instead, my heart pounded, my skin overheated, and a liquid warmth swirled and roiled deep inside me, desperate for release.

"You're not wearing anything weird, are you?" I asked him, my cheeks flushing with the question, but I had to know. "Like some sort of strange pheromone thing that I'm reacting to?"

Liam side-eyed me with genuine curiosity. "I'm not, but that, my friend, is a fantastic new product idea. Probably not ethically right, as I think about it, but that's totally something I should put a patent on..."

He cast his gaze skyward again, and we kept walking as he spent the next couple of minutes discussing the potential uses of a magically enhanced, sexually stimulating cologne or wearable tech. By the time we got to my apartment, he'd dismissed the idea as a possible avenue for development because of the almost certain likelihood of it being used for nefarious purposes. "But of course the obvious corollary to said dastardly invention is to create something that…"

"Defends you against such a product," I finished for him. "Basically some sort of magical cockblocker."

His eyes lit up with delight. "That would be exactly what I would call it. If you're a member of the magical community and you're nervous about getting swayed into liking some creepazoid who simply has better magical skills than you? Have I got the product for you."

His grin faded as he caught me staring up the street. Without turning to see what I was looking at, he asked, "What is it?"

I made a face. "It's nothing—or I don't think it's anything. It's just that there's a light shining in a window on the third floor of my apartment building, and I don't think I've ever seen anyone in that unit. I'm so used to coming home at all hours of the night and the place is dead. I just don't know, it's weird. And given the fact that Zach found about a dozen cameras in my place, I can't help but think that, you know, maybe people on the third floor isn't such a great thing."

"Agreed." Liam kept his focus on me. "Where's the light in relation to your apartment?"

"Right beneath it." I shot him a glance. "That's bad, isn't it? That's probably bad."

"It's not great, most likely, but it does keep things interesting. What all do you have in your apartment that we need to bring back to campus? You already dumped off your lockbox with the letter and all that. What else could they be interested in?"

"Honestly, not a hell of a lot. Clothes and shoes, a few knives and other stuff from when I was growing up. Like random iron totems I kept in my pockets when I found them, more for superstition than anything else."

I frowned, thinking about that. Only yesterday, I'd come across a similar token that I tried to pick up and pocket, only to discard it because it gave me the creeps. A small silver bead that had proven to be a tool of particular value against the demons that had hit campus in search of Zach. A bead that Grim had known what to do with...much like he'd been able to identify the elves by name. The old world tracker of our monster hunting collective was proving that he had depths far beyond Hulk-smashing things. I wasn't sure how I felt about that.

"Superstitious totems are exactly the kind of things we need to get out of your place pronto, scary people who live beneath you or not," Liam said, scattering my thoughts. I looked up to see him peering at my apartment. He swung around his backpack, unzipping it without looking down. "Fortunately, I've got an app for that. In this case, app as in apparition ward."

My brows lifted as he rifled through his bag with one hand. "An apparition ward? Like a ghost illusion?"

"Exactly like that." He grinned, glancing at me with such warmth, I felt my cheeks heat all over again. "So let's say we've got company on the third floor. We put this ward in play, nobody can hear or see us—not directly, anyway. We look like no more than a shadow. We're not totally silent, but I've got other toys to cover that. Trouble is, all these things use a ton of energy, so they're only good for short bursts, got it? We need to get in, out, and down the street in...well, fast."

"Fast." I narrowed my eyes at him. "Do you know how fast?"

He shrugged, arching his eyebrows in challenge. "Not even remotely. You ready to give it a try?" Without waiting for me to answer, he pulled out two small metal cuffs, handing me one. "You slide it over your wrist just like your anti-Zach bracelet, and when I tap mine, it goes into effect. With my other tools in play, we can yell as much as we want, we can run, we can laugh, we can bang off walls, nobody can tell. We're ghosts in the machine, baby."

I made a face, turning to peer at my apartment and the brightly lit space beneath it. "Okay, but again, how long does that last? What happens if they stop working midway?"

He zipped up his pack and repositioned it on his shoulders. "We improvise. You ready? Because I'm ready. I'm totally ready. I'm ready to rock it. Hit your cuff."

Obligingly, I gripped my cuff with my hand, and Liam slapped his. A jolt of electricity blew through me, quick and hot. "*Wait,*" I tried as Liam gave a short, loud whoop. "Why do I feel like this is a really bad—"

But Liam was already running. "*Leeeeeeeroy Jennnnnnk-ins,*" he howled.

I took off after him.

10

Despite his hollering at the start, Liam shut up quickly as we pounded our way toward my brownstone. We galloped up the front steps of the building, and I ripped my keys out of my skirt pocket. I used the key card to get through the front door, then we both hustled up the stairs. I found myself wanting to tiptoe past the apartment on the third floor, but Liam urged me on.

"They can't hear us, they can't see us, unless our cuffs short out and then we're fucked, so choppity choppity," he insisted.

I redoubled my speed, and a few seconds later, we reached my front door. Fueled by panic, I unlocked the various locks in less than seven seconds, and then we were inside, the door slamming behind us. I arrowed a glance at him as he blew out a harsh breath.

"They couldn't hear that? It felt like the whole building shook."

"Move," he said tightly, and I realized for the first time that beneath the excitement, there were genuine nerves.

"I'm moving," I said, defensive as I started for the back

room of the apartment, past my tweed chaise, which was virtually the only piece of furniture in the living room. "Seriously, you've never tested these cuffs?"

"Nope," Liam confirmed, his head on a swivel as we moved through the apartment, not that there was much to see. A tidied kitchen, a bathroom with a lot of medical supplies, an empty hallway. The apartment of a monster hunter, outfitted for function, not finesse.

"A lot of what I pick up is single-use-only kind of stuff," Liam continued. "These cuffs, I had three of them to start, and the first one I shorted out way too fast, but that wasn't exactly my fault because I ended up jumping into a pool... Never mind. Bottom line, I don't know how long they're going to last."

"You jumped into a pool? Like a swimming pool?"

"Yeah from about five stories up. Not my brightest move, but, you know. Desperate times."

We paused at the entry to my bedroom, which had an armoire, a mirror, and my rolled-up sleeping bag tidily stacked on a folded square of plastic sheeting. Nothing else on the floor, nothing on the walls.

"So you spend a lot of time decorating is what you're telling me," Liam said drily, and I shouldered him out of the way as we both tried to enter the bedroom at the same time. "I do love a girl who accessorizes with plastic sheeting."

There was nothing I could say to that, so I went directly to the armoire as he kept going. "No, seriously. Do you cut up dead bodies in here, or is this just to catch your own blood when you've had a particularly busy night?"

"The latter," I said, dropping to my knees in front of the armoire and rifling through the clothes on the floor of the closet. I pulled out my boots and another pair of jeans, plus a half dozen tank tops and a few hoodies. I took a second to strip out of my blouse and miniskirt and re-dress in more intelligent gear—jeans and boots, a tank top and a hoodie. "Most of this I probably don't need—"

"But it's yours," he said simply, unzipping his pack. "I've got a kind of vacuum sealer in here—lemme...here."

He settled the bag on the floor, and opened it wide. In went my boots and jeans, then he stuffed the shirts down, his gaze on the last item in the closet, a velvet bag I'd scored from...somewhere. The back of Mom's closet, probably.

"Sweet pouch," Liam drawled, hefting his pack up, its open top angled toward me. "Why do I think there are no sex toys in there?"

I snorted, and pulled the bag free—it was heavy, but that wasn't surprising. "Weapons, mostly. Some junk too." I made to pull the drawstring open, but he waved me off, the glint of his cuff catching the light.

"Negative on the show-and-tell. Remember, we're on a time limit."

I jolted. "Oh. Right." I dropped the bag into the pack and Liam's hands jerked down, the weight transfer taking him so much by surprise that he dropped the pack to the floor. It made a loud thunk as it hit, the room shaking as much as it had with the slammed door. A glass shattered in the kitchen, and Liam blinked at me. His mouth quirked up at one corner as his eyes lit with excitement.

"Thing one, I suspect those weapons and trinkets are more magical than you think. Thing two, it appears our cuffs have shorted out."

"*What?*" I spluttered as he rolled to his feet and hauled the pack over his shoulders. He staggered a little, clearly trying to readjust for the weight.

"Is there another way out of here?" he asked, ratcheting up my nerves.

69

"No, there's not another way out of here," I snapped. "This is my apartment. It has a front door and a fire escape down the hallway, that's it."

"Windows it is, then." He strode quickly to the wall and pulled the cellular blinds out of the way, then lifted the casement window as high as it would go.

"Are you nuts?" I hissed as he leaned out over the sidewalk. There was nobody on the street below us, and he whirled back toward me, smiling broadly.

"You didn't hear that, did you? Opening the window, that was totally silent? Am I right? Because I have a theory."

"Yeah, it was silent, but—"

We froze as the front door to my apartment rattled against its hinges.

"I have my own locks," I whispered. "My landlord doesn't have the key to those."

Liam made a face. "That's not going to stop him for long."

Sure enough, a large boom sounded from the front door, and Liam grabbed my hand, speaking quickly as he pulled me over to the window.

"My theory: whoever possesses your bag of crazy weapons-n-stuff wins. You picked them up easily, but the transfer to me was a bitch—and left you vulnerable. Sorry about that. I can carry them now more easily thirty seconds later. I'm still invisible, silent, my wards still working. So I'm going to jump out first and hope I don't break my ankles. If I don't, I'll turn around and catch you, because once again, your bag of goodies doesn't want to be found. You get that, yes? The bag wants to keep itself safe. That's the game."

There wasn't time to argue as the door slammed open at the far end of the apartment. Liam didn't hesitate. In one smooth move, he slid his legs over the window sash and dropped out of sight, leaving me staring after him for a long second as dimly I registered the sound of running footsteps behind me. I stuck my head out the window, and shockingly, Liam was beneath me, his arms out as if he could catch my weight from three stories high.

He was a lunatic, but I didn't have any other choice. I slid my legs through the opening and then turned around to cling to the wall. I hung from the window, barely peeking over the sill. I had to see. I had to know.

A tall, pale, gray-suited man burst into the room, and even if I hadn't planned on it, I couldn't hold on. My fingers had gone numb with shock. I dropped like a stone into the darkness—

And crashed into Liam, driving him to the ground. As we slammed to the pavement, Liam's backpack exploded around us like a car's airbag, an enormous balloon ejecting beneath him, extending out several feet in each direction. We bobbed on top of it for a heart-stopping three seconds, then it collapsed again—and completely poofed out of existence with a rushing gasp of air. Leaving me sprawled on Liam's body as he arched awkwardly over the top of his pack.

He grunted, shifting beneath me. "You sure do know how to make an entrance."

"Oh my God, are you okay?" I asked. I tried to roll off him, but he held me tight.

"Wards," he muttered as he narrowed his eyes on the window far above us. Sure enough, two figures crowded into the window, then the blinds crashed back down, cutting off the view.

"Was that friggin' Dean *Robbins*?" Liam hissed, and I sagged against him, grateful for the embrace for a second longer as he confirmed my own shock.

"That's who I thought it was," I said. "I mean, it could have been somebody with some sort of crazy illusion spell, but it looked like Dean Robbins, and the guy beside him was my landlord, Mr. Bellows. Which...I don't even know what to make of that."

"Same. But we gotta split. I'm going to roll over to my right until you're beneath me, and then I'm going to get up while still holding on to you, okay?"

"Um...sure?" I didn't see how that was going to work at all, but didn't say anything more as Liam wrapped his arms around me and pulled me in tight. Once again, the flood of desire swept through me—quick, hot, and completely inappropriate for a public sidewalk.

With a strength I wouldn't have expected, Liam did exactly as he'd explained, rolling me over and somehow managing to lift me in his arms as he braced his legs beneath him and stood straight again. Without missing a beat, he bent to scoop up his pack, then strode quickly across the street and down the sidewalk, ducking down the nearest alley. I stayed silent, willing myself to be as light as possible, but he didn't seem to be concerned. Maybe he had some sort of levitation tool in his pack?

When he finally settled me onto the street, he lifted a finger to his lips, while his other hand held me fast. "Stay connected to me," he murmured, and I nodded.

Together we crept back to the corner, and I waited until Liam had satisfied himself that we weren't being followed. He turned back to me and lifted his brows at my expression. "What?"

"Ah...exactly how much weight lifting have you done and how is it your body isn't as big as Grim's with a move like that?" I asked.

He laughed. "I get a little help, and I've been lugging this pack around for a long time. You learn how to make momentum work for you."

"Right." It was becoming clear to me that Liam had made downplaying his own abilities into an art form, but as he glanced around the corner again, I frowned at his back. "How long do we have to stay connected?" I asked.

He shrugged. "Long enough to...hold up a sec. Shh."

I pressed myself closer to him, peeking around the corner to see the front door bang open on the brownstone. Dean Robbins trotted down the stairs, looking fussy but unconcerned. He had a phone up to his ear, and even from this distance I could hear him talking with the kind of oily, soothing tones that were required for any high level university official. He was either apologizing or defending himself to somebody, but Liam straightened and stepped carefully backward, making me move as well.

"Slow and steady," he directed. He turned and drew me close to him, the two of us arm in arm as we angled toward campus. "I'm not sure how long or how aggressively your weapons kit is going to protect us, but it's doing a damn fine job so far. I haven't had time to uncork any of the other goodies I have in my pack, so we're not going to look a gift bag of toys in the mouth."

I shook my head, trying to parse his words, but at the moment, all I could really think about was the fact that we were walking hand in hand away from my apartment, our mission accomplished, all my relevant worldly belongings safe in Liam's pack and...we were holding hands. The connection between us fairly crackled with energy, but I couldn't quite figure it out. It didn't have the earth-shattering urgency of Tyler or the time-stopping otherworldliness of Zach, but it was full of possibility, potential...and, once again, *danger*, in a way I didn't quite understand.

"Exactly what are your magical abilities—like your innate ones?" I blurted without looking directly at him, emboldened by our close embrace. "Zach can read minds and sense magic in the area, Tyler can hurl some serious spells, and Grim, besides being a one-man killing machine, can track like nobody's business. So what's your deal?"

Liam's huffed breath sounded remarkably sad, and he didn't say anything for another half a block. "Well, that's a funny thing," he finally sighed. "I don't actually have any innate magical skills."

I swiveled my head, narrowing my eyes at him. His profile was resolute, a small blood vessel jumping in his temple—I'd never noticed that before, but then again, I hadn't been looking. It struck me that a lot of people probably didn't notice things about Liam, by his careful design. "What? That's totally not true."

"*Au contraire,*" he countered ruefully. "I am, by all accounts the runt of my family's litter. My folks and their folks before them and on down the Graham line have all been high-level wizards, but every once in a while, every few generations, in fact, there's an outcast of the family tree, an apple that dropped too far away and kept rolling. I'm this generation's bad apple. Gotta hand it to my folks, they weren't quitters. They kept at me to see what I might develop, and even augmented me to the point that they could."

"The electricity over your shoulders," I said. "I saw it in the chapel."

His lips twisted. "Insertables. They're not just for rock bands anymore. I have a dozen different rods inserted at various points in my body that are supposed to tune me up, if you will. To help me access the ambient magic in the room."

"Yikes. Did that hurt?" I asked, and he shot me a look.

"More than I wanted it to, but significantly less than not having access to any magic at all. Tyler has known about the tuners for a long time, and Zach figured it out before we all warded ourselves against him. Grim probably knows too, because he's an asshole. But Frost doesn't, and nobody else at the academy does either. The fam has kept it on the down low because, well, I'm an embarrassment."

I couldn't help myself, I rolled my eyes. "You're insane. You are probably the most valuable member of this entire team. You have to know that."

He let out a long sigh. "Definitely not the case," he said. "But maybe, I mean..."

A new flare of awareness shot through me, and I understood exactly where his mind was going. Maybe if we hooked up, that could be the trigger to help Liam access his innate magic? A guy who I was already jonesing for so much, I was squeezing his hand to within an inch of its life? Sign. Me. Up.

Liam, of course, had no idea that my butterflies had started doing their own anticipatory Macarena. "I mean, it looks like you've already leveled up after your time with Zach," he said, measuring his words out carefully. "So for reals, you don't have any obligation—"

"Yes," I cut him off. "Yes, absolutely we should. Immediately. Or as soon as possible. But yes, we should do that. Whatever it takes."

He blinked at me, and there was no denying the interest flaring in his eyes. "You're serious?"

"I could not be more serious—" I began, but Liam's eyes had already gone slightly unfocused, his mind obviously spinning ahead.

"Because honestly, if we're going to do this, we should

approach it from a purely scientific standpoint. I mean, for the sake of research, we should do it the right way."

Um, what? I frowned at him, but he wasn't paying me any direct attention. "Ah... Scientific?"

He nodded quickly, and I realized his pace had picked up too. We were speed walking through Back Bay at midnight, tucked together like two conspirators bent on a mission spiraling out of control.

"I mean, think about it, when are we going to have the opportunity to really test and see empirically exactly how the whole male-female collective thing works, right? I mean this is a fantastic opportunity. It's epic!"

Epic. I frowned as Liam chattered on, roughing out a three-part testing protocol of different levels of intimate contact, emotional and physical, and ways to empirically test the outcomes of each in a controlled environment. Here I was experiencing a profound need to make out on a street corner while all he most wanted to do was set up an experiment suitable for peer review. Was he joking? He had to be joking.

I opened my mouth to respond—and our phones blared.

11

___

"Oh shit," Liam groaned, shaking me loose to grab his phone. I shoved my hands in my own pockets, trying to focus. "I didn't tell the guys you're safe. My bad."

His fingers flew over the screen, but he didn't stop talking. "You're going to need to reassure them as well. Let them know... Well, maybe don't let them know, now that I think about it. If Robbins is in on the surveillance stunt in your apartment, he could be tapping into other networks. I haven't debugged our phones in a while. Which, dammit, is a whole new thing we need to figure out."

"Right," I said, trying not to feel cheated that Liam and I had somehow already moved off the idea of kissing. Or touching. Or engaging in the scientific process. Because my body was still reacting to the very distinct and real possibility of all those things coming to pass, and Liam was right here, right now. I stuffed down my desire and reluctantly pulled out my phone, chiming in on the group text that Liam had reached me, and all was well, and that...

I looked up. "What should I say we're doing? Are we going back to Fowlers Hall?"

To my relief, he hesitated. But not for the reason I wanted. "You know... I think that would be a bad idea. There's a lot of crazy energy there, and we need to see exactly what weapons you've got in your kit."

"My kit."

He nodded with emphasis. "Absolutely. I mean, you said there were knives, right? And some totems?"

"Yeah..." I frowned. I rarely used anything but my standard iron knife, but there were other things in that bag, sure. "I mean, it's all kinds of basic stuff."

"Well, that's what you *thought*—but something in there is heavy-duty, and I can't wait to check it out. So let's get to Lowell Library. Remember that basement room where Frost had all his toys hidden? I found a way to get in there, and that place is a freaking bunker. It would be perfect to test out your toys. I've even stored some of my own stuff down there."

I peered at him in the semidarkness of the street. With his gleaming eyes and cocky grin, briefly caught in the glare of a car's passing headlights, Liam was in his element. He looked like he'd been born to the half-light of streetlamps and shadowed corners, always poking his nose into the unexplored fringes that everyone else passed right by. "You have stuff? I mean, more stuff than your bag?"

"Dude, of course." He stowed his phone in his pocket, and retook my hand. The move irritated me because it made me feel so much better, but I didn't pull my hand away. One had to respect the scientific process, after all. "I've had to repack this bag eighteen different times in the last couple of weeks, it feels like. That forced me to take full inventory of everything I own."

Something in his voice tipped me off, and I slanted him another curious look. "Because why, exactly?" I asked. Liam reddened, but I knew instinctively he was going to tell me the truth. He always answered when somebody had put a direct question to him. I'd never really thought about that before now, but while he would skirt a response with a joke or a redirection, he never truly lied. Was that a choice? A compulsion?

Those questions were chased away by Liam's next words. "Well, mostly because of you. Things have stayed relatively stable in the monster hunting minor for the last couple of years. Ever since we created our collective, we've learned, we've fought, we've bitched about the administration, but we've sort of kept our heads down and ground through it. Then you showed up with a Tarken land worm on your ass, and everything went into overdrive."

I made a face. "Because I'm monster bait."

"You are so much more than that," he assured me earnestly—then winked and gave me a knowing grin. "But the monster bait part is clutch. All of a sudden, Dean Robbins kicks everything up to a new level of harassment— and that was even before we noticed he may have had a hand in the academy's unofficial off-campus neighborhood watch program. We've got monsters jumping out everywhere, even coming onto campus grounds. We've got old bluestocking donors popping up like daisies everywhere we turn. And that's not all. There's a weird energy going on around campus, something I can't quite explain."

I frowned at him. "Tell me about that," I said as we headed away from Newbury Street toward the school. Somebody else had said something about a new energy. Commander Frost, maybe? "You think Wellington's energy fluctuation is tied to me?"

"In this case, not exactly," Liam said. "I don't think it's attached to you so much as you triggered it. Again going back to the whole harbinger thing. And there are books down in Frost's basement. I found his archive. The answer's got to be in one of them."

"Right," I said. Grim had said that too. That I was some sort of trigger. But if there was information in the library we could use... "You're talking about the Apocrypha? The book that wasn't there, given how much of it has been hacked out."

Liam flinched. "Ah, well—not just the Apocrypha. Frost's got a ton of old books from some highly interesting places, jam-packed with information. There's gotta be more information about you in them."

"Then why hasn't Frost found it?"

Liam tugged me along, walking faster now. "Because Dean Robbins has been keeping him dancing as fast as he can, and we've had a few monsters to wrestle down in the past few days. You've been here less than two weeks, and I think Frost and Robbins have been in meetings for most of them, whenever we haven't been outright fighting monsters. And it's not just Robbins who's all up in Frost's grill. Our fearless commander's getting emails and phone calls around the clock from the first families, and the search for the other monster hunters went so badly so quickly that he had to explain that as well."

I pressed my lips together, the last embers of my attraction to Liam getting banked, at least temporarily. This was a mess. "We've got to find answers to all this."

Liam cocked a brow at me. "Well, there is a way for us to do that, yes? There's always a way. There's always a tool, a trick, or a gadget to get the job done. Always."

I snorted. "What is that, the Graham family motto?"

"No, just mine. The Graham family doesn't have an issue accessing magic. I have to get more creative."

"And you have."

"I have," he said definitively. "But first, we need to get your kit safely into Lowell Library and open that bad boy up. So let's kick it up a notch."

The campus was far quieter than it had been when I'd left it a few short hours earlier, though there were still some students roaming along the brightly lit sidewalks. As we passed beneath the gargoyle studded archway, I felt a strange chill steal over me. Liam's phone pinged again, and he muttered a curse as he pulled it out, then glanced my way.

"Hang on a second," he said and he moved off from me a couple of feet, letting me linger in the shadows. The trees had grown tall here, and I drifted toward them, wanting their embrace. I reached out my mind to see if I could determine any sort of amped-up energy like what Frost and Liam were talking about, but I felt nothing but a strange, hollow loneliness, the sense of feeling incomplete. An overlay of loss, despair, and aching pain. Distracted, I patted my front pocket where I'd stuffed Grim's lanyard...

I stopped. "Oh, *shit*," I muttered, shoving my hand deeper into my pocket, but of course there was nothing there. Had I dropped Grim's key card? Had it fallen out during Liam's and my crazy trip to get my weapons? I'd thought it was pushed down pretty deep, and I certainly had it at the coffee shop. Had I lost it after I'd let Liam try to wrap his hand around it?

Another finger of cool breeze drifted across my forehead, and I angrily brushed it away, then caught a movement deeper in the woods. Light reflecting off a pale flash of color. Instantly, I thought of Grim. Was he back there? Had

81

he pickpocketed me to get his key card back instead of, you know, coming up to me like any normal guy? I mean, seriously. What was *wrong* with him?

"Hey," Liam said, and I turned back to him, surprised to see his manner tenser now, more focused. "Sorry about that. Let's go."

"What is it?" I asked, and he waved me off.

"Nothing major, just my family being my family." He turned back toward Lowell Library, and I fell into step with him.

"I'm not really sure if I know what that's like," I offered, not knowing what else to say. "My mom and I had a good life, or I thought we did. But ever since she died, I don't know anymore. It's like she was this whole different person before I came into her world, and she never once shared any of that life with me, not even when she got sick and knew she was going to die. I guess I still have a hard time understanding that."

Liam sighed beside me, and his hand closed over mine again, the heat that flared between us equal parts shared emotion and...something more. At least something more for me.

"I have a hard time believing it too," he said. "Man, we sure ended up with a messed up group of parents. Yours with the secrecy, mine—don't even get me started, Zach's with his family curse..."

I huffed a soft laugh. "Yeah. None of us really ended up with parents of the year."

Liam squeezed my hand. "We don't know anything about Grim though," he said, a hint of a smile returning to his voice. "He might have had seven other brothers and sisters all as big and feral as he is, lined up around the kitchen table wolfing down cookies and hot cocoa."

I thought about the flash of pale white hair I'd seen against the trees, the soft chill that surrounded me. "Now that's something I would like to see."

We reached the library a few minutes later, closed up for the night. Liam didn't enter through the front door but moved around to the side of the building, sliding his pack forward. He pulled out a small device as we approached the door, and I lifted my brows.

"You have a lockpick for the *library*? That has to be the nerdiest thing I've ever seen."

Liam laughed, unperturbed. "When your library is as cool as Lowell, you're damn right I have a lockpick. If I have to enter it from the outside, it's the quickest way possible to get in—and that was before I knew about Frost's secret hidey-hole in the subbasement. I thought I'd mapped out this place pretty well, but this was one case where I was happy to be wrong."

I quirked him a glance as he bent toward the side door to the library, nearly invisible in the shadows. "You've mapped the library?"

A lock clicked, and Liam straightened again, gesturing me forward. "I've mapped the whole friggin' campus—and believe me, what goes on beneath this place is a hell of a lot more interesting than what happens up top."

My further questions were stymied as we stepped into the darkened library and Liam lifted a finger to his lips. He waved for me to follow him and didn't waste any time. Striding quickly and almost soundlessly, he hurried down the long polished hallway, not even glancing at the main section of the library, but heading deeper into the building. We made three left turns, then a right, cutting down a side hallway barely illuminated by flickering sconces set high into the wall. Then we emerged into a hallway I recognized and, a few moments later, arrived at the elevator bay. Liam summoned the elevator, and when the doors swished open, he stepped inside first. I followed, my heart beginning to thump with anticipation. We'd been down this elevator once before, all the way to a hidden basement, and he struck the B key three sharp times with authority.

"You don't have the key to get down to the secret storage room, do you?"

He flashed the same device. "Consider this an all-access pass. Frost should never have let me see that room. I already had stuff hidden throughout the library, but down underneath, where nobody could get to it who didn't know how the campus was originally set up, just makes so much more sense."

Sure enough, the elevator paused only briefly at the basement, then kept going down what felt like easily two more levels. When the doors opened, however, it was to a different room from the one that Frost had shown us earlier.

I stepped out of the elevator, looking around. "What is this place?"

Liam exhaled with genuine excitement as he joined me. "Best I can tell? Some kind of underground bunker, though not exactly intended to protect you against a nuclear attack. Not even really enough to protect you from a monster attack. It's more of a storage place of last resort. There's electricity and plumbing, but the accommodations sort of suck otherwise."

He gestured to the makeshift bed in the corner, little more than a few sleeping bags piled on each other, an electric lamp and clock, and a small refrigerator unit. Still, the space looked remarkably...cozy.

I narrowed my eyes at him. "Do you sleep down here? Like on a regular basis?"

Liam shrugged, then gave me a rueful grin. "I only found it the other day, remember. But since then, yeah. I've started spending a lot of time here, and it's quiet enough for me to think. Plus, I have all Frost's books and the entire library to access if I need to."

"And no observers for any mad-scientist experiments you might want to conduct as well, I take it?"

The gibe was intended as a joke, but Liam turned toward me, his cocky smile returning.

"I'll have you know I am *exceptional* at mad scientist experiments, I have several in mind for us when the time comes." I started with surprise, a flare of now-familiar interest tingling inside me, but Liam pushed on.

"First things first," he said. "Let's check out your weapons of mass destruction."

Swinging his pack around, he moved toward the large wooden table pushed up against the wall. He set the pack on the table, flipped on a gooseneck lamp I hadn't noticed hovering to the side, and unzipped the top of the pack. Slowly, almost reverently, he pulled the heavy cloth bag out of the pack, transferring it to the table with a loud thunk. He flipped open the top of the pouch and slid out the first thing his fingers could reach, a long, skinny blade, like an old-timey scalpel. It'd fit perfectly in my little-kid hands when I'd started striking back at the monsters that'd come after me, but it couldn't cause much damage. I hadn't used it in years.

I folded my arms tightly to my stomach as he dipped into the bag again, pulling out a tin sheriff's badge. Mom had gotten me that when I'd killed my first monster. A ripple of sadness slid through me, pricking my nerves. "I don't know what you think you're going to find in there. It's just a couple of knives and some iron things I picked up. Nothing even expensive."

Something in my voice penetrated Liam's science-guy fugue, because he looked up sharply, then pushed back from the table.

"Hey," he said, walking over to me and leaning down a little to look directly in my eyes. "It's going to be okay. You know that, right? It's all gonna be okay, no matter what's in this pouch or what's in that iron box upstairs. You're part of us now. We'll protect you."

"I don't need your protection," I snapped, then immediately felt bad when Liam grimaced with concern. "No, that's not true. I hate needing your protection, I guess."

He gave me a sad smile. "There's nothing wrong with asking for help sometimes."

"I know." I blew out a sigh. "And I do think I was supposed to come here, I just...I don't know. None of this should be happening. Mom should never have died, I should never have been designated as monster bait or a harbinger—any of it. We were doing fine. She was doing fine. How she could have had a family who never once tried to find her..."

"Hey," he said again. He lifted his hands to my face, brushing away tears I hadn't realized had slipped free. Slowly, he leaned forward and his mouth touched mine, and everything horrible and broken in the world slipped away. For one impossible second, it was me and Liam with our lips touching, our breath mingling. Need, fierce and sure, scorched through my core, sizzling along my veins and practically electrifying my nerve endings. Nothing shook outside of us, and we weren't swept far away and somewhere else, but I felt like I might *explode*.

Liam jerked away, his sandy hair standing on end, his

bright eyes wide and dazed. "Holy *crap*," he breathed. "That was *way* more reaction than last time. Did you feel it? Does that happen—I mean, was it like that with the others?"

"No," I answered shakily. "No. With them, it was powerful, but...um, different."

"Oh, man. That is so *awesome*." His gaze cleared, and he fairly danced on his toes. "But I can't get distracted. We have to be serious here." He turned back to the table with excitement. "We've got more tools to get through, and I happen to be a master at deciphering ciphers and unraveling mysteries. So don't tell me anything about your stash, okay? I'd rather take it all in with fresh eyes."

I sighed. Apparently, unraveling the mysteries of our sexual attraction took second place to my childhood scraps and memories. "Have at it," I said, standing back.

Liam seated himself at the table and leaned forward, peering down at the knives. Then he leaned forward a little farther, his mouth moving, his eyes scanning back and forth rapidly. With a startled huff, he pitched forward even more, his face dropping all the way down to the surface of the table, the move so strange that it caught me off guard.

"Um...you okay?" I asked, stepping forward to touch his shoulder—before jerking back at the arc of electricity that leapt up from his body to my hand. "Whoa!"

Liam lay slumped on the table, out cold.

12

"Liam!" I surged forward, stopping just short of touching him again, my hand poised over his back. Should I shake him? Wake him up? Would that cause some sort of problem?

His head partially covered the velvet bag, his hands curled beside his head on the table's wooden surface. I could see the barest edge of something shiny sticking out from beneath his mop of hair, and I gingerly reached down and teased the item out. As it slid into view, my brows went up.

The hilt of my beloved Renaissance Faire-purchased athame stuck out from the bag. Seeing it made my heart tug a little, despite the fact that I should be worried about Liam. I glanced back at him, but he was breathing easily now, apparently dead to the world but not otherwise harmed. I took an extra second to pull the athame out of its pouch and study it.

It was a pretty trinket, mass-produced by the thousands and sold around the country to gullible festival goers like me, but I didn't care. When I'd been twelve years old and had saved up enough money and gone to the local Ren Faire to buy it, I'd been full of hope that it would not only take out the monsters in my path, but give me magical powers to make them go away for good. The woman who'd sold me the knife had been a festival worker, maybe twenty years old, dressed in swirling robes, with heavily lined eyes and bracelets that jingled whenever she moved. But it had been the store's proprietor who'd stopped me on the way out of the colorful tent, frowning down at my purchase in its little organza bag.

"You're kind of young to be playing with knives," he'd observed, and at the time, I hadn't realized who he was. I'd bristled, my shoulders going back.

"It's not a knife," I'd informed him with all of the authority of a twelve-year-old monster warrior. "It's an *athame*, and it's going to protect me."

He'd gotten a strange, almost angry look in his eye at that point, which had flustered me, and when he'd asked to see the blade, I'd given it up willingly. He turned it over in his hand, his gaze roaming from it and back to me as he weighed it.

"What sort of things do you need protection from?" he asked carefully, and I realized my unintentional error.

"Oh no," I said, giving him a wide smile. "I'm not being bullied, my mother loves me, and I'm okay. I mean like protection from, you know...monsters."

I expected him to laugh that off, chalk it up to me being a kid. That was what generally had happened before when I'd slipped up around adults. Instead, he nodded somberly, looked down at the blade again, and murmured something to himself. Then he'd told me that for a job like that, the blade should be sharpened.

To my surprise, he led me next door to a similarly festive

89

tent, this one set up to show the process of making chain-mail armor. Shoppers could purchase everything from delicate little ankle bracelets to full shirts of mail, and sure enough, they sold old-timey weapons too. Axes and swords and even maces. All those were blunted, but in the back of the tent, there was a table with several long files. Using a round cylinder, he'd scraped the blade several times until by the time he returned it to me, it gleamed with a wicked edge. I had been over the moon.

"You come back here next year if you need it sharpened again," he told me.

I hadn't, of course. I'd learned quickly enough that while the athame was pretty, it was too light and the wrong size to be much use in fighting monsters. I had to be economical with the weapons I carried around with me. Still, I'd kept it in my stash because it made me smile whenever I looked at it.

Now I slanted a glance toward Liam. Should I have warned him? How was I to know what random crap from my past would knock him out?

I set the blade back down and hesitantly laid my hands on Liam's shoulders. He sighed in his slumber as if somehow recognizing my touch, but he didn't wake. I frowned, then pulled him back more or less upright in his chair, bracing myself to keep him from tumbling over. I couldn't just leave him like that, so I heaved him out of the chair, stumbling over to the makeshift bed he'd built for himself and flopping Liam down on it like a rag doll.

He still didn't wake up.

I knelt beside him, stretching out his limbs and smoothing the hair from his head. He appeared unhurt, but why wasn't he waking up? Why didn't I have more skills when it came to helping these guys?

Not knowing what else to do, I settled with my back against the wall and angled his head into my lap. He sighed again, more contentedly this time, and I smiled. I wished I'd had the time to go through a few more classes before the semester ended. If I'd been able to take some sort of magical first aid class beyond getting the syllabus and a stack of books, I could be useful here. There had to be some sort of spell or magical whozit or...

My gaze lifted to the table where Liam had dropped his pack. He'd had smelling salts in there the first time I'd met him, right? It was reasonable the pack had them now. Should I go through it? Was that some sort of breach of privacy?

As I studied the pack across the room, it seemed to shiver a bit, a burst of sparks and some smoke flickering at its mouth. My eyes widened. Was that an invitation or a warning?

Beneath me, Liam sighed again, turning over slightly to make himself more comfortable. I sank my head against the wall, unreasonably tired. Smelling salts would probably be a good idea. I'd close my eyes for a second, and then...

When I awoke hours later, if my phone were to be believed, Liam and I lay in almost the exact same position. He'd curled into me more tightly and had somewhere along the line scored a blanket, but he was resting comfortably from what I could tell. I, on the other hand, was pretty sure I needed traction. I slid out from beneath Liam, muscles screaming, glad when he murmured something unintelligible but normal sounding, and stood. My entire left leg tingled with outrage at being woken up, and I was *ravenous*. I squinted around the small room, but there was no food here.

I wondered if Liam would be aghast at the idea of eating

in his secret lair. My stomach rumbled. Well, too bad. This wasn't my secret lair, and I was starved. I had no idea how to get out, though, or how to get back in.

I knelt down again next to Liam.

"Hey," I whispered. "How're you doing?"

"Mmmph," he managed, making me grin. Then he opened his eyes and squinted at me. "Um...what're we doing on the bed?"

Not nearly enough, I wanted to say, but instead, I pulled the blanket up higher around his shoulders. "My childhood mementoes bored the crap out of you, I think. You passed the hell out, and I dragged you over here."

"Bored...?" He clearly wasn't tracking fully, but at least he wasn't in a coma. Progress.

"Yeah—but now I want to get some food. How do I find this place again?"

Liam grunted, waving vaguely at his pack. "Inside the cover of the pack, homing device. It'll bring you back. To get out, use the elevator."

"Oh." The elevator, of course. Another quick check of my phone verified it was only 6:00 a.m., a good three hours before anyone was supposed to assemble at Lowell Library. I could get out and back again before anyone noticed.

Liam seemed to be thinking the same thing. "Coffee," he sighed, apparently not that concerned about food in his hidey-hole after all. Or at least not caffeine.

I set out on my quest, amused that it almost felt like a game. Then again, Liam made everything feel like an adventure, even when he'd apparently been knocked out.

How often did he knock himself out when he was on his own? I suddenly wondered. I got the sinking feeling this might not be an unusual situation. Who found him—took care of him—when he got in too far over his head? Did he have friends beyond the guys?

None of the guys seemed like they had much in the way of friends outside of the collective, now that I thought of it. Then again, neither did I. Was that a function of being a monster hunter? Or just who we were as people? Which came first, the antisocial nature, or the monsters wanting to eat you?

I stepped into the library's gleaming hallway, rolling more questions around in my head. Did Liam get lonely? I didn't think Zach did, with the constant murmur of voices in his mind. Then again, I knew all about being alone in a crowd. Was that how Zach and Liam felt too? All the guys?

I frowned, mulling over these thoughts but not focusing long enough on any one of them to get pulled under. I'd made it all the way out to one of the cafés on the edge of campus and almost back again, with two coffees and break-fast sandwiches in tow, when a startled voice called my name.

"Nina?"

I turned around to see Merry Williams standing at the corner of Cabot Hall. Tall, willowy, and way too pretty for six thirty in the freaking morning, with bouncy auburn hair and striking green eyes, Merry sported her usual uniform of perfectly pressed academy attire—blouse, plaid skirt, knee-high socks and boots. Something was off about her, though. Her hands were clasped around her own insulated coffee cup, but she didn't burst into her usual babble of chatter. In fact, she seemed a little lost.

"Hey," I said, changing my trajectory to head toward her. "How are you doing?"

The last time I'd seen Merry, she'd been captured by demons while carrying a megaphone. We'd left her in the safe hands of the first responders to the fire at Bellamy Chapel, but I realized with chagrin I hadn't checked up on her since then. Then again, had that only been yesterday? Time seemed to be rushing by way too quickly.

"Were you hurt in the fire?" I continued when Merry didn't respond.

"What?" She refocused on me, as if my words had reached me from a far distance. "Oh. Oh, gosh no. Not really." She shook her head, lifting a hand to tuck a lock of her hair behind her ear, and I blinked in surprise. A thick band of white hair now shot its way back from Merry's forehead, mingling with the heavy mane of rich auburn. The effect was undeniably stunning, but I wondered if Merry realized it'd happened yet. She seemed to be a bit in a daze.

"The paramedics said I'd probably gotten concussed in a fall," she confided, confirming my suspicions. "But they couldn't find any evidence of injury. They told me to go home and sleep it off, and I've just now rolled out to get some coffee."

She raised her cup to me. "Great minds think alike."

I nodded, but a strange unease drifted through me. Even with a knock to her head, Merry was far too subdued. "Maybe you should get some more sleep?" I asked, and she smiled a little wistfully, then glanced up toward the sun peeking over the tree line.

"No, I think I'm going to walk in the sunshine for a little bit. I don't feel quite right."

"Do you want me to walk with you?" I really needed to get back to Liam, but there was something forlorn about Merry that struck me to the core. The only reason she'd been at Bellamy Chapel yesterday was to protest the poor treatment of monsters. The monsters hadn't treated her very well in return.

Now she offered me a distracted smile. "I'm good, really. I just sort of feel a little cold. I might be under the weather, or heck, maybe I did hit my head. I think the sunshine will help."

I glanced around. It was an absolutely beautiful day, I had to admit. And I knew she was right. It would take some time for her to recover from her close encounter with demons, and sunshine sounded like the best tonic for that.

Still, seeing Merry so affected made my heart hurt. I stood for a while watching her wander off, her steps far less enthusiastic than I'd ever seen them before, and scowled. We needed to figure out why monsters were attacking Wellington. The old walls of the academy weren't enough to keep them out anymore, and everywhere I turned, it felt like I was being watched. Studied. Assessed. If I was the harbinger of some great monster battle of the ages, then the fight needed to get here, and pronto.

I turned back toward the library, newly resolved. First we'd figure out if there was any real magic in the weapons I'd collected as a kid...and there had to be *something* there if they'd knocked Liam out cold. And then we'd make a plan. As long as that plan included taking down the monsters of Wellington Academy once and for all—without hurting any of the guys—then that was good enough for me.

It was time for us to kick some monster tail.

13

When I stepped back into Liam's little hideaway room, I found him standing over the velvet pouch, his hands clasped behind his back. He looked up with a quick smile as I entered.

"Man, I totally passed out last night, didn't I? Did you see it happen? I can't decide if I was just wiped out, or if one of your weapons did me in."

I glanced down at the table, noting the gleaming athame lined up with the other tools, looking as innocent as a magical RenFest blade possibly could. "I'm pretty sure it was one of the weapons, though I was pretty exhausted too. I zonked out just on general principles, but as for you—that athame was one of the things you were handling from the bag when you collapsed onto the table. I didn't know if you were allergic to medieval festivals or something."

"Aha! Ye olde dreaded cursed blade," Liam agreed, reaching for it. I tensed when he picked it up, but as he rotated it in his hand, he seemed to suffer no ill effects. "I'm getting nothing from it now. Maybe a single-use blade? Or maybe it exhausted itself knocking me out?"

"Ahhh...maybe?" I offered, a little lamely. "I got it for protection back in the day. But I didn't maintain it. It's not even sharp now."

"Well, that's just disrespectful," Liam chided, and though I knew he was joking, I frowned over at the athame. Did ceremonial knives have feelings? Did normal people ask these questions of themselves?

"I didn't mean to make it feel bad—" I started, but Liam waved me off, reaching for the sandwich bag.

"Not to worry. You couldn't know what you didn't know, right? I've got a sharpener in my bag. We'll get you set up."

"Oh. Ah... Good."

Liam took a giant bite of the first sandwich he pulled free of its paper, then gestured with it toward the lineup of weapons. "Pretty nice kit, but it's not the athame that's got the juice—or at least that isn't what tripped my magical Geiger counter this morning."

"You've got a...never mind." I shook my head as he grinned. He downed half a sandwich in one bite, then pointed to a small separate pouch next to the weapons, with half a dozen little silver animals resting on top of it. "Where'd you get that?"

I frowned down at the bag. "I-I mean, they're toys. I've had them since I was a little girl." I picked up the largest of the animals, a leopard, and turned it over in my fingers. "I'm pretty sure Mom gave them to me for Christmas one year. They were gray metal, so they rated high for me. But I never used them in any sort of monster fight."

"Don't think that's what they're for," Liam said around a mouthful of food. He picked up the coffee cup and took a generous swig, then made a face. "No sugar?"

"Sugar's bad for you," I said automatically, sounding so much like my mother, I jerked a little.

"Maybe in your world." Liam chuckled. He moved over to his bag where, sure enough, he liberated a couple of sugar packets and dumped them into his coffee. He turned back to me, leaning one hip against the table. "Anyway, these little guys are packed with major wards. The lion, leopard, and wolf most of all, but all of them bring something to the party. They're place wards more than people wards, and I'm thinking *they're* why the cameras went kablooey in your apartment, not so much your harbinger-ness. Though your harbinger-ness probably didn't hurt."

"Really?" I lifted my brows. "Mom never said anything about them being protector animals, but—that's kind of cool."

"She probably felt safe knowing that you kept them in your little secret bag of weapons. You'd carry that bag pretty much anywhere if you moved somewhere different, and you were living at home on top of that. So you were covered."

"That makes sense." I pressed my lips together, trying to repress the surge of sadness that welled up within me. "It would've been a lot easier if she'd just told me, you know, *any* of this."

"Yeah, I've been thinking about that," Liam said, taking another impressive bite of his sandwich. "So there's gotta be only two, maybe three answers to the question of Why the Big Secret, and none of them are awesome. Frost may know more by now, but to my mind, you've got option A, your dad was a shit and your mom was afraid of him, so she hid you away. Option B, your mom's family was a bunch of assholes and couldn't handle her getting pregnant, so she ran away. Either way, she was super proud of you, which is why she wrote the *This is Nina's Life* letter, but never sent it. She wanted you to know that she understood you were awesome."

98

"Yeah..." I frowned, shoving my hands in my jeans pockets. "Do I want to know what option C is?"

Having finished his sandwich, Liam waved his coffee cup at me. "Not really. But option C is that your mom was the bad guy in this equation, and she stole you away from your loving father and family, and raised you on her own. Assuming, you know, that she was your mother in the first place, and not some jealous nanny or batshit crazy bystander who wanted the cute little monster-hunting baby for herself."

I coughed a sharp laugh, the tension easing in my chest. "I think we can pretty much rule out that last one. Nobody would have put up with me the way she did, all the monsters and everything, unless she was blood. There's no way."

Liam tilted his head, considering that. "Maybe. But don't forget, you're the harbinger. If she knew what that meant, that changes things."

"Yeah, well. *We* don't know what that means, so that doesn't get us very far."

Liam straightened and set down his coffee cup just as both our phones buzzed. "Oh, come on," he muttered, diving for his pack. I looked down at mine as well, confirming the text had come from Frost. "He's completely too early."

"Do you think he knows you're down here?"

"Not a chance. He's good, but when it comes to place wards and sneaking around, I'm better. Only Grim has ever shown up someplace I didn't think anyone could—like the chapel—but I don't mind that so much. He's a different kind of cat. But come on. They're all upstairs."

I gestured to the weapons bag. "Should I bring these? Will they be safe?"

"They'll be totally safe down here. Upstairs, we've got the box and your letter. They're the stars of the show, I'm thinking. These won't matter much. They're place wards."

"Okay..." I moved toward the pouch anyway, putting all the weapons back in the velvet bag, patting the athame awkwardly. It didn't feel right leaving them out. "You guys protect us," I whispered to the tiny leopard, just like I had when I was a little girl, even hearing the high-pitched, earnest voice I'd used, as soft as a whisper in my mind. Liam was already at the door, and without him noticing, I stuffed the little bag into my own pocket. Even if it was a place ward and not a people ward, I just didn't feel right leaving it down here. I turned to go—then turned back, scooping up the child-sized athame and tucking it into my back pocket. Hopefully I didn't gouge myself to death with it, but at least it wasn't sharp.

Liam didn't notice my sleight of hand—or if he did, he didn't comment on it. By the time we got to the war room of Lowell Library, the other guys had assembled. Tyler and Zach both had wet hair and looked like they'd gotten a good night's sleep, while Grim looked as gritty as I felt. He didn't look at me, though both Tyler and Zach grinned and gestured to a pile of food and coffee on one of the shelves along the wall.

As Liam had suggested, my mother's iron box was set up on the long table in the center of the room, the books and laptops that typically occupied the space shoved to the side, but Frost lifted a quelling hand as Liam started forward.

"Hold up," Frost said. "We need to cover some other issues first."

This morning, the commander looked fit and a little fierce, his burly Paul Bunyan frame outfitted in a workman's light denim shirt and heavy brown work pants. He'd trimmed his beard recently, something I hadn't noticed the night before, and I wondered about the meetings Liam had mentioned.

"Dean Robbins," Tyler put in, folding his hands over his chest, his brown eyes narrowing. "Namely, what the fuck was he doing in Nina's apartment last night, not two hours after our meeting where he acted like he was our best buddy and that we'd be graduating early with full honors, per the Wellington board of directors."

"Wait, what?" Liam turned toward Tyler, the box momentarily forgotten. "He said that to you? Who got that to happen?"

"It's bullshit," Grim muttered, and even Zach looked dubious, while Frost just heaved a sigh.

"I'm inclined to side with Mr. Lockton on this one, but the facts remain that Dean Robbins did put forth the assertion that the graduation ritual would be moved up, specifically to ensure that you were all prepared, and I quote, to defend the campus."

I frowned. "Defend it from what? Monsters?"

"On the surface, that's what they're saying," Tyler said, rocking up on his toes. "But I'm getting the feeling that it's more some sort of weird internal first-families fight. It's not in a monster's nature to attack unprovoked. That means someone's driving them to it. And think about it, the first monster wasn't even a monster, but my Great-Uncle William called back from the crypt by some asshole necromancer who remains in the wind. Zach's demons were their own special kind of crazy, but—"

"But it wasn't just my own demons that hit campus," Zach said. "They brought along a party, and they were amped. That whole scene at Bellamy Chapel, with the students protesting and getting sucked into the fight, I don't think that was tied to my demons. It was more a collateral excitement of the horde."

"Which would imply that something major is cooking," Liam put in. "An uptick in the energy."

I shot a look to Frost. He'd said much the same thing to me, and God knew I felt the uneasiness all over campus. I thought again about Merry and frowned.

"So, Dean Robbins is behind this?" I hazarded.

That brought a round of scoffs and rolled eyes. "No way," Tyler said emphatically.

"I can't really see that," Zach agreed.

"He's a douche," Liam put in.

Grim merely breathed out a judgmental "hmmm."

"The most likely scenario is that Dean Robbins serves more as an intermediary between the school and outside parties," Frost said. "Mr. Bellows works with Mr. Symmes and the board of directors here at Wellington, but he gave Symmes no indication that either he or Robbins had been at Nina's apartment last night. Bellows advised he'd been home the entire evening. So at a minimum, he's working directly with Robbins, but I suspect there's more to it than that."

"Right, okay," I said. "So Dean Robbins is a bad guy—except when he isn't, like when he's letting us know you guys might graduate early."

"You too," Tyler said, shaking his head as I turned to him. "I know. It's insane. You haven't even been here two weeks. But—something's got them spooked."

"Which takes us back, of course, to you and your family, Nina," Frost said. "There's still nothing on the facial recognition software to link you to any former students, nothing on the DNA scans."

"You took a sample of my DNA?" I asked, genuinely surprised. "When—How?"

"Bellamy Chapel—we all got scraped up," Liam put in with such a matter-of-fact nonchalance that I accepted it and moved on. When it came to today's roll call of the bizarre, unexpected DNA sampling was way down the list.

"And you're telling me I'm not in your database," I said. "I'm a true, I don't know, rogue. An outlier."

"Bait," Grim taunted, but I wasn't going to let him push me into a reply. Instead, I swung my attention to Frost.

"We need to open the box," I pressed. "Nobody's ever bothered it. I didn't know it existed until I found it after Mom died. She left the pass code on a Post-it note stuck to the box—and her handwriting was pretty shaky. It was near the end."

My words were flat, clinical, almost like someone else was saying them, but I forced myself over to the box. It took me a couple of unsteady tries, but I got the combination correct. The lid popped open, and there they were. The pathetically few mementos of my mother's life. A necklace with a semi-precious yellow stone in the center of a teardrop of diamond chips, some handmade earrings of sea glass, financial documents, a dozen or so photographs, and the letter.

This was my mother's legacy. These pictures, this letter, these scraps of jewelry.

"Wow," Liam said, edging closer. "I have a feeling we're probably going to learn more from the box than we are from your mom's letter, no offense. It's a custom-made device. Now that it's open, I can see the wards written into the corners. This box wasn't bothered because it was set up not to be bothered. That's a high-end piece of equipment you got right there." He didn't mention my magical Protector

Zoo I now carried in my pocket, for which I was grateful, and I quelled a small sigh.

Liam wasn't done, though. He'd leaned closer, his hands lifted in defense if the box would potentially bite him, and peered intently at it with an expression almost of awe on his face.

"This just gets better and better," he breathed. "I hate to break this to you, Nina, but this is serious first-family shit. I don't even have a lockbox like this at my house, and we've bought our way into just about every corner of the Magic Kingdom that we could. Can you take the letter out? Carefully?"

I nodded, feeling strangely apprehensive as I reached into the box, sliding the photographs to the side and picking up the letter. It seemed smaller than I remembered it, but I pulled the pages free of their envelope and counted them quickly. They were all there, fourteen sheets of closely scribed writing in my mother's academic hand.

"You want to read it?" I asked, and Liam nodded. He held up his phone. "First I want to photograph it. I'm surprised you never did."

Now it was my turn to shrug, though my cheeks warmed a little with embarrassment at the obvious oversight. "The letter wasn't for me. I don't even understand it. It's written in such a way that it's not like a conversation from my mom. It's more like, I don't know, some kind of report. I don't want to keep it, I just want to deliver it." I made a face. "Or I did, anyway."

"Fair enough." Liam watched as I set the pages out in neat order, then he reached into his pack, bringing out two handfuls of quartz shards, each the size of my thumb. He transferred them to me, and I grunted with their unexpected weight. "Place one of these on each page, to keep them in place," he directed.

When I did that and stepped back, Liam leaned over the first page, positioning his phone to take the first picture. He turned the device around and scowled down at the screen.

"Oh, for fuck's sake. It's warded," he complained. "I've seen this sort of thing before. It's basically ink that doesn't have enough contrast to be seen by a camera's eye, even if it can be read by the *human* eye. You won't be able to copy this unless you do it by hand, so that leaves reading it. I'm pretty fast, but—that's what we're looking at."

"We can analyze it later in detail," Frost said. "Hit the high points."

"Noted." Liam dropped his finger until it was only a couple of inches off the page and started skim reading the words I'd gone through myself more than a dozen times. I folded my arms, then unfolded them and shoved my fists into my pockets, reassuring myself that the small pouch was still there, then pulled my hands free and shook them out, hooking my thumb into my back pocket to feel the heavy weight of the dull-bladed athame as Liam finally spoke.

"Okay, we start with a Dear Mom and Dad kind of feel, though there's no name used. Then she immediately goes into Nina's exploits as a little girl, all of it normal—walking, talking, learning fast, typical Mom shit... Kind of strikes me as a 'look how normal my little girl is' speech."

"Maybe I *was* normal then," I suggested. "The first time I saw a monster, I was old enough to know what it was—or at least that it wasn't ordinary. I could definitely talk and understand my surroundings."

"Yup, agreed. Second entry seems to be several months later, and then we've got a break, here."

He flapped a hand at no one in particular, and Frost

stepped forward, handing him a stack of cards. Tyler tossed a pen across the table, and Liam picked it up, his gaze never leaving the letter as he scrawled a note. "Same entry, but her handwriting shifts, gets more intense. Nina's first monster attack outside the house, looks like."

"How old?" Grim asked abruptly. I looked up to find all the guys staring at me.

"I honestly don't know. That one I remember, but not well. It was some sort of giant spider—we had several of them in the shed behind the house that I'd always thought were enormous. But this one kept coming for me, and once it got all the way into the light, I figured out it was anything but normal."

Liam whistled softly beneath his breath, scanning the page. "Maybe four years old? It's not dated, but given the way she's describing your motor skills, even if you were an early bloomer, four sounds about right."

"Okay," I agreed. "Is that significant?"

"No. Your Mom is writing with more agitation, but pride. A lot of pride. And then we've got some math equations outta nowhere that make zero sense..." Liam scrawled down more notes. "Then we have another fight, this one talking about a concerted response on your part, Nina. Mom was pissed here."

I smiled a little ruefully. "I got hurt pretty bad. I...can't remember that one at all. Those scars are some of the ones that never healed."

I could feel the guys' focus on me, but I kept my gaze on Liam. "I don't remember her being as mad as she seemed in that letter, for the record. She started training me more after that, finding YouTube videos, getting weapons, but that's it. I was maybe...six or so?"

Liam made a note and kept scanning. The rest of the

letter read more of the same. Reports of my improving skills written sometimes with defiant tones, sometimes almost apologetic, and then more equations and even bits of gobbledy-gook words that Liam duly recorded as he encountered them. Nothing, in all of it, indicated who Mom was writing to or anything about her past.

He'd almost gotten to the twelfth page when Zach huffed out a soft breath. "Don't move. We've got monsters at the door."

I froze. The guys did too, only our eyes swiveling. "How in the hell..." Frost growled. "That shouldn't be possible."

"On several levels," Liam agreed. Once again, he sounded more excited than concerned, but then—Liam.

Given where I was standing, it took me longer than the others to fully pivot toward the door. As I did, the thing shifted forward. Grim muttered a curse, and Tyler gave a low, dark chuckle.

"Looks like your spiders missed you, Nina," he murmured, and I stared in absolute shock as a spider the size of a smart car spilled into the doorway to the war room, its long, hairy legs waving, its mandibles clicking with sharp, percussive urgency.

Tyler spoke a harsh-edged Latin curse. Fire slashed toward the door.

"No!" I shouted, but it was too late. The abdomen of the spider ripped open—and a dozen spiders the size of bowling balls hurtled into the room.

14

___

"*Crap!*"

That exclamation was all I could manage before the spider tsunami engulfed us. I couldn't even pull my athame out—let alone free up my real knife—before I was forced back against the table, the spiders churning, crawling, leaping over each other to gain purchase on my boots and legs. Scrabbling up onto the tabletop, I grabbed the nearest heavy crystals weighing down the last few pages of my mother's letter and started whacking at the creatures as Tyler continued shouting in Latin and Liam's hands burst into flames.

Did Liam have insertables in his wrists that allowed him to shoot fire? If so, I was definitely a fan, as he let fly with two jagged flaming bolts that swept the floor, incinerating the nearest spiders. Unfortunately, they kept coming. Only Grim and Frost could make meaningful headway toward the mother spider as they punched baby spiders to the left and right, fists flying as they struggled forward. The two of them converged on the giant spider in the center, pushing it out into the main library and sending it sprawling across the floor.

Unfortunately, that wasn't the end of our troubles. As the spider flopped over, a second wave of arachnids poured out of it, these barely larger than our fists, and twice as fast as their bowling ball cousins. I squeaked in alarm as this new tide flowed out, racing not just toward the four of us, but spreading out over the room, crawling up the stacks of books and skittering across the shelves.

"You're gonna need one hell of an exterminator," Zach shouted, his grim humor punctuating the fight. I finally ditched the crystals and went for my blades—both the athame and my regular iron knife. We kept bashing, stomping, and murdering spiders while Tyler's Latin spells grew longer and more complex. More effective too. Spiders started erupting in a grid-like pattern, blasting upward and then dissolving in a shatter of sparks.

"Mind the books!" Frost reminded him.

Tyler huffed a sharp laugh. "Everyone's a critic."

"Guys!" Liam said, drawing our attention back to him despite all the whacking, burning, and exploding going on. He stood over the corpse of the spider mother, a corpse that gave every appearance of still being alive. It twitched and convulsed toward him, making him jerk back, his hands going up in defense.

"I don't think she's finished yet," he warned, and sure enough, a new ripple shuddered across what was left of the spider's abdomen. From the gaping rip in her belly, a sea of tiny heads and scurrying legs broke free.

"Wait a minute," Liam blurted, and he turned and sprinted back into the war room, leaving us to contend with the third wave of spiderlings. He was back within seconds holding a blinking electronic gadget high. "I bet..." He depressed a button on the gadget and...the spider disappeared.

Not just collapsed or expired, but *disappeared*, along with all its baby spiders, from the itsy-bitsy bastards to the few remaining bowling ballers.

As quickly as the battle had begun, it was over.

Liam looked across the room at us.

"Anyone hurt?" he asked.

"Other than my heart about stopping, no, I think I'm good," Zach said, checking his arms for spider bites. To my surprise, I hadn't been bitten either, which, considering the swarm and the size of our attackers, was kind of remarkable.

Grim put a name to it first. "Illusion magic," he said, sounding disgusted. He excelled at that.

"*Powerful* illusion magic," Liam agreed. "Able to be cast inside the library. Which, I gotta tell you—"

"Is warded to its foundation," Frost bit off.

"More to the point," Tyler said slowly, "illusion magic is forbidden on campus."

I frowned at him. "What do you mean, forbidden?" I asked. "I thought you guys were an equal opportunity magic academy."

Tyler shook his head. "That sounds like a good idea, but think about our original charter, to fight monsters. Back in the day, we had lots of other magical disciplines on campus as well, and some of our founding fathers were gifted illusionists. It's considered one of the highest forms of magic to create something that isn't there and make someone believe in it."

"I've had entire relationships based on that principle," Liam said drily, and Tyler grinned at him, then kept going.

"But on a monster campus, it was all too easy to create

monsters, much like what we just had here, to distract the hell out of the students, and once that was done..."

"The illusionists took advantage? Like, what—they stole stuff?" A sharp jab of anxiety poked at me, and I glanced over to the war room. "Oh, no."

Everyone had the same idea I did, and we all pivoted as one. Liam, the closest to the door, dove into the room. His curse told the story.

"What the actual *fuck*?" he snarled. "Someone has stolen Nina's letter."

We all crowded in behind him as he emerged from behind the table, holding up two pages. "These were on the ground, blown off somehow."

I grimaced. "I took the crystals off them at the start of the fight. Sorry, I needed weapons."

"Don't apologize—at least we still have these." Liam scowled down at the sheets. "Fuck."

"But who?" Zach demanded. "How?"

"How is right," Frost followed up, sounding even more pissed.

"That's the entire nature of illusion magic," Tyler put in, sounding thoughtful. "To distract you and then strike."

"No. You don't understand," Frost said angrily. "Nobody can break down the wards of Lowell Library. This building has existed since the academy was founded. It has the best security of any building on campus other than the main administration building and the arena. You just don't waltz in here and throw magic around."

"I hate to be the contrarian here," Zach put in, "but we just had a full-on demon attack in the library, like, yesterday. I doubt that was allowed in the original charter either."

"That's different. The horde came in on the backs of students and their professor," Frost said. "Students and staff are trackable. Eventually, we would be able to go through and identify which ones were possessed, but possessions aren't really a danger to the library as much as they are to the persons being possessed. The demons had limited power over anything except the students. The library wards were created primarily to protect the contents of the building, not its occupants at any given time."

"Well, good to see that we have our priorities in order," Liam observed drily.

"You're missing the point," Frost began, but Liam waved him off.

"Oh no, I get exactly what you're saying. We've had a breach in a place that shouldn't be able to be breached. By an individual we didn't see, and who I'm betting won't show up on the cameras, if their magic is as good as I think it is."

"Our necromancer?" Tyler asked. "The asshole behind the Boston Brahmin attacks from last week? Those originated out of Boston Public Garden, so right in our backyard."

"Very possibly, but it's worse than that," Frost said. "I don't think anyone strong enough to breach the halls of Lowell Library constrains themselves to one type of magic."

"So you're saying we have a multihyphenate. How very first family of us," Liam drawled.

Once again, Liam's sense of humor pricked Frost's nerves. He glared at Liam across the room. "I'm saying that the only person who could do such a thing is either a member of the first families or someone hired by a first family. Either way, it's not a good situation. The academy wasn't built to defend itself against its own."

We all digested that for a second. It wasn't a tasty consideration.

"Who on campus will know about this breach, or who would ordinarily know?" Tyler asked at length.

"The board, typically," Frost said. "This one, of course, won't show up on any computer scan since it didn't trip any of our wards. The intruder was essentially a ghost. *Not* an actual ghost," he snapped as Liam opened his mouth, then shut it with a smirk.

Tyler considered the doorway to the war room. "So the only people who know we've been breached are in this room and the bad guy."

"Correct," Frost said. "I don't see how that helps us, though."

But Liam was already turning toward Tyler, his eyes gleaming. "You think we can set a trap," he said.

Tyler nodded. "We still have the last two pages of Nina's letter. Whoever stole the rest of it may well realize that, especially if it cuts off in the middle of a passage."

"Which it does," Liam said, studying the letter. "Unfortunately, it cuts off at a kind of important moment, all about how Nina is going to grow up to be the biggest, baddest monster hunter the world has ever seen. Depending on the mood of the person reading the letter, that could be good or bad news. Anyone reading that would assume there's gonna be a clear and present danger with Nina coming to Boston. That might pull someone out of the woodwork on its own, no trap required."

"But they already know about me, right?" I protested. "I mean, the illusionist came into the library for a reason. Wouldn't that reason be to steal my mom's letter?"

"Possibly, or it was just a crime of opportunity. Somebody trying to mess with us."

"Well, they succeeded," Frost muttered.

"I mean, think about it," Liam said, returning the final

two pages of the letter to the table, then tapping them. "Bad guy makes it into the library, sees us all heads down over this thing, and devises a plan on the spot. Once he or she reads the letter, maybe he'll sell it, maybe he'll contact us for ransom, maybe he'll burn it in effigy on the central quad."

"Oh my God," I muttered. I hadn't thought about the letter being destroyed. The very idea of that made my stomach pitch.

"You think they'd do that?" Tyler asked, and Liam shook his head.

"Not even remotely. Most likely this guy is from a very old, very badass family, given his mad skillz at breaking down the library's wards. He may know who Janet Cross was or have the magic to suss it out. And that, unfortunately, puts him a giant step ahead of us, which isn't great, but he won't destroy the letter. If anything, he'll kick his own ass for not securing the whole thing."

He dropped his gaze to the remaining pages of the letter, scanning quickly. "More of the same—proud, almost defiant warnings about Nina's developing skills, and even a note of hope here, that...hmm. This doesn't make sense."

I nodded, knowing this part of the letter by heart. "*She's not what you think she is. She's more, she's stronger. She could change everything—for us, too. Think about that,*" I finished for him. "I have no freaking idea what that means. It's almost, I don't know..."

"Mercenary," Grim put in, and I winced, my cheeks heating as I endeavored not to look at anyone in the room.

"It does sound...kind of calculating," Zach agreed. I felt him push at the barriers in my mind, seeking to comfort me. I didn't want comfort, though. I only wanted answers.

"Yeah, I know." I nodded. "It didn't exactly leave me

warm and fuzzy. And that's the last thing she said. The letter ends after that."

"Hmm..." Liam said, his gaze back on the sheets, rereading.

Frost's phone chimed, an insistent, high-pitched alert tone I hadn't heard before, impossible to ignore. He issued a sharp, expressive curse as he fished the device out of his pants pocket. His mood didn't improve as he scanned the screen.

"What in fuck's name are they thinking?" he groused.

Before Liam could provide a potential response, Frost gestured his phone toward us. "We've been called into a meeting with Symmes and his cronies at Wellesley Hall. All of us. Let's go."

15

This was my first visit to Wellesley Hall, a small, unassuming building just off the main quad of campus. By my reckoning, it was the exact center of the old campus, including the monster quad. The building was made of gray, rugged-looking stone and possessed only one story with a high pitched roof. Gargoyles presided over the two visible corners of the roofline, and were positioned over the front door as well. As with many of the other buildings on campus, embedded strips of wrought iron flanked the doorway and lined the porch.

"This is nice," I allowed as we approached. Liam nodded beside me, looking up with a similar air of appreciation, though I had no doubt he'd been in and out of this building dozens of times during his years on campus. He seemed to study everything as if for the first time, no matter how familiar it was to him. It was a good trait.

"Believe it or not, this wasn't the first building they built on campus. That was a barracks for hunters, which they put up right after the," he said. "When Wellington Academy was founded, Boston was in the middle of being overrun with magic. Something about the city proved particularly tasty to monsters, and the academies evolved to handle it. First Twyst, then Wellington, then a handful of others. Some of them still exist, some have died out, and some have gone underground."

I slanted him a glance. "More underground than Wellington Academy? It's not like you guys do much advertising."

He snorted. "No, but those who need to know can find out about us easily enough. You did, after all. And maybe your mom before you, even if she wasn't a student. It's just not reasonable that someone with your monster hunting abilities doesn't have any connection with the academy. That may be why we've been called here now."

Frost huffed an irritated sigh beside us, the first noise he'd made since ordering us to Wellesley Hall. "I sincerely wish that were the case. It would be far more useful. Still, I expect there will be something to learn here. Just don't argue with them, and let's get through it. We need to return to Lowell Library as soon as possible to secure it. I don't like the idea that its wards were so easily breached."

"Maybe not so easily," Liam countered. "Maybe we're just facing a magician of epic skills."

"As always, Mr. Graham, your insights fail to uplift me. I suggest you endeavor to listen more than you talk."

Behind Frost's back, Liam and Tyler exchanged a smirk, but they didn't say anything more as we entered the building. There was no attendant to greet us and barely any sound at all in the old building, except for the faint murmur of conversation deeper within. We moved down a long hallway, and I noted several sitting rooms off to either side, all of them decorated in a stuffy Victorian style. Exactly what you would expect in an academy that had been founded in the

1800s and maintained by people who wished we were still living in the 1800s, I suspected.

"Commander Frost." I looked ahead to see Mr. Symmes standing at the end of the hallway in front of a wide doorway.

Frost nodded. "Mr. Symmes," he acknowledged. Tall, thin, and well-dressed, a man of harsh angles from the cut of his suit to the sharpness of his features, Symmes looked at the rest of us as we approached, but his face remained impassive. There was no excitement in his gaze or even concern. He looked resolute. Satisfied, I decided. A man who'd been waiting for this moment for a long time and was now happy it had arrived. He gestured us into the room, and the only indication I had about the unusual nature of the group assembled beyond was the sharp intake of breath from both Tyler and Liam. Coincidentally, Tyler and Liam were also the two members of our group who had family in the area. In the *very immediate* area, as it happened.

Theodore Perkins stood before a bank of windows at the far end of the room, ramrod straight in an impeccably tailored black suit with an honest-to-God cravat at his neck. Somehow, he managed to pull off the incredibly pretentious style, and he nodded at Tyler, assessing his son with shrewd eyes. If the elder Perkins hadn't noticed Tyler's development before now, I got the feeling he picked up on it as we'd entered the room.

Since Tyler and I had first met, he'd leveled up both in skills and in physical appearance. He was bigger, stronger, and exuded an air of charisma that was unmistakable to me —and apparently to his father as well. I'd helped Tyler reach that new level, too. I straightened my own shoulders, lifting my chin. I might be a rogue, untrained monster hunter, but I was an important part of this team.

The scrutiny Liam received, however, was nowhere near as approving. An older, slender woman with a pronounced similarity in features to Liam, dressed in an elegant, champagne-colored suit, her caramel-and-blonde hair perfectly styled in a long bob, gave him little more than a passing glance before focusing on Tyler. She too seemed to notice the difference in Tyler, and her mouth tightened. Then her gaze went to Zach and Grim, and rested finally on me. If she was surprised that I stared right back at her, clearly having watched her assessment of the room, she didn't seem to care. Her brows lifted slightly, her gaze imperious. She said nothing.

The other members of the room, I hadn't seen before. I'd halfway expected Mrs. Pendleton of the neighborhood watch squad to be here, but apparently she was merely a lieutenant and these players all generals. Two men and another woman regarded us with a frosty hauteur that had probably been ingrained in them since birth. Mr. Symmes made the introductions.

"I believe most of you know Tyler's father, Theodore Perkins, and Claudia Graham as well, Liam's mother," he said quickly, dispensing with more formal speech, something that Mr. Perkins seemed to take in stride, but Mrs. Graham noticed with disapproval, her lips thinning slightly.

"In addition we have Meredith Choate, Marcus Wellesley, and Anderson Reid, all of whom we are indebted to, and their families before them, for the academy's strength and security."

He leveled a look at Frost. "Security which now appears to be in your hands, pitched against an enemy who is rapidly approaching."

Beside me, I could tell Liam was almost bursting to ask the questions for which he desperately needed answers. He visibly restrained himself as Frost replied, "The collective is ready to serve."

The word collective made the entire group stiffen, and I watched with interest as the old guard of Wellington Academy exchanged glances. Did they know what the collective meant? Did they know specifically what *my* involvement with the collective meant? I deeply hoped not.

"We have fast-tracked waiving your team's requirements for graduation," Symmes said briskly. "Since you are effectively fighting monsters now, there's no need for anything but the final ritual. We're moving ahead with that now."

"Alastair, no. Traditions must be honored," Claudia Graham insisted. "You cut corners at your peril. You always have. The presentation must take place, at the very least. Only then can we proceed with the graduation ritual. That rule is inviolate. And now more than ever, we need to abide by them."

Mrs. Choate grimaced, but Mr. Reid nodded with resignation and Mr. Wellesley stepped forward slightly to emphasize his agreement. "Claudia is right. We don't know what other families are in play, but you can rest assured they will hold us accountable if we don't follow the protocols and something goes awry." His words were rough and graveled, as if he wasn't used to speaking, and Symmes sighed.

"We've gone over this," he said. "There isn't enough time."

"Of course there's time," Claudia sniffed. "You simply haven't applied yourself to the organization of it. I will take charge."

Nobody argued with her. I got the feeling nobody ever argued with her much.

She didn't stop there either. She turned and pinned

Liam with a stern look. "You were attacked," she said. "Recently. What was the nature of that assault?"

I barely managed not to gape at her as I processed how she could possibly have known about what had happened to Liam. Then again, he'd been inserted with any number of toys to help augment his magic. How difficult would it have been for one of those toys to be a monster-attack tracker as well?

Answer? Not very difficult at all. I suddenly developed an intense and deep dislike of Claudia Graham, but Liam answered without rancor, his voice polite and even.

"An illusionist," he said.

Much like the term collective, the reference to an illusionist elicited an immediate response from the room. Frost tightened his lips, clearly pissed that Liam had dropped this piece of information, whereas Symmes's eyes widened. Liam's mother and Wellesley drew themselves up almost painfully, and Meredith Choate gave a small, startled cry.

"The Hallowell family?" she squeaked. "Is it possible?"

"No, it's *not* possible," Mr. Reid answered heavily. "Their line has long since removed themselves from any magical undertakings with the academy so that they can function in private industry, which they have done quite successfully. There would be no reason for them to trouble us here. The agreements that were struck are set in stone."

He spoke with such authority that it was clear he intended his words to be taken as gospel. Too bad this wasn't a group of true believers. More to the point, a strange shiver rolled through me at the name of the family he mentioned. *Hallowell.* Deep in my mind, my mother's cry resurfaced, warning me away from the very collective I'd recently joined. Four warriors, bonded as a team, working together. I needed to run if I ever encountered them, and run fast. *Hallowell.*

As if she could hear my thoughts, Claudia turned her gaze to me and spoke. "But the girl here is looking for her family. A girl of unusual talent and ability. Who better to be that family than one who basically owned all things magical in Boston back when all the trouble began?"

"That's ridiculous," Symmes insisted, batting her suggestion away. "By your own logic, if the Hallowells had lost one of their own, don't you think they would have moved heaven and earth to find her? And we haven't been completely remiss. We have our own agents in place watching the Hallowells and their activities. Much as we assume they are watching us as well, all is fair in business. But Anderson is right. The agreements that were struck with the Hallowell family were executed amicably to great mutual benefit. If they had any issue with the academy, they would simply raise it in the normal course of action and we would accommodate them. They know this as well as you do."

I felt a different set of eyes on me and turned to see Theodore Perkins studying me with new interest. Apparently, he wasn't convinced my arrival had nothing to do with the Hallowell family.

"Well, where does the Hallowell family live?" I asked, unable to keep the hope from my voice. "Are they still in Boston?"

"Absolutely not," Symmes said, throttling my enthusiasm. "They relocated to upstate New York at the time of the agreement, a century ago. The only conversation we've had with them since then has been through intermediaries, as the agreement dictated."

"Well, if not them, then who?" Claudia demanded. "It's

not as if we have master-level illusionists coming out our ears."

"And thank God for that," Wellesley put in.

"We will search the rolls." Symmes turned to Liam. "This is excellent information. An illusionist on the level of the Hallowell family explains a lot. The recent monster sightings, the demon attack and subsequent destruction on campus... Some of that could have been mere fantasy, conjured up to keep us hopping. We'll need to act fast."

"What if it's not fantasy?" Tyler countered. "What if there really is a monster invasion on the way?"

Symmes exhaled. "Time was, I wouldn't have thought it possible. For all your disdain for your Dean Robbins, his information is not incorrect. Monster sightings and interactions have gone down dramatically these past generations. Not enough to remove the minor entirely, but certainly enough to limit the way we behave. I can't say the same for powerful magicians. Perhaps those are the monsters we should be fighting against."

Grim muttered something under his breath that I couldn't quite catch, and no one paid him any attention. In fact, it seemed as if the old guard of Wellington Academy were doing their level best not to look at him at all.

"So Dean Robbins *is* working with you?" Tyler asked abruptly. "You trust him?"

"Of course we trust him," Symmes said, his tone measured. "His loyalty is impeccable, and his discretion inviolate."

Tyler looked like he was going to argue when Frost cut in. "We'll start the search. We'll also explore every avenue to determine the identity of the illusionist, including any potential connection with the Perkins family since he used you all to make his initial point."

Theodore Perkins nodded sharply. "That slight was personal, and we have made our share of enemies. That should narrow the list."

Symmes glanced back to Frost. "Excellent. Meanwhile, despite my misgivings, I'm forced to agree with Claudia. To ensure you're all prepared for the battle to come, your graduation requirements will be waived for all but two inviolate elements: the presentation and the final ritual."

I wrinkled my brow at the repeated word. "Presentation? Like some kind of a parade?"

To my surprise, Symmes nodded gravely. "Exactly like a parade, Ms. Cross. We are a product of our Victorian-era founding, and Victorians enjoyed nothing more than a grand show of strength—and if music and dancing were involved, so much the better. We'll get you the information you need to prepare as soon as possible. In the meantime, keep a sharp eye. Whether we're being attacked by magic or monsters, the enemy is at our very door."

16

We had barely exited Wellesley Hall when Frost began giving orders. "Tyler and Liam, I need you back at Lowell Library," he began.

Liam raised a hand. "That would be negatory. Family matters to attend to first. You may not have picked up on Claudia's death glare, but you can bet I did."

"What are you talking about?" Frost blustered, but Liam waved him off, his face grim.

"You can bet if the old battle-ax wants to talk to me, it's going to have some bearing on our upcoming monster campaign. Permission to take Nina with me? Because I have a feeling she's going to want to learn it too. She may even make my mom unbend a little, which would be a miracle of the modern age."

Frost breathed out an irritated breath. "Okay. But I need you back at the library as early as possible. We've got things to do."

"And may I remind you that you have two amazingly elevated monster hunters, courtesy of one Nina Cross, already at your disposal. I suggest, if you're not doing anything else, that you figure out exactly how super special their powers now are. Because I'd be willing to bet they're way bright shinier than mine, even in the ward-building department."

It was as close as I'd ever heard Liam get to insubordination, and he sounded genuinely rattled. Frost apparently thought so too. He scowled at Liam. "Are you okay?"

Liam shrugged. "I will be once I get to the bottom of things," he said. "You go handle your crazy, and I'll handle mine."

That seemed to satisfy Frost, and he jabbed a sharp finger at Zach. "What do you know about electronics?" he asked, and I stifled a laugh. Zach had single-handedly dismantled Mrs. Pendleton's camera brigade in my apartment. I was pretty sure he'd be able to handle anything Frost threw at him.

Grim didn't wait for an assignment.

"I'm going to check the perimeter," he said. "If we have an illusionist at work, he should have been caught well before he reached Lowell Library."

"Agreed." Frost turned to him. "Report back whatever you find, as soon as you find it. And keep in touch. Also, I don't buy the bullshit that Dean Robbins is on the up-and-up. Symmes and the others may think he's their flunky, but that doesn't sit right. There's something else going on, and until we figure it out, don't underestimate him. Try to avoid him even more."

The guys all nodded at that, and the three groups peeled away—Frost, Zach, and Tyler heading back to Lowell Library, Grim heading for some obscure "perimeter," and Liam and me heading...I had no idea where.

Liam seemed to have a plan, though, and he set off at a quick stride, not looking back. We didn't talk until we'd reached the gates of Wellington Academy and stepped onto the public sidewalk.

"Sorry about that," he finally said. "But I needed to shake them, stat. I didn't feel like playing Frost's flunky while he shored up library security. I honestly don't think the illusionist is going to bother with that place again. He got what he wanted."

"The letter," I sighed.

"Actually, I think that was just a collateral win for him. Like I said, a crime of opportunity. I think the main goal of the illusionist was to get under our skin. The whole thing kind of smacked of a taunt more than anything else. Nobody was hurt, you know? Even with illusion magic, you can pack a punch that takes out a person, and our guy didn't do that. He's playing with us because he can."

"You think so?"

"I do think so, because it's exactly what I'd do if I had the opportunity. People who are smart like to show off. It's a hazard of the profession."

"So where does that leave us? Where are we going?"

"You tell me." He turned and grinned at me, cocking a Sherlockian brow. "You're the one who had the answer all along. You just didn't know it. I didn't know it either because I didn't make the connection, which proves I'm not as smart as I think I am. I've got some catching up to do."

I made a face. "Once more for the cheap seats?"

"When you first met Tyler and you guys ended up fighting the *Magla Gušter*, you took Tyler back to your place right? Remember that?"

"Vaguely," I allowed. "I was a little beat up that night."

"Yup, you were. Back then, we were still trying to figure out what your deal was, so Tyler told me about your conversation and the stuff about your mom."

"Okayyy." I couldn't summon up annoyance at Tyler's betrayal of my confidence, because what I told him hadn't been in confidence, exactly. I'd given the guy my life story, more or less. Of course he wanted to share it with his best friend. "I told him how she died and what little I knew about her past in Boston, if that's what you're getting at."

"The second part, absolutely." Liam nodded. "Her time up here in Boston. She said she was a teacher, and the school she mentioned was..."

I blinked at him, suddenly getting my bearings of where we were headed, both in conversation and on foot. "Beacon Hill Preparatory Academy," I said "Well, I hate to break it to you, but that school is a nonstarter. It's been closed for over a hundred years."

"It was closed almost *exactly* a hundred years ago," Liam said cheerfully. "Funny you should mention that. You know what else happened a hundred years ago? The Hallowell family left town. They ran the Beacon Hill Preparatory Academy for Exceptional Women. It was synonymous with the family, at least among our exceptionally exclusive circle. I can't say as to whether or not any of the women who graduated from there were truly all that exceptional, but it wasn't for lack of trying."

By this time, I was staring at him. "Are you serious? Beacon Hill Prep was run by the Hallowell family?"

"Yup. A little-known fact of the great and magical families of Boston, of which I know far too much, courtesy of one overzealous Claudia Graham. I know every family in the city with ties to the magic academies. Hell, I probably know the evil bad illusionist-slash-necromancer-slash-all-around-asshole that we're looking for right now who is supposedly about to bring a monster apocalypse to our door. If I were a little smarter, I'd already be able to give you his name, but at the very least, we can figure out your connection—or at least your mom's connection—to the Hallowell family. I'm an idiot for not thinking of it sooner."

"Well, how would you?" I countered. "My mom's name was Janet Cross, not Hallowell."

"Yup, and I'd convinced myself that much of what she'd told you about your past was a lie—but I forgot that the best lies are those that contain a kernel of truth. And I think this particular kernel may turn into a nugget of gold."

We argued back and forth about what the possibilities could be as we made our way across the sun-drenched, tree-lined streets of the Beacon Hill district. It was another predictably gorgeous day in Boston, with lots of people out and about, the streets choked with cars. But walking by Liam's side, it was as if there was nobody but the two of us, arguing arcane mysteries from a century ago. The attraction I had for him stirred up all my slumbering butterflies, but I snapped off the overhead light in their cage just as quickly. This wasn't the time.

Liam seemed to be struggling with no such concerns. "I'm telling you, it's gotta be one or the other. Either your mom was somehow connected to a long-lost remnant of the Hallowells and she believed you were a throwback to their former greatness, or her connection is much more recent than that. She didn't just pick this school out of thin air to mention to you. She didn't write that letter for no reason. That letter makes perfect sense if you wanted to impress a family that was known as one of the top magic makers in Boston. Believe me, I'm a member of such a family, and we love nothing more than to impress each other and ourselves. Like Reid said, it doesn't make a hell of a lot of sense that she's some randomly missing daughter, like from the last twenty years. The Hallowell family wouldn't exactly lose their own kid."

"But there's that headstone," I reminded him.

"*Somebody* knew about her, yeah. But the more I think about that, the more I'm convinced that's also the work of our friendly neighborhood illusionist. The rock itself was real, but how closely did we look at the thing to make sure the name was etched on it or merely affixed there as an overlay glamour? Some of those can be pretty sophisticated, and Grim beat the shit out of the headstone before we got a chance to look too closely."

"He did," I agreed. "But back to Mom. Why the cloak-and-dagger, then? If she wanted her family to know about me, why didn't she just tell them? They sound like they're kind of rich and awesome."

"That would be the million-dollar question," Liam agreed. "Because you're right. The Hallowells are rich, awesome, and insanely powerful. That said, if your mom had done something to piss them off, like oh, say, steal their granddaughter away, she may have been a little uncertain of their reception of her. Especially since she didn't try to reach out when she got sick."

I stumbled, Liam's comment catching me off guard.

"Crap, you're right. She had cancer. She was the daughter of a magical family and she got cancer, and she didn't reach out for help. Not even to her family who, at a minimum, would have been able to get her the best care money could buy."

"That and more," Liam agreed. "They may even have been able to magically reverse the illness, though cancer is a bitch no matter what your superpowers are. She also didn't reach out to your dad, assuming she knew who he was, which I'm betting she did."

"She didn't contact him," I agreed. "Or anyone, really. She didn't even like going to the doctor, because she didn't like people in her business. They told me that she had a high concentration of heavy metals in her system they couldn't quite explain, but that wasn't what killed her."

"Heavy metals," Liam said. "Huh."

That train of thought was effectively derailed as we came around the final corner to the disheveled section of Beacon Hill that housed the Beacon Hill Preparatory Academy. In the daylight it looked only slightly more civilized than it had when I'd used it as a backdrop for hacking up a ghoul. The rioting overgrowth that spilled over the stone wall looked merely quaint, not creepy, and the metal placard that announced the name of the academy remained barely visible where I'd pushed away the greenery.

Liam moved up to the gate and tried it. It was, of course, locked tight.

"I don't suppose you have a lockpick that works on century-old gates, do you?" I asked, only half joking. Liam nodded, which was why I was only half joking.

"It's an equal-opportunity lockpick set. Something else I need to put a patent on, the moment I get a chance."

He brought his pack around and pulled out the small set of tools. It took him longer to find the lock on the rusted old gate than it did to jimmy it free, and he pushed the gate open with a rebellious creak.

"This is where things get a little trickier," he said as we stepped through. "I've got my own set of personal wards, and they're good, but these are the Hallowells we're talking about. They would have some protections in place to keep out any assholes."

We continued walking, our steps slow and measured along a cobblestone street that was now overgrown with weeds sticking up through the seams in the stones. The air was close and quiet here, the trees pressing in from either side of the narrow lane.

"What sort of protections?" I asked. "Like a security team? Some sort of alert system?"

Liam shook his head. "Nothing that obvious," he said, stepping from stone to stone. "The Hallowells prized secrecy over everything else. They didn't want anybody in their business."

I snorted. "They're sounding more and more like my mom all the time."

"Exactly. So anything they would put in place would be tailor-made to hide the evidence. Something like…"

He stepped forward, and a strange whoosh of air burst up as he sank ever so slightly down.

"Oh, *shit*—" he began.

The street dropped away beneath us.

17

We fell for what seemed like way too long and landed hard on a floor that thankfully had a blessed amount of give to it. In fact, it wasn't even a floor, but more like...

"Wood chips," Liam blurted, feeling around in the dark. I heard the shooshing of fabric that betrayed him pulling his pack around, and a second later, a powerful flashlight flared to life.

"Wood chips," he repeated, "and I can't tell how old they are. But clearly, the Hallowells didn't want to kill anybody from the fall alone, so score one for them."

I peered up, confused at the inky blackness that arched over us. "There was a hole. We fell into a hole," I protested. "How come it's dark?"

Liam angled his light up, revealing that the roof was very much intact over us.

"Hmmm. It must have been a hinged mechanism. We didn't hear it snap shut, maybe because we were too busy wondering if we were going to die."

He flashed his light over toward me, making me flinch.

"Hey, congratulations to us. We didn't die. Though this wasn't exactly what I meant when I said I wanted to get to the bottom of things."

I grimaced. "Okay, but...how do we get out of here?"

"Ordinarily, I'd say we wouldn't. The groundskeepers would have sent up the alert to the Hallowells the next time they did their rounds, and we'd be collected in due course. I suspect this particular property hasn't had groundskeepers for a long time. That argues for a more mechanized alert system, probably with cameras, because if some sort of wild boar...wait a minute. No."

I could almost picture Liam tilting his head in thought, while my gaze tracked the flow of the beam as it swiped across the featureless walls. He continued, his tone more thoughtful.

"I bet the stones were geared for human weight, not kid or animal weight, so anything over, like, a hundred pounds. It would be interesting to see if they were counterbalanced against something heavier, like a car, but then again, we are talking magic..."

"Earth to Liam," I said a little sharply. "How do we get out of here?"

The insistence in my tone brought him back to the present and more pressing issue.

"Once again, my first thought is that we don't," he said. "This is an oubliette. It's where you stick somebody if you want to forget about them, as the saying goes, but certainly the intention is to keep them trapped until you make the decision on what to do."

I stared at him. "An oubliette? That seems...not awesome. I don't want to stick around here waiting to be found."

"Agreed," he said, sounding way too cheerful. A second

later, I understood why. He pulled out a gadget from his pack that looked like one of those stud finders my mom had used to hang paintings.

I peered at it. "You planning to decorate while we're here?"

Liam's response was a little rueful. "I have a habit, you could say, of getting lost in dark places. But this isn't one of those times. Little-known fact about my growing up, I spent a *lot* of time in basements. My folks stuck me down there because they didn't know what else to do with me, and I frustrated them to look at."

He spoke the words easily, but I stared at him in the darkness, unable to see his face past the glare of the light. "Your *parents* did that?" I asked, aghast. I bit my lip, wanting to cry. How was it that every time Liam let drop a detail of his past, it was more awful than the one before?

"Yup," he said, though he'd already stood and was feeling his way along the nearest wall. "But it wasn't all bad. Those basements led to subbasements that, happily enough, led to the tunnels the first families and their masons had carved into the bedrock of Boston."

"Let me know when you get to the part about them not being so bad."

He snorted. "I know I make them sound like monsters—"

I made a face, though I knew he wasn't looking at me. "Honestly? That's kind of doing a disservice to monsters."

"Well, bottom line, they really *weren't* all that bad. And I really *did* frustrate them a lot. But anyway, I also had no issue with not doing what I was told, especially when it came to cooling my heels in a basement."

He leaned down, and from the shushing sound that followed, I decided he was brushing wood chips away from the wall. "I started to explore those lower levels, and then I started to create better tools for exploration. Now I'm never without them, because, well..."

He broke off, and the answer to whatever he was going to say flowed into my mind as if I was talking to Zach, not Liam. I might not be mind melding, but I knew I was right.

"You never knew when they were going to do it, did you?" I asked, my heart twisting all over again. "That's why you always carry that backpack with you. Because you never wanted to be caught unprepared for when your family decided to be a bunch of dickheads."

"Again, it's not like I didn't understand where they were coming from. I just didn't necessarily agree with their solution to the problem."

"Ya think?"

The device in his hand gave a tiny, hushed beep, and Liam wagged his flashlight, beckoning me over.

"Bingo," he said as I hurried to his side. I peered into the darkness, seeing, well, nothing but a stone wall in front of my face.

"And bingo would be...?"

Liam tapped the softly beeping gizmo. "This little guy likes to find holes behind walls that shouldn't be there. Most of these old passageways that were man-made have false fronts, exit doors, if you will, because well, my family wasn't the first set of rich old magicians to be a bunch of douchebags. A lot of times, they'd forget people were down here working for them, hollowing out the subterranean passages of Boston's richest neighborhoods, and people could die before somebody remembered to go check on the help. Workers weren't stupid, especially those who had the modest level of power needed for these kind of jobs. They put back doors in place to protect themselves."

Well, that certainly explained why he hadn't been nervous about the fall. But the wall looked pretty solid to me, solid and made of *rock*, not wood.

"Okay," I allowed. "So do you have a lockpick for a bunch of stones jammed together?"

"I do not, as it happens, but we don't need one. Our guys were smart enough to realize they might get stuck here without the benefit of tools. If they were really smart, or really stupid, take your pick, they might also have thought they might come back one dark and murky night and hit the school for ransacking, in which case they'd want to give the combination to their buddies who were going to help them."

"Ransacking? Was that a thing?"

"More than you might think. My family might have been obnoxious, but again, it wasn't like they were the only rich people with shit to hide. What ended up happening was an old family would move out of a house and not share its secrets with those who came next. In the interim, if they'd been foolish enough to leave anything behind, maybe forgetting it altogether, which also happened more than you might think, people could get in and steal stuff they didn't understand. That's how most magical totems get set loose in the world, and it could be a bitch to get them back. Think about the necklace that caused Zach's family all the trouble with the demon horde right along with giving them supernatural skills."

I frowned. "That was a necklace his great-great-grandfather had gotten from a tinker or something, I thought." Though Liam was right. That chance acquisition had become a life-changing event for the Williams clan, creating a line of cursed demon hunters that had extended all the way down to Zach.

"Sure, but how do you think the tinker came across it?

Somewhere along the line, that thing was stolen, and a lot of times it was by the people who'd been contracted to work for the rich and spoiled. Step a little closer, and I'll show you."

While he'd been talking, Liam had been tapping the stones one at a time, moving upward in a straight line. Or not quite a straight line, actually—he was alternating stones, almost like...

"Footsteps," I blurted as he tapped the same stone he had before.

"Yup," he agreed. "Double-checked for safety, but this is the right block." He pressed his palm into the stone. It pushed in easily. A second later, a rusty set of gears turned, and a door opened in the glare of the flashlight beam with an exhale of moldy air.

"Boom," Liam said. "Measuring from the ground up, this stone marks the number of steps it took for us to get from the iron gates to the point in the street where we fell through."

I stared at him. "You were tracking the number of our *steps* while we were walking?"

"Not consciously, but yeah. Everything is a pattern, a series. When you break it down that way for as long as I have, it just becomes second nature."

"Maybe for you," I said, and he chuckled.

"Bottom line, there's a reason why it's always good to find a guy who'll hold the door open for you." He waggled his brows. "Only in this case, I'm going to need a little extra help."

He gestured me forward, and together we pushed the door open the rest of the way, then stepped into a dank passageway. We closed the door behind us, my heart giving a little lurch as the door clicked shut. "Okay, then," I muttered.

Liam flashed his light around. "You don't have anything to worry about. Where we are is infinitely better than where we were, which was a hole that could be opened up by a bad guy at any time. So we're already making progress. Best I can tell, we have about two hundred yards to the front door of the school, and I'm betting there won't be much in our way between here and there. You ready to find out?"

He didn't wait for me to answer, but tucked his gizmo back into his pack, then reached for my hand. I felt the spark of energy arc as we connected, like a string of Christmas lights flaring to life, but Liam didn't hesitate. He set off at a fast pace, hunched over with one hand carrying the flashlight, his arm stretched high and in front of him. Not only did that position the light at an ideal angle, it turned his hand into an early warning system in case the passage got tighter—which it did, twice. Score one for the benefits of experience.

"All right, here we go," he murmured. By now, we were moving more slowly, almost hunched over, but the corridor terminated in an actual door this time, complete with a lock. "Not a complete back door—these people expected to be bringing whatever fell through the street back, just not in a way that anyone could tell. That's...interesting."

I made a face in the gloom as he fished out his lockpicks. "You mean the girls, don't you? Some of their young women who maybe were tired of being exceptional and wanted out?"

"Maybe. Though I'd expect word would get out pretty quickly to the students to avoid the main entry street if they were going to make a break for it. But this passageway is too uniform and long—and it ends in a door. It had to have been used all the time."

He made short work of the lock, and this time when he opened the doorway, there was an actual floor on the other side. We stepped into a cool, mildew-smelling basement lined with empty metal shelves. There were windows set high into the walls that let in a thin trickle of light through the thick, dirty glass, and Liam clucked as if recognizing an old friend.

"You never forget that smell," he muttered, and I squeezed his hand in solidarity.

The gesture seemed to catch him off guard, and he stopped, swiveling back to me.

"Hey, I'm sorry, I didn't even ask. Are you okay? This isn't freaking you out, is it?"

"Not at all," I began, though I was so happy to have his undivided attention, I regretted my words immediately. Liam stared at me, his cheeks flushed, his body practically quivering with excitement. "I think it might be scary if you weren't here, but—you are."

"I am," he murmured, and, as if he suddenly realized we were alone, safe, and out of the dark and cramped passageway, he gave me a slow grin. "Don't get me wrong, though. Things could still get dangerous here—"

The ceiling dissolved into a sea of screeching bats.

18

"Duck!" Liam didn't have time to say any more as the creatures from the ceiling descended upon us. They were less bats than winged insects, but insects the size of small rodents, their segmented bodies and flying legs creating a gruesome counterpoint to their rapidly buzzing wings.

"What the *hell*?" I shrieked, bobbing and weaving to avoid the creatures' sharp stingers. I yanked my knives out again, but they weren't all that useful. Unlike the spiders in the library, these bastards had some bite to them, and every few feet, I yelped in pain as one of them scored a direct hit.

"This way!" Liam directed, and I followed him willingly, blindly, some distant part of my brain registering the fact that no matter how great a monster hunter I thought I was, it was impossible to combat a swarm with a couple of knives. Even if I graduated with the guys the way Symmes seemed to think we would, I *needed* those classes in spell craft.

As if reading my mind, Liam yanked me around the corner, then pivoted back, his hands going out. As it had in the library, fire erupted from his palms, and he sprayed the room beyond in three quick bursts. Instantly, the smell of roasting bugs flowed toward us, and Liam collapsed back against me, his hands practically smoking.

"Are you hurt?" I asked, and the lack of his response, mocking or otherwise, was all the answer I needed. Nothing else buzzed from the basement storage room, so I stowed my knives, then guided Liam down the hallway by the elbow until we reached the stairs. He half fell, half sat on the closest stair, resting his elbows on his knees. His palms were raw and blistered the color of charcoal.

"Um, I don't remember that from last time," I said. "What happened?"

"Nothing really," he managed with a tight smile. "I've never tried to use that particular trick twice in one day, is all. It stings a little."

"A little," I echoed. "Exactly how often do you do this to yourself? Push yourself until you bleed, or break something, or dislocate a joint, or burn your skin black?"

He shrugged, but didn't meet my gaze. "I don't really look at it that way—"

"How often?" I asked again.

Another shrug, and Liam dipped his head, the grown-up echo of the little boy who'd been shoved into basements, injected with arcane devices, tested and rejected, forgotten, belittled, tortured, and demeaned. "As often as it takes," he finally admitted, and my own throat closed up as I forced myself to swallow the sob that wanted to break free, even as his mouth creased into an achingly weary smile. "Trust me, I'm not usually the one to break first."

"I'm sure," I whispered. Swallowing hard, I reached for his backpack. "I can get in this okay, right, to get you some salve or something? You don't have your stuff password protected or anything weird like that?"

He shook his head, looking relieved to focus on anything but himself. There was no doubt this was yet another defense mechanism, one that had made him into the deceptively careless, smart-assed, shrewdly observant and yet brutally wounded warrior slumped in front of me. "You should be good. You'll want the inside pocket to the right, zipped shut. A tube of goo, not a vial. Probably close to the top, within easy reach. Just reach inside with intention. It's thought-responsive."

"Roger that," I said. Stuffing down everything else I wanted to say in favor of healing his hands more quickly, I unzipped the pocket of the pack and found an assortment of small tubes and vials. No sooner had I tucked my hand inside, than I felt one of the tubes nudge my fingers. That explained how he was able to access his toys so quickly, I thought. This was one high-tech bag.

Pulling out the tube of salve, I cracked the seal and squeezed the thick, cloudy liquid over his outstretched palms, watching as the goo dropped onto his skin and instantly liquefied, spreading fast and deep into the blistered cracks. Liam groaned.

"I don't want to say that feels better than sex, but..."

I laughed. "I get the picture." I sat beside him, peering down at the charred remains of bugs that littered the floor outside the doorway to the basement room. I didn't want to bother Liam while he was healing, but I couldn't stop the dread gnawing at my stomach.

"What the hell was that? Our illusionist again?"

"I don't think so," he sighed, surprising me. "There's the fact that the bites from these creatures genuinely hurt, and we legit seemed to startle them out of a slumber, as opposed to then swarming in with a focused attack. They looked like a variant of musk bees, sort of like rats with wings."

"Charming," I drawled.

"But most of the time, relatively harmless, although no one ever would want to stumble onto a swarm of them like we just did. They aren't aggressive, except when startled. And then, they usually seek to neutralize the threat. Enough of those bites would have rendered us unconscious, but after that..." He paused, tilting his head. "You know, I'm not sure if they'd try to eat us or not."

"Kind of an important detail, just saying."

"Either way, it's not the illusionist's work," he insisted. "Remember, that baby-making spider machine approached us. It showed up on our doorstep, not the other way around. That's the difference."

"Right." I glanced down at Liam's hands, but they still appeared as black and angry as they had a few seconds ago. "How long does it take that stuff to work?"

Liam flexed his hands and winced. "I'm still working out the formula," he admitted. "The numbing agent works like a champ, but from the looks of things, the healing side doesn't seem to be taking quite so quickly. Of the two, I'm happy enough to be numb right now."

"Agreed." I peered at his hands, frowning. "So, how did you become all Captain Flamethrower, anyway? Did you embed little chutes in your skin, and they, what, drew on your inner magic to make fire? Or how do you recharge them?"

He glanced up at me, offering me a cocky grin. "Well, I should tell you that a magician never reveals his secrets... but yeah. I've found a way to synthesize whatever magic that my tuners pull together into a highly combustible liquid, which ignites when I direct it out of my skin. Hurts like hell, so not a perfect setup, but it works."

"No pain, no flame, I guess," I muttered. "Is there anything I can do to help it heal faster?"

"Ah…" He blinked at me as our gazes met, and he looked surprised and more than a little taken aback.

"What is it?" I asked quickly. "What's wrong?"

"Nothing. Nothing's wrong. It's just…I think it's the first time someone has offered to help me."

His response was so unexpected that I gaped at him, my heart lurching sideways again. Here was this guy, this MacGyver of the collective, that everybody knew could handle himself, as long as he had his trusty pack, or, failing the pack itself, his quick wits and resourceful attitude would save the day. But even though I'd only known Liam a short while, I knew he spoke the truth. People didn't help Liam; he helped them. Ever and always.

"You're a victim of your own success," I offered softly, not knowing what else to say. "No one ever thinks you need help, I bet."

"True enough. I try pretty hard to keep it that way," he admitted, then fixed me with a warm gaze. "You didn't hesitate, though. You're always looking to help other people too."

"Well, you know. Monster hunter," I murmured, but he watched me with his soft hazel eyes as I sat back on my heels to look at his ruined hands more closely. I felt uncertain, even awkward beneath his frank gaze, the energy rolling off him intimate and intense…but vulnerable too, the two of us caught in this moment outside of time, where no one else could judge us, no one else could see.

My cheeks flushed as I lifted his hands gently, feeling the zing of energy spark from his ruined skin. "That must be kind of strange," I said, glancing up at him only to have him look quickly away. "Not having the use of your hands. Especially you."

"Yeah, it is." He flexed his fingers and winced a little. "It will take probably twenty minutes for the healing mechanism to start. I never realized how much of a liability that would be, or I would've kept tinkering with it to get that time down."

"Twenty minutes?" I frowned. "Do you think it's safe for us to be out here in the open like this, or should we try to find some place to hunker down?"

Liam blew out a breath. "Good question," he said, turning back to me and nodding to his pack. "Hit the side pocket. Let's see what the meter reader says."

Obligingly, I open his pack again, following his directions to access the reader. It was a small key-fob-size device, and I pulled it out and showed it to him.

"Button on the back," he directed, and I depressed the small button, turning the fob back over to see it register a compass-like image. The pointing arrow spun around and around, eventually settling on Liam. The register number that popped up was 95.

I blinked. "Whoa. Is that out of a hundred?"

"Ignore that. It does that all the time, an initial false reading," he said dismissively. "My subcutaneous bionic-man circuits throw it off. But what that *does* tell me is that there's nothing else stronger than me in the area. Which is good except it's not registering you either, which could mean we're screwed."

He sounded unreasonably tired, and I squinted at him. "You know, why don't we go ahead and get out of sight anyway," I said. "Or at least get to someplace where we can mount a defense if need be."

He didn't object, and I helped him to his feet again, the

two of us automatically moving up the stairs. I suspected Liam had spent more than enough time in basements for any one person, and I was a big fan of heading to a floor that at least held the possibility of a window or a door to the outside.

We ended up emerging into a surprisingly clean, barren hallway, the stark walls and dust-covered hardwood floor echoing with long-ago wealth, the walls doubtlessly once hung with gilded frames, the floor gleaming. I could *almost* see how beautiful it must have been, and I bit my lip.

"So, this illusionist thing. Tell me about that. Was that something that the Hallowells taught here as well?"

"Honestly? I have no idea," Liam said. "I knew about this school because of my parents' history lessons, but nobody had much to say about it. The exceptional young women were either quietly married off or never existed to begin with, and the whole thing was a front. But a front for what, I don't know. Our families weren't tight, mainly because the Hallowells were at a higher rung on the social ladder. Most families were."

"Yeah?" I asked, though I recalled Tyler making a similar comment about the Grahams. "I thought you guys were super magical."

"Oh we are," Liam said. "But the meritocracy of the first families goes only so far. If we'd been part of the original group that had come to Boston, we doubtless would be pretty high in the pecking order, but we came a little too late. And you better believe we've spent the last hundred and fifty years trying to make up for it. But it's not all bad. The upside is that we work harder and appreciate our successes more. We've had some pretty powerful magicians in our family, and I can't help but think we wouldn't have if we'd had a few more things handed to us. Just the nature of the beast, I guess."

"Fair enough..." We tried the first door that we came to, and it was unlocked. It opened on to a standard-size classroom with swiveling stools lined up next to dusty hardwood tables, as if the students might return at any moment to take their positions. I helped Liam to the closest table, and he sighed with genuine relief as he slid onto the stool, swiveling to rest his weight on his elbows.

"It hurts more than it should," he muttered, and I grimaced.

"Is there anything else I can do?"

His sigh was tight and a little pained. "Nah, I just need to distract myself and suck it up."

The comment was innocent enough, but it was all that was needed to spark the dormant dancing butterflies I'd been trying to shush ever since we'd left the meeting with Symmes. Wordlessly, I swiveled Liam's knees around until he faced me again, and then stepped forward, positioning myself between his knees.

"Whoa there," he said, his eyes going wide. I lifted a brow.

"I thought you wanted to be distracted?"

Before he could object, I leaned forward and brushed my lips over his.

19

The connection between us was electric, literally. Sparks jumped, and I forced myself not to lurch back, even as I savored the prickly heat.

"That's different," I murmured, and Liam huffed, his breath coming more quickly.

"I'm totally going to need to study that more," he agreed.

I kissed him again, more firmly this time, and sighed as the flow of warmth raced along my skin, heat flushing my cheeks. I lifted my hands to either side of his face, hesitating only slightly before laying my fingers on his skin. This time, there was no electrical charge, more a tingling, and I pulled back to see Liam's hazel eyes alight with interest.

"Any idea why we're doing the whole electro-twins thing?" I asked, and he shook his head.

"It doesn't hurt, though, does it?" He searched my face as if half expecting to find scorch marks. "It doesn't hurt me, though there's a bit of a bite at first. It's more surprising, I guess."

"Hmmm..." I kissed him again, more firmly this time, and touched the tip of my tongue against his lips. They parted easily at my gentle pressure, and when our tongues met, the electrical jolt was enough that we both lurched back.

"Hey!" Liam burst out with a startled laugh, though his smile was wide. "No pain, but—wow. Let's try that one again."

"Yeah?" I breathed out, but I couldn't deny that I wanted to give it another go as well. "It didn't hurt, but it—I mean, did I burn you?"

"I don't..." Liam stuck his tongue out, his eyes practically crossing as he tried to see its tip and failed miserably. I started giggling, but could at least assure him on one count.

"Your tongue isn't even a little bit red. What about mine?"

I obligingly stuck my own tongue out, and he grinned. "Not even close. So..." He tilted his head in thought, his eyes going slightly unfocused. "We're basically an electrical conduit. But a conduit for what? Has to be our innate magic, yes? It's not like we've got batteries inside us. Why would we be conducting energy that way? And how is it *I'm* conducting energy at all? I don't have innate magic. That's my whole problem. You might, you likely do, but I don't. So I can see me reacting to you, but you're feeling this too, and—"

I waited until he was finally forced to take a break in his monologue to breathe, then silenced him completely with a long and searching kiss. This time, the zing of electricity was diminished, even when our tongues tangled. If anything, we seemed to press closer together in search of that spark again, my fingers threading through his hair as Liam spread his arms wide, holding his hands clear as I dropped my hands down his back, reveling in the heat of him. Drawing my hands around his body to the front of him, I palmed the flat planes of his chest and torso, then slid my fingers down to his waist.

By then, I'd started trembling, my breath growing short and halting, my skin flushing for an entirely different reason than our strange electrostatic connection. Biting my lip, I pulled back my head as I dropped my hands lower. I watched their progress while Liam sucked in a sharp breath, his abs going taut beneath his shirt. That made it easy for me to dip my fingers into the waistband of his jeans. I glanced up to see him staring at me, the intensity in his eyes sending an entirely new heat rolling through me.

"Nina," he murmured throatily, and I smiled at the tremor in his voice, a flicker of confidence building in me. With Tyler, the earth had shaken when we'd kissed. With Zach, we'd stepped out of time, but this...was different. Power licked through me like fire and roared in my blood as I met Liam's gaze.

"So... I mean, I don't want to be forward, but..." As I spoke, I flipped the button of his jeans, reveling in Liam's sharp intake of breath. There was no question that he liked what I was doing, liked it a lot, and that only supercharged my need to do more.

"I suppose there's no need for me to tell you that you don't have to do this, right?" Liam asked, his words equal parts stressed and hesitant, though his body fairly quivered beneath my hands.

I snorted, meeting his gaze resolutely. "If I haven't made this abundantly clear, I totally want to do this. I only feel bad about taking advantage of you when you're, you know, injured."

"Well, about that," he said and he shifted, waving his hands a little to draw my attention. I followed the movement —and blinked with surprise. A tiny flare of sparks zipped along the tips of Liam's left fingers, and the deep burns in the palm of that hand seemed less violent than the right.

I whipped my gaze back to meet his. "You have got to be kidding me."

He raised a professorial eyebrow. "I can't say for sure that what you're doing is expediting the healing process, but, let me just say that for the record, if that's what's happening here, I'm a big fan. Huge."

I nodded as somberly as I could manage. "Well, I'm inclined to believe your hypothesis is correct. And it would be a travesty of the scientific process if we didn't continue to explore this line of inquiry down to its natural conclusion."

As I spoke, I moved my fingers along Liam's waistband, but he didn't make any move to stop me. In fact, he didn't do anything but groan expressively as I urged his hips nearer to me and unzipped his jeans completely. He stood, and it only took another sharp tug to drop his pants past his hipbones and stretch them across his thighs. Fortunately, Liam didn't go for the skinny jeans look, and it was short work to free him from his boxer briefs.

"Good to see that the rest of your body is onboard with our experiment," I observed as I widened my own stance, lifting Liam's shirt higher so I could trace the curves of his abdomen with a trail of kisses.

Whether Liam was no longer capable of response or simply felt the question needed no answer, I didn't know, but he didn't say anything until I reached the wispy trail of hair that pointed down to the V between his thighs. I followed the direction that trail led me, until I was dipping low against his surprisingly muscular right thigh, the soft edge of his shaft brushing my cheek.

"I really hate that I can't use my hands right now to touch you," Liam said, his words a little choked.

I murmured something supportive in response, but the truth was, *I* didn't hate that he couldn't touch me. I absolutely didn't hate being so in control. It was a new experience for me, fun and powerful and freeing in a way I'd never felt with a guy. Energy arced up inside me the closer I got to Liam's shaft, and when I finally drifted my lips over the curve of his head, I couldn't hide the way my body jerked as the electrical charge zipped through me.

"Jesus, are you okay?" Liam asked, or I think he asked. I didn't much care. I plunged down over him, reveling in the burst of sparks exploding deep inside me. Something about this guy literally set me on fire, and I could not get enough. A storm of emotions and sensations cascaded through me, and I lifted my head to meet his gaze—joy, excitement, and pure unfettered delight flowing through me.

"This is freaking amazing," I said, and he blinked at me in unfeigned surprise.

"Are you serious?" he asked with such shock that I couldn't help but laugh. But I wasn't going to let this moment pass.

"You're okay? You're good? I'm not hurting you?" I asked.

"Uh—*no.* Definitely not hurting me." He waved his right hand, distracting me. I stared as tiny pinpoints of light danced along those fingers, running down the grooves of his skin, his hands visibly healing in front of my eyes.

He sighed in absolute wonder. "This is awesome on so many levels, I can't even—"

I didn't let him finish. I dropped down again, taking him fully into my mouth and delighting in his groan of pure pleasure. Or maybe that groan was all me. I could feel the tension building inside him as I moved, thoroughly enjoying what had to be the world's *best* scientific experiment, my own excitement spiraling up and up until my heart was pounding, the blood rushing through my ears an almost deafening roar.

The only warning I had of Liam's impending release was the hiss of my name through his lips. Then he convulsed in climax, and I barely held on without blacking out. I came fully back online several heartbeats later, pulling back as Liam sagged against the table, his hands still spread wide, fire racing over his palms, and then everything slowed, slowed—the sparks around his hands finally dimming, then winking out completely as we both stared at each other, then down at his hands.

"My *God*, Nina," he murmured in total awe. "I totally need to put a patent on that."

20

"So....now that my hands are better," Liam began after another few seconds, but his words were cut off almost immediately with a sharp crash that sounded from somewhere down the hall. We both jumped, this time for far less pleasurable reasons. Liam hopped off the stool, straightening his clothes, talking quickly the whole time.

"Nobody knows we're here. There's probably nothing else in here with us, but given the insect swarm we incited downstairs, I don't think we can take anything for granted. So I'm going to ask for a rain check on our experimentation here—as much as that seriously pains me—and we're going to go get what we need, then get the hell out."

"What is it you think we're going to find in here?"

Liam was at the door now, and peeked out into the hallway before glancing back. "I told you, this place was run by the Hallowells. There are records they would have left behind, more or less."

"Oh, come on. There's no way that's true. They would have taken any books and materials with them. There wouldn't be anything worth reading still here, not after all these years."

"Like I said, it'll be there...more or less," Liam countered. "You'll see."

He poked his head out of the room again, but there was nothing there to greet us, fortunately, and silence reigned again. He glanced back toward the stairway, then ahead again, as if trying to get his bearings. He nodded quickly.

"Mom told me about the school once, how secretive it was. There was only one room that visitors got to see when they came to check on the students here. It was a formal sitting room, gorgeously outfitted, and the Hallowells took great pride in it. All their history and knowledge was on display for the paying customers."

"But..." I still couldn't understand how there would be any record of these people after so long, but Liam was already moving fast. He trotted down the long hallway, toward what I assumed was the front of the building, and sure enough, there was a set of double doors standing off to one side of the corridor, literally flaked in gold.

"Proud group," Liam observed drily. He tried the double door, and it slid apart at his touch, the wood stiff but still remembering its tracks as it receded into pockets in the wall. We stepped into a parlor that was completely devoid of even one stick of furniture. There was nothing on the walls, no shelves, no furniture. It was empty.

I looked at him. "And this proves what?" I asked, but Liam had already dropped his pack to the floor and was rummaging through it, bringing out another square box, this one with a tiny fluttering blue light.

"Energy is the game here, yeah? I want to see what these people looked like. I want to see who they were and what they did—and most especially, what they *read*."

He depressed a button on the machine, and a tiny light projector extended up and whirled, rotating its beam around the room, filling in the empty spaces.

As I watched, shelves appeared in stripes of flickering light, chairs, a gorgeous buffet bar with a full set of crystal, and shelves upon shelves of books. Books that looked remarkably real, though of course they were only illusions. Or at least that's what I thought until Liam darted forward, opening up the glass doors to one of the bookcases and pulling several books free.

"What the hell are you doing?" I blurted.

"Think of it as a 3D rendering of memories," Liam said quickly. "These books are magic. Magic leaves an imprint, and a 3D printer can reproduce what they were, kind of pulling it out of the very atmosphere. The effect doesn't last long, but while it lasts, it's friggin' awesome. Come on, we need to look at these."

I hustled over to him, and he handed me a thick tome. "What are we looking for?"

"Pride, for starters," Liam muttered. "There has to be a connection between the Hallowells and the Perkins family. Some slight, some issue. If we can tie them to that, then we may have a reason to point the finger at them."

"Okay." I accepted that and began paging through the books. They were journals, written in a beautiful hand, and I caught myself skimming passages detailing students and teachers at the academy, progress and exams and courses in etiquette. I didn't see anything about the Perkinses, though, so I turned another page, and heart quickened. The page grew more insubstantial as I flipped it.

"How long does the illusion last?"

"First time I've ever tested it." Liam shrugged, confirming my worst fears. "Why, you got anything?"

"No, I..." My words broke off as my gaze landed on a name.

"Oh my God," I breathed. "Janet Cross."

"You're kidding," Liam said. "What's it say? Read quick."

"She was a teacher. She definitely was a teacher here. But...that doesn't make any sense. Why would she be a teacher here over a hundred years ago? The dates are in 1889, for God's sake. How could that be possible?"

"It's not possible. It just means your mom was smart. She took the name of a teacher who taught here for a reason. Who did she teach? Does it say anything about her students?"

"Just that it seemed like she had the more, I guess, wilder students. There's all sorts of entries about her needing to improve their discipline, their control. I don't really understand it, but...I just don't understand."

"Well, I'm coming up with nothing here. From what I can tell, we've got no connection—no mention at all of the Perkins family. I totally thought we would. It's the only thing that makes sense."

By this point, Liam was muttering under his breath, and he turned to pull another book off the shelves. Scanning it quickly, he shook his head in exasperation. "Girls, girls, girls, nothing but girls." He looked back at me, his brows knitting together. "That's kind of interesting don't you think? Wellington Academy has some women, but not a lot when you think about it. Not even when monster hunting was more of a focus of the academy. How come?"

"I don't know. Maybe you need to be big and strong to fight monsters?"

"That hasn't stopped you," he pointed out, and I nodded.

"Fair enough, but this was the 1800s. Women weren't allowed to do a lot of things."

"Fair, but in the magical families, that kind of sexist bullshit didn't really play. It really was more of a meritocracy, and if these young women were gifted and the Hallowells had a school...there's something there, something I'm missing. I don't know what it is yet, but there's—"

He broke off as the illusion around us flickered.

"Fuck," he muttered. "I need more time."

More time was not in the cards, however, as the machine in the center of the room gave a final sigh, and the illusion petered out completely.

Liam moved back toward his pack, pulling out what looked like a compass. "Well, that was fun while it lasted. But I really need to do a better job with my power supplies. First time I've ever had the chance to test these things in the wild, but they're not much good if they flake before anything interesting happens. Come on."

He held the compass aloft and reached for my hand. Once again when my fingers clasped his, I felt the zing of electricity between us. He did too, and he gave me a smile. "Don't think we're not going to pick up where we left off back there. But we need to get back to Fowlers Hall. I need to recharge a little myself."

I lifted my brows as he glanced down at the compass again.

"Recharge in what way?" I asked, and he just shrugged.

"In the way you're probably thinking. When my parents decided to trick out my insides, they didn't give much thought to the effort it would take to keep everything working without causing problems to my system. It...it takes a lot out of me, you could say. Anyway, way too much information. Let's go."

Following the compass, we moved back down the hallway, then turned down a side hallway that we'd passed earlier, and eventually angled into a room that looked like a kitchen.

"It's always the kitchens with these people," he murmured, though the room looked as barren as the rest of the building. He went over to a large pantry and pulled it open. A platform lay on the other side, heavy and wooden, and Liam leaned over it, testing it with his hands.

"I've fallen through my share of these, but this one looks sturdy enough," he decided.

I frowned. "Sturdy enough for what?"

"Come on. It's going to be tight with both of us in here, but I don't want to leave you up here." He crawled into the closet and beckoned me to join him. The two of us barely fit in the small space, and Liam reached up and opened a panel in the ceiling, revealing a wheel with a deep track, an old, oiled rope threaded through it.

"I don't have time to mess around with this," he muttered. He flipped out his wrist, and fire smoked out of some hidden port while he hissed out a sharp curse.

It leapt onto the twine, which immediately began to fray.

"Wait a minute," I blurted. "If you're cutting that, aren't we going to—"

"Brace yourself," Liam shouted back, shoving his hands against the sides of the cabinet. "Hang on!"

I'd barely gotten my hands up in time when, with a sickening lurch, the cabinet dropped easily a couple of floors, landing with a thud and dumping us onto a straw-covered floor.

We lay there for a moment, stunned. Liam spoke first. "These things always had braces in the bottom. Falls happened more often than you might think, and they didn't want to smash dishes or, you know, kill people."

Sure enough, there were thick bales of moldering straw

stacked beneath the platform. I stood and staggered a little anyway, trying to get my bearings. "So where is this?"

He waved his compass. "This is the way out. I've tailored this compass to latch into the subterranean network of passageways that extend throughout Boston. It doesn't do much for getting me to new places, but it can always point me home, which is a lot more useful than you might think."

"Home as in your parents' house?"

He shrugged. "Originally, but I reset it to Fowlers Hall. That's home to me now, more of a home than my own place ever was. Let's go."

We headed out, making our way through passageways that varied between little more than narrow alleys to tunnels that seemed like they'd once been part of the underground rail system, Liam keeping up a chattering commentary the whole way. It took us about twenty minutes until he turned down a particularly well-kept passage, which led to a steep flight of stairs.

"Here we are," he said, the grin obvious in his voice, though I couldn't see his face. "Fowlers Hall has a basement, but as you might imagine, I'm not a big fan of basements. So up we go."

He headed up the stairs, and when it ended at a short landing with a door cut into the wall, he keyed in a code on a surprisingly modern-looking keypad. The door opened to a bright cheerful room.

"Welcome to my humble domain," he said.

21

I'd seen both Tyler's and Zach's dorm rooms at Fowlers Hall—both of them way more luxurious than any ordinary college dorm room. Tyler's had been twice the size of Zach's and reasonably tidy, and I honestly couldn't remember Zach's that much, given the fire and brimstone I'd had to fight through in order to get to his bed.

Liam's room was a revelation.

The room was enormous, partitioned into sections separated by a wide, gleaming wood floor. The right side of the room was dominated by a dozen floor-to-ceiling bookshelves that jutted into the room perpendicular to the wall, with tall rolling ladders positioned at the near edges of the shelving units that were stacked with books on every shelf. A large, comfortable-looking recliner peeked out from behind the last shelf, also surrounded with books. The left wall was given over to a desk with three laptop computers faintly gleaming in sleep mode, and the far end of the room boasted a large door—what I assumed was the main entry.

"Where's your bed? Or do you just sleep in that recliner?"

Liam turned and pointed to a series of doors on the same wall from which we'd just emerged. "This door goes to the stairway we just came up—there are lots of other corners and nooks down there, but the footprint is only about the size of a closet. Bedroom's there, bathroom's over there."

Sure enough, I could see the corner of a bed through the open door, the room looking like a bomb went off in it. I suspected Liam didn't spend too much time worrying about housekeeping—not when there were all these books to read.

"How did you get a room this amazing? It looks like it was designed specifically for you."

"Well...it kind of was. When I knew I was going to come to Wellington Academy, I broke into Fowlers Hall from beneath, and searched the entire place."

I stared at him. "Nobody noticed?"

"Not even a little bit." He grinned. "Remember, the monster hunting major has been on the decline for a *while*. This part of the building is farthest away from the front doors. I think only Grim's quarters are tougher to get to. Not generally a great option if you have to go back and forth to class a lot. I scouted out the rooms and found the one I wanted to fix up mainly by virtue of the fact that it led to the most interesting places."

"Your subterranean network."

"Yup. Once I figured that out, it wasn't that hard to arrange for the shelving to be put in and then the desk set up. It was all there by the time I officially joined the school, and frankly, nobody cared that I wanted this room. I kind of thought they would, thought someone would make a comment about it, but they didn't."

Once again, there was a sense of isolation in Liam's tone

that I didn't miss, but he rushed on before I could call him on it. "I've got books in here on just about everything you could imagine," he confided. "Anything you could possibly want."

I gazed around. "Yeah? How about a phone book of my family tree?"

"You laugh, but I've got something close to it—a history of the magical families of Boston, all the way back to the founding fathers of Wellington. I started looking through it after you arrived, but we haven't had that much downtime. Still..."

He muttered something under his breath, and a whirring sound emanated from the depths of the stacks. A few moments later, a series of drones flew out into the center of the room, their hanging clawlike appendages carrying books. They whooshed over to the broad desk and laid the books gently down.

"Okay, well, that's kind of cool," I allowed.

He nodded. "Pretty much anything you can imagine, I've figured out how to do. And I'm not going to lie, the last several days, I've sort of wondered what *you* could imagine, you specifically."

I blinked at him. "Me? What do you mean?"

"Oh, you know, like what would impress Nina Cross, specifically? What is something you'd want that I could maybe give you? An experience, a piece of information other than your elusive family ties, a spell? What's the thing you feel like you missed out on, living your life as a monster hunter?"

The last question caught me off guard, and I looked around the room, not seeing shelves and books and laptops anymore, but actually the floor.

"Honestly?" I blushed, surprising myself by sharing the

first answer that came to mind. "This floor reminds me of the gym in our school. The hardwood was darker than most gyms. They hadn't gotten around to replacing it with the new bouncy floors they use now, and they'd overvarnished it, making it dark like this. That's where we were going to have our prom senior year, or I guess where we *did* have our prom. I just didn't go."

He frowned at me. "You didn't go to your own prom?"

"Nah. I'd almost gone to the one the year before, but on our way there, we kind of ran into a bit of a monster problem. My date didn't take it really well after I hacked a bugbear to death in front of him. It sort of ruined the night, and he moved schools before the next semester started. I felt pretty bad about that. I didn't even make the attempt my senior year."

"Really," Liam said. "Well, we need to fix that. Every girl should have a ball thrown for her."

He'd moved over to one of the shelves, leaning against it casually. Too casually, I thought. He was up to something, but I didn't mind so much.

"Well, we're going to have this presentation thing and Mr. Symmes said there'd be music there, right?" I asked. "That sounds like a dance to me, so it looks like I'm going to get my chance."

"Oh that," Liam said, rolling his eyes. "Don't expect much dancing. There's a long formal...I guess you'd call it a walk or some sort of promenade where the monster hunters and their dates, which I guess in this case will just be you, go through this superweird parade, totally ridiculous and not at all fun. It's not like there's going to be a glitter ball and photo opportunity with sequins and streamers. You're also not going to wear a dress like a princess, but you should."

He pulled something off the shelf, a small remote control, and fluttered his fingers over it.

I watched him as he worked, the coiled intensity of his body, his sandy-brown hair skimmed back from his tanned face, his newly healed hands moving fast. He was leanly muscled, and surprisingly strong, and if I squinted hard, I could almost see the flare of electricity shimmering along his shoulders and collarbones, crackling at his wrists. He was an enchanted Iron Man, part machine and part magic, with a heart that could probably beat a million times a minute without failing if that's what it took to reach his goals, protect his friends, or defeat the evil bad.

I sighed, and when he glanced up to wink at me, I let all my butterflies stutter and flutter to life, and no longer tried to stop them. I knew he was trying to impress me, though he legit didn't need to, and a part of me wanted to tell him that he didn't need to bother. A larger part wanted to let him, though, wanted to see what he'd do.

Liam Graham was the kind of guy who'd pull out all the stops for something he wanted, not doing anything by half measures. He'd build a castle for a weekend and gather an orchestra to perform original music where most guys would opt for takeout and a Spotify playlist. He already made me feel like a princess, and he hadn't even started trying yet.

"Here we go," he murmured. I felt the flare of energy drape around me, not close enough to constrict my movements, but an almost fabric-like field. I turned and looked down, then drew in a sharp breath.

"What the hell is this?" I no longer stood in my jeans, T-shirt, and boots. Instead, I appeared to be wearing a flowing pink silk gown with an enormous skirt that extended out all around me. My arms were covered in long white silk gloves, and as I pivoted in a circle, I could feel the weight of something on my head. I reached up, but there was nothing there. As I turned back toward Liam, though, I could see that the far wall was now taken up with a large mirror, standing in front of where his desk had been...and I could see myself in that mirror, looking like I never had in my entire life.

"I'm pretty sure I wasn't going to dress up for prom like Cinderella, complete with crown." I laughed, but I held out my arms anyway and twirled a little, the hem of my illusionary dress lifting off the floor to reveal an honest-to-God pair of glass slippers—or at least really sparkly ones.

He sighed with what sounded like real pleasure. "Something I've been playing with, and it came together way easier than I expected it to. Kinda makes you understand why illusion magic was such a powerful draw for the Hallowells, yeah?" Liam's voice had gotten a little deeper, and I turned to him—then stared.

"Oh my God..."

Liam stood tall in a suit any prince would have been honored to wear, his sandy-brown hair brushed back from his tanned skin, his eyes bright and gleaming, his body encased in a black tuxedo with tails, framing a snowy-white shirt. He wore some sort of tight-fitting pants, almost tights, and the look was finished off with tall, shiny boots. I couldn't remember what the prince wore in Cinderella, but frankly, I didn't care.

Liam strode toward me, then held out his hand like a real Prince Charming, and as our fingers touched, the arc of electricity danced along my gloves, not muted at all by the illusion. As we stepped closer to each other, a straight-up glitter ball appeared above us, casting off a kaleidoscope of color that swirled around the room, in time to an instrumental song I couldn't possibly name.

"I'm afraid I'm not really up on my prom music," I said, blinking away a totally unexpected wash of tears.

"I don't expect you to know this one," he said. "I wrote it."

With that, he swept me around, and the music built as we danced, or really just sort of moved in sync with each other. I'd never learned how to dance, of course, but with Liam, like so many other things, it just felt right to be in his arms. He stared at me as if I were a dream come true, the girl he'd been waiting for his entire life. I didn't know if that was simply part of the prom illusion he was creating for me or anything real, but once again, I didn't care. Before, in the Beacon Hill Prep Academy classroom, I'd felt powerful and in control. Now, here in his arms, I felt something equally unique. I felt safe. I felt loved.

"Do you do this for all the girls?" I managed, and he chuckled.

"Just the ones who are chased into my life by a Tarken land worm, and who make me feel like I can do anything," he said and his lips came down on mine.

The burst of sparks that erupted in my stomach at his kiss should have caught all my butterflies on fire, but instead merely sent them into a frenzy of excitement. I shuddered in Liam's arms, and he tightened his hold on me, deepening his kiss. I leaned into it eagerly, welcoming the rush of heat and limitless energy that swept through me. I didn't understand this, I didn't understand *him*, but I didn't need to understand it. I just wanted to experience it. Music flowed around us, and he twirled me in a wider arc, breaking the kiss only enough to stare down at me, an expression of naked wonder in his eyes.

"Are you feeling what I'm feeling?" he asked. "It's like everything in my body is firing at once, and you're doing this, Nina. You're waking up my magic, no extra tools required."

The disbelieving joy in his voice made my throat constrict. "This isn't me, it's you," I whispered, and I fully believed that. With Zach and Tyler, there'd been no real hint as to what would happen when we struck our intimate bond. But with Liam, I knew. I wanted him to fully experience the furthest limits of his magical abilities, the best of everything he could be.

The swell of music swept us past the open door to his bedroom, and I noticed the illusion he was casting didn't extend so far into that room. It was still a wreck. For that reason alone, I wanted to explore it.

I tugged him toward it, and he hesitated. "It's not set up for the show," he said, and I laughed.

"Good. I don't know how to get out of this dress anyway."

We stepped across the threshold, and as promised, my gown disappeared like Cinderella's at midnight, and his suit did as well—actually, everything did. The music still played loudly in the other room, the glitter ball still threw off its kaleidoscope of lights, but we stood completely naked next to his bed.

"How did you..."

But I honestly didn't care as Liam leapt for me. Laughing, he pushed me back into the bed, and we lost ourselves in the sheets and the mountain of pillows for a second, rolling around like idiots. Then we stopped, lungs heaving, and he levered himself over me, staring down. I looked down at myself as well and saw what he saw. The scars, the bruises, the rough and ragged skin. It didn't seem to bother him, and I hadn't expected it to. Liam, like all the guys, accepted me for what I was—hell, he celebrated it. Which was a beautiful thing.

Fortunately, I didn't need him to provide a formal assessment of me as a test subject. The look of straight-up lust in his eyes was all the information I needed. I reached for him, the sparking fire within me resuming as we kissed. As with everything with Liam, there was no hesitation once he decided what he wanted. He shifted himself to align his body perfectly with mine, and I obligingly lifted my knees and locked my legs around his narrow hips.

He groaned with heartfelt pleasure as he sank into me, and I arched upright, half in willing pleasure, half to counter the river of fire that burst through me at our intimate bond. I drowned in our connection, sinking into a world gone fiery hot, forged in power that we traded back and forth, an endless circuit that exposed new circuits and pathways every time the cycle renewed.

I wasn't even sure who shouted first, but our voices echoed off the walls of Liam's bedroom over and over again, each new climax that we shared ebbing just long enough for a new one to build, each valley of boneless sensation lasting only long enough for us to miss climbing the peaks of sensation, and we'd start the process all over again.

I had no idea what time it was by the time we finally collapsed at each other's sides, tangled in the sheets, breathing heavily. It was...incredible. Unbelievable. Perfect.

"This is really the way they should do the presentation," Liam said. "Way better than a parade."

I grinned at the image, but despite my deep longing to remain lost in his arms, my eyes popped wide.

I angled myself up on one elbow and stared down at him. "Um...so something just occurred to me. What do people wear to this presentation?"

For once, Liam didn't meet my gaze. His lids remained comfortably closed, his breathing deep and even. "Oh you know, little black dress for the girls, rando suits for the guys. The usual."

The usual. I grimaced. It might be the usual for a group of Ivy League elites used to running with Boston's rich and magical families, but it wasn't the usual for me. I didn't have a little black dress. I didn't have any dresses. It wasn't really the attire of choice for fighting monsters, so it didn't make the cut. My mind churned, trying to come up with a solution, but there was really only one.

"I'm gonna be right back," I said.

"Bathroom to the right," Liam called out, but I paused to scoop up my phone first. Hours had passed since we'd left Wellesley Hall, and the day was quickly turning to night. I didn't have time to waste, though. It was going to take more than a trip to the ladies' to get me ready for the presentation of Wellington Academy monster hunters.

I slid out my phone and texted Merry Williams.

22

When I arrived at Merry's dorm room, she took one look at me, made a horrified, exaggerated face, and yanked me inside.

"Okay, you're staying the night, right?" she asked. "You're totally staying the night because of course there's nowhere else you could possibly be thinking of staying."

"Ah...I guess I hadn't really thought about it. I mean..." I frowned and pulled out my phone. There was nothing more from Commander Frost or any of the guys, and I knew for a fact that Liam wasn't going anywhere soon. "I mean, sure? I can spend the night. I don't want to put you out, though."

"The only way you would put me out is if you forced me to do anything with your face the way you look right now. My God, girl, when is the last time you took a nap?"

"I..." I honestly couldn't remember, but since I'd spent the night before with Liam collapsed beside me in the library, it was probably reasonable that I wasn't looking my best. Merry steered me into her second bedroom and pulled out academy-logoed pajamas when we got there, handing them over to me.

"I don't even want to see you until tomorrow morning when the sun is up. The actual sun, that big yellow thing that goes up in the sky, which it looks like you haven't seen in way too long. My God, your coloring, girl. What the hell happened to you?"

I laughed, then realized why I felt such an unreasonable surge of relief at her extreme and pointed criticism about my appearance. This was the Merry I knew. I grinned at her enthusiasm, despite her exasperation.

"What happened to *you*? When I saw you last, you were nowhere near this, I guess, happy. You were walking around like zombie central, and that was only a few hours ago."

"I know, I know," she groaned. "The sunshine helped a lot, and so did a quick visit to the demonology department. I walked right into one of their little demon club meetings, and everyone was so nice, I snapped right out of it. Heck, I may even have a date for Saturday night." She grinned.

"Seriously?"

She tugged on the lock of white hair. "Apparently, streaks of white hair are total turn-ons to demonology guys. And not gonna lie, some of those guys are super—"

"Do *not* say it."

"Hot!" she finished triumphantly, then burst into a peal of delighted laughter that did more than a full night's sleep ever could to lift my heart. "Anyway, it took me a minute, but I feel better, I really do. But you, girl—"

"Okay, okay." I lifted my hands in surrender. "I get the picture. I haven't been getting a lot of sleep and there's been a lot going on."

"Oh, *whatever*." Merry rolled her eyes. "It's the end of the semester, and the demons are all gone. Don't you monster hunting freaks know when to take a break?"

"I guess not." I sighed, the fatigue of the day finally

hitting me as I slid into my borrowed pajamas. Merry continued chattering as she handed me a toothbrush still in its original packaging and pointed me toward the bathroom.

I stared from it to her. "You have extra toothbrushes on hand? For what, drop-in guests?"

She only grinned. "Yo—it pays to be prepared, and don't you forget it."

By the time I got back to Merry's guest bedroom, I barely remembered brushing my teeth. I hit the bed hard, practically asleep before I landed.

When I awoke next, the room was bathed in light. I sighed, snuggling into the blankets as I flickered open my eyes. And screamed.

"Hey!" A fully dressed, coiffed, and excessively alert-looking Merry jerked back from her position on the floor, surrounded by no fewer than four different piles of clothes. "Well, it's about time, sleepyhead. The sun has been up for totally an hour, and we've got work to do. But you do look way better, so go grab a shower and do something with your hair, because my *God*, and get back here. When do you have to be anywhere, do you know?"

"Um... No?" I admitted. "Not anytime soon. At least, I don't think so."

"Yeah, well, based on everything I've seen from your monster hunting friends, I'm going to call bullshit on that idea. I bet we have less time than you can possibly imagine. So step it up. There's coffee in the kitchen, and bagels and fruit, but grab it on your way to getting a shower. We have work to do."

Less than twenty minutes later, I was back in the bedroom, where Merry had not only made up my bed with fresh sheets, but the clothes had been transferred to that higher vantage point. Four different cocktail dresses were laid out for me, in four different colors—black, red, white—which was an immediate no—and hot pink.

I looked from the last dress to her. "Are you serious?"

"You're just lucky I didn't have more time. Some girls I know have been to the presentation as dates for past monster hunters, but there hasn't been an actual graduate who's been a female in, like, I don't even know how long. Back then, they were wearing prom gowns, so count yourself lucky we didn't need to find serious formal wear. But even with all that, you still want to look great. I'm thinking probably not the white."

"You're thinking correctly so far," I agreed, and she patted the dress affectionately. "It *is* beautiful, but you spill something on that and your evening is over. You do need to try on the hot pink, even if you hate the idea of the color, because I pretty much just have to see you in hot pink."

I couldn't help but laugh, and obligingly tried on the shift, which was far too dramatic for me, even after I'd reluctantly nixed wearing it with my sports bra.

"Do you even have a bra that's not double-enforced spandex?" Merry demanded after she'd demanded I hand it over, and I shrugged.

"I dress for function."

"You dress for World War Three." She tilted her head, studying me. "Okay, well, I don't have your assets, so we're going to have to figure something out about that, but let's see you anyway."

She turned me toward the mirror, and I grimaced. "This is way too tight."

"Nope. This is exactly the right amount of tight, especially for your body, which is perfect for it. I'm giving it to you."

I shot her a bemused look. "C'mon, Merry, no. I'm never going to wear it."

"And that is where you're wrong." She wagged a finger at me. "Because this is an incredible dress that you need to wear when you want to have it end up on the floor."

She pushed on as I snorted a laugh. "I am *not* kidding you. I got that thing at a remnant sale when I was still at Twyst Academy, and there's something about the fabric that is flat-out dangerous. It's maybe a monster all on its own, and it looks way better on you than it ever did on me, so you need to take it home and—feed it, or something. I'm just saying."

I didn't know what else to say to that, so I shimmied out of the thing and tried both the red and black cocktail dresses on next.

Merry sighed with real feeling. "My heart wants to say the red for you. It's gorgeous, you're gorgeous, and it has a built-in bra so I don't have to worry about your girls' situation. But you look like you're standing in your mother's wedding dress in it. Totally lost. Whereas the black one..."

I looked down at myself, then back at the mirror. The black dress was ridiculously simple, a scoop-necked tank-style bodice, sleek and formfitting, that flowed down to a lightly ruffled skirt that flared out at the knees. Somehow Merry had managed to find shoes in my size, and the shiny black pumps were elegant, yet still walkable. I wouldn't want to fight any monsters wearing this dress, but the monsters that awaited me at a fancy college presentation? Those I felt like I could take on.

"You really don't mind me wearing these?" I asked.

"Not at all. The one you have on was a dress I wore my freshman year, believe it or not, so I'm thrilled that somebody else can get use out of it. It's pretty, isn't it? You look good in it."

Something had shifted in Merry's voice, and I glanced back at her. A shadow had crept across her face, and the way she tilted her head, I could see the white streak again, more pronounced than ever.

"I know you think I don't believe in monsters," she said, fixing me with her gaze, "but that isn't exactly right—I definitely have a greater respect for demons, and I know there are monsters everywhere. They had them at Twyst, they have them here. I don't think they deserve our fear, but I'm beginning to understand that some of them are dangerous. The guys at the demonology department, they told me some of what happened at Bellamy Chapel. Things I didn't remember at all. That, more than anything, broke through to me, you know?"

I grimaced. I didn't know—I couldn't imagine what this all must be like for Merry, who hadn't spent her entire life fighting monsters.

"I'm glad you came to Wellington, Nina," she continued, lifting her hand to brush my hair away from my forehead, tucking the errant strand behind my ear. "You and the guys are trying to fight monsters that are going to come for the rest of us if we're not careful. We can't avoid all the monsters out there, but knowing you're willing to face them head-on... that matters. It's important, and it's right that it's happening now, with you. Thank you for fighting for us—for me. I get the feeling you've always been the one willing to fight."

My throat got a little scratchy, and I blinked hard, a swell of unexpected emotion pushing against the backs of my eyes. "I must be more tired than I thought," I managed, and Merry smiled, her eyes also suspiciously bright.

"Me too," she said, nodding quickly. "Take the dress and the shoes. Take the sex dress too—and don't say I never gave you a good time. But now...brace yourself. We need to do something with your face."

23

By the time I returned to Fowlers Hall, hours had passed, and any thought of trying on the hot-pink dress for Liam was quickly extinguished. Commander Frost waited at the door for me, with keys to an assigned dorm room all my own.

"Stay in your room until tonight," he said, handing over the keys. "It's on the second floor. You have the whole south wing."

"I do?" I took the shiny card, frowning down at it. "I'm pretty sure I don't need all that—"

"The presentation is tonight," Frost cut me off, waving at my dress bag. "If that's what I think it is, good job on finding clothes. Everything's moving too fast for sense right now, but we're not going to be able to stop it. Not with Symmes so up in arms. And as far as I'm concerned, the sooner we get you all through this graduation bullshit, the better."

"Tonight," I echoed. Merry's concern for moving quickly on my makeover was apparently well-founded. "Do the guys know?"

"They do—and that brings me to the next idiotic thing

we have to deal with. Wellington Academy has rules for the presentation of monster hunters, arcane and frankly unnecessary, but we need to play this one by the book. You don't see the guys, don't see anyone, until tonight. Stay in your room, and whatever you're wearing, cover it up with the cape that'll be waiting for you there. The cape is enormous —you won't be able to miss it."

"Okay..."

"At eight o'clock sharp, you'll be met at the front door of Fowlers Hall by a member of the board, but you won't see the other members of the collective until you reach Guild Hall. You know that building?"

I frowned, but I couldn't place any Guild Hall. "Should I?"

"I guess..." He blew out a breath. "No. I forget you've only been here a short while. It's in the same section of campus as Wellesley, though, so all that should look familiar. Stay with your escort, try not to talk to anyone. Wearing that giant smock, it'll be hard not to feel ridiculous, but fortunately, it's a short walk."

Frost seemed unreasonably preoccupied, and I didn't feel like talking much more after this list of bizarre instructions, so I didn't ask any questions. With my hot-pink and black dresses in tow and all my thousand and one questions, I was eager to see Liam—only, of course, I couldn't.

Instead, I returned to my room. I laid out my dresses and shoes, stripped myself of my iron knife, athame, and Protector Zoo, and examined the cape of doom. Commander Frost was right—no one would be able to see anything of my outfit beneath it. The cape wasn't really a cape at all, but a long, shapeless pup-tent-size garment of heavy, dark purple wool, with a neck wide enough to sit on my collarbone and two armholes slit in the front. The armholes should have been a bonus, but they turned out to be unusable for anything but sticking your hand through briefly to open a door or shake someone's hand. When I put the cape on, I looked like a gumdrop with feet.

"There'd better not be any monsters waiting for us tonight," I muttered. I pulled off the cape and laid it out on the bed again, then tried not to mess up my face until 8:00 p.m. For the record, that was way harder than I expected it to be.

Night had fallen by the time I arrived at the front of Fowlers Hall at my appointed hour—only to find Liam's mother, Claudia Graham, waiting for me, her frosted hair teased into a helmet of old-money sophistication, and her own outfit covered by a long cape only slightly less ridiculous than mine. *Great.* No wonder the whole campus rolled their eyes at monster hunters.

I entertained brief, fervent hopes that we would simply stroll across the campus without speaking, but no such luck. No sooner had we cleared the bright lights around Fowlers Hall than Claudia laid into me.

"It's highly irregular that there is absolutely no information about you, Ms. Cross. You do understand that, correct?"

I thought about what Liam had said about his mother, how proud she was of her ability to parse out the various family lines of Wellington Academy, carefully ranking the position of everyone up and down the social ladder, and blew out a long breath. She might be obnoxious, but she wasn't wrong. "Nobody wants to find my family more than I do," I said, not even bothering to hide the resignation in my voice. "Liam still thinks there's a possibility that it's the Hallowells, but—"

Claudia finished for me, because of course she did. "The Hallowells would never have left you alone for these past couple of weeks. If *we* knew about you with our very basic surveillance techniques, then *they* know about you. There would be no reason for them to stay their hand. They're not your family. It's possible they know who your family *is*, however. You'll need to keep a sharp eye out tonight."

I frowned at her. "Why?"

"Because the Hallowells will be in attendance." She clucked her tongue at my obvious surprise. "Please. You can't imagine they would stay away, with the shred of possibility that you might be a relation? Even if by some miracle they hadn't caught wind of you before the events of these past few days, they're well aware of you now. So you should take good care. If any of them speak to you, if they mention any other names at all, pay attention. There are families who no longer interact with the academy, who have run afoul of our governing laws. If your people belong to one of those outcast groups, we can work through it, but it will be complicated."

I shot her a curious glance. "Ah...what's there to work through?"

"You can't imagine that your association with the other members of the collective will be sanctioned postgraduation if you're found to be a member of an undesirable line," she informed me coolly. "The monster hunting minor has had enough bad press. An entire swath of our graduates have managed to get themselves killed it would seem, and don't think we're not trying to get to the bottom of that either. If your family has had anything to do with the adverse activities plaguing the minor, then no matter what good acts you've performed, there will be a reckoning. I'd really rather avoid that, if possible."

I looked at her in confusion. "Are you even listening to yourself right now?" I hadn't exactly meant to ask that question out loud, but I clearly did, and Claudia leveled me with a look that would pulverize concrete.

"Just because you've been brought up outside the realm of polite society doesn't mean that you will not abide by our rules and comport yourself with a modicum of respect for those who have come before you, Ms. Cross."

"The only one who's come before me is my mom, and she's not around to care anymore," I shot right back. "After that, I pretty much don't give a shit."

Claudia turned her focus forward at that, which was okay by me. I couldn't look at her without thinking about the tuning rods she'd inserted into Liam, all in some sort of a terrible bid to enhance his magical abilities. He was plenty magical all on his own.

I tilted my head as that thought struck me, taken aback. Had Liam leveled up after last night? I'd spent the day in virtual isolation, and he hadn't reached out. None of the guys had. I supposed none of them were allowed to, all part of the supersecret presentation rules, but still... For the first time, it occurred to me that graduating from the school would be a relief. All the benefits of monster hunting power, none of the bullshit.

"Just keep a sharp eye out," Claudia instructed, still not looking at me. "You never know who your enemies could turn out to be."

Fair enough. And some of them were much closer to home than they should be, though I had the grace not to share this particular view out loud. I didn't know Liam's family, I didn't know the challenges they'd faced over time. I couldn't begin to imagine being in a place where you felt justified doing things to him that apparently his mother had —his own *mother*! But this was not the time to explore any of that.

Oblivious to my judgment, Claudia drew in a deep breath, seeming to center herself. "I'm going to assume that you're woefully unprepared for what's about to happen. Commander Frost has many talents, but explaining the details of Wellington Academy's social obligations isn't one of them. I'll be brief. Given the musical component, the presentation appears to be like a dance, but it's not a dance at all, not in the conventional sense."

"Liam told me," I said, lifting a hand. "It sounds like we're going to do more like a fancy parade?"

To my surprise she favored me with a small smile. "That's not a bad way to describe it. The four male members of the collective will take turns accompanying you through a series of steps. You'll be walking along a pathway that's marked into the floor, etched into the very marble of Guild Hall. There will be turns and pivots, but nothing that requires any sort of advanced dance skills. Most people get by just by walking with a moderate amount of grace."

I grimaced. "I'll do my best."

She nodded, accepting that. "The order of the young men in the collective is typically determined by strength, though I suspect they won't follow that particular tradition this year." Her tone was a little grim. "They wouldn't want to embarrass me."

Once again, a flare of irritation spurted up. "You know, you act like Liam has no innate magic, but that's not true. I've fought alongside him. He's way more skilled than you think."

Claudia's lips tightened, and a haunted look slipped across her face. Then her expression cleared again, and she spoke in softer, more measured tones. "I appreciate your loyalty to my son. When his father was still alive, we moved heaven and earth to help Liam find his way, but our hopes were dashed at every turn. George took him to see every specialist he knew and kept me away from him as much as he could, though I never wanted that. And then George died, and I realized quite quickly that our efforts to help Liam had not been without their own consequences. But he has found his way, and he's a valuable member of the monster hunting collective. For that, I'm very glad."

I barely managed not to grab the woman and shake her. She had it all backward, about what was important about Liam and how skilled he really was, but I didn't miss the pain in her tone, the hesitation. *Consequences.* How well did she even know her son anymore? How well would she ever?

"Ah," she said, refocusing me as she gestured up the street. "Guild Hall. Brace yourself."

I peered at the tall foursquare building, surprised at how pretty it was. I truly hadn't noticed it before, which probably wasn't all that surprising since I'd only been on the campus a hot minute. But with its rose granite walls and bright white stone trim, not to mention its wide marble stairs, it looked like something out of an *Architectural Digest* magazine.

Claudia ushered me up the stairs, pausing only briefly at the top to hold out her arms. "Your cape," she directed.

I shouldered off the heavy garment happily enough, which left me in my black cocktail dress and pumps. Claudia surveyed me with a shrewd eye that was mercifully approving.

"Close," she said. "But missing something, I think."

She lifted her hands to her own neck and unclasped the string of pearls that lay in the hollow of her throat. Giving me a curt gesture, she waited until I turned around, then clasped the beads around my neck. I felt a curiously soothing energy wash through me, though whether that was magic or simply the shock of being touched by this strange and mercurial woman, I couldn't say. Claudia didn't give me time to think about it.

"That will do. With your hair down, nobody will see your ears to know whether you have earrings or not."

"I don't have pierced ears," I said. "Kind of a liability when things are trying to eat you. You don't want to give them anything to latch on to."

She pressed her lips together but made no further comment as the doors opened and light spilled out of the foyer. A man who looked like some sort of usher or major-domo stood just inside on the heavily polished floor, and music played down the hallway from a room past two open doors.

"Chin up," Claudia advised. "Know you will be scrutinized at every turn, and the Hallowells are all tall, patrician looking, and pale. Paler than you, actually, by a fair margin."

"Maybe I get my coloring from my dad's side," I said, wanting to be rid of the woman.

She nodded, taking my comment seriously. "It's the only explanation. I don't know who your father was, but he must have some magic to him, for you to remain hidden all these years. There's simply no other explanation for it. The Hallowells aren't the only exceptional magic family. Anyone of note could have found you, yet they didn't. Something else—or someone else—is protecting you."

She said nothing further, however, merely waved me on, the majordomo relieving her of her cape as well to reveal a long, glittering formal gown, also in a rich champagne hue. The woman knew what she liked. At the door, she moved gracefully ahead of me, and I could hear the hushed lift of conversation in the room beyond as she entered what I assumed was some sort of ballroom. The music changed cadence, becoming more of a dreamy, meandering waltz type of tune, and the majordomo nodded gravely at me.

I stepped into the room.

The first thing that struck me was how crowded it was. I'd expected the people from the meeting with Mr. Symmes to be in attendance, and they were, each with another person who I assumed was a spouse or sibling. But there were also people I'd never seen before. A gamut of snowy-haired aristocracy with only a few younger members of the magical families represented, and even those were no younger than forty-five or so to my eye.

I saw the guys too, starting with Tyler, all of them facing the front of the room despite my obvious entrance. They didn't turn around. I felt instantly out of my depth, as if I should have been given more information than to simply wing it, but there was no time to worry about that now. The majordomo positioned himself beside me, and together, we moved toward Tyler.

"Chin up," I heard Claudia murmur again as I walked by her, and I flushed, but belatedly followed her direction.

As if drawn by an invisible string, my gaze settled on a particularly imperious group who stood near the front of the room, all of them looking at me with determined disinterest, as if they knew they had to look, but they weren't impressed with what they saw. I understood without asking that these were the Hallowells. An older, stern-looking man, a stunningly beautiful woman of about forty years old, and a man who could have been her twin, with deep-black hair and cold gray eyes. He was every bit as attractive as his... sister? Wife? But my attention was drawn inexorably toward the woman. Was this my relative? My aunt, maybe a distant cousin? I couldn't see it. And clearly, they couldn't either, judging by the faint air of boredom on their faces as they returned my gaze.

Then the music shifted once more as I reached Tyler's side. He turned to me at last, his eyes going wide as he took in my appearance.

Wow, he mouthed, though there was no sound to the word, and he lifted his hand. I pressed my fingers into his palm, and together, we turned and walked very formally with slow steps. All I needed to do, apparently, was follow his lead. At one point, ten steps in, he turned to me and placed his arm around my waist, walking me in a slow circle. I suddenly felt like I was the top entry at a dog show, and I bit my lip not to laugh, though across the room, Zach suddenly coughed out a sharp laugh as well.

"You're not wrong," he said in my mind. *"I witnessed one of these as a freshman, and it's the dumbest thing I've ever seen."*

By now, Tyler had reached Liam, who offered me a cocky grin as he took the handoff from Tyler. The music shifted, and for this section of the parade, Liam held me so close, we might as well have been lovers walking in the shadows. No twirling this time, but just having him close beside me, our secret exchange of electricity sparking along my nerves, felt right. Then it was Zach's turn, who accepted the handoff from Liam with a somber nod and clasped my hands in his, facing me as we turned in a slow circle, my eyes wide as I had absolutely no clue what significance any of this had.

"You don't feel it, but there's a hell of a lot of magic bombarding all five of us," Zach said, once again in my mind. *"If we weren't bonded as a collective, we'd probably be in a fair amount of pain. But Frost said that our bond is what's being tested. We could just as easily be playing hopscotch and the result*

would be the same. This part isn't about us. It's just to give them time to throw shit at us."

"I don't feel any of that," I thought right back to him, and he nodded.

"Good, then. Here you go. Try not to let Grim eat you."

He turned me to the side, handed me off to Grim, and I realized how accurate his warning was. Beneath his carefully braided, thick, white-blond hair, Grim looked ferocious, his jaw set, his pale-gold eyes burning bright, every muscle in his body straining. I wanted to ask him if he was okay, but he hissed out a warning breath, and instead, I lifted my hand to his face, and brushed it along his jaw.

I had no idea the significance of any of this—or what possessed me to touch the guy so intimately—but it seemed to be the right thing to do. Grim jolted, his gaze meeting mine, and the tension in his muscles relaxed.

Then he turned me, folding me into his large body, and walked sedately past the last group of spectators, the Hallowells. I could feel the intensity of their glare as we passed, but they said nothing and I didn't look at them directly. If they were my family, that certainly would make this process easier. I could leave Boston tomorrow a happy girl and never see them again.

The parade route finished, Grim stopped in front of Mr. Symmes, who had been joined by Claudia Graham, the music finally ebbing away as Liam, Zach, and Tyler stepped into line beside us.

"Well. That *was* impressive, wasn't it?"

It was the forty-something, dark-haired Hallowell woman who spoke, her voice ringing out before Symmes could utter whatever ponderous pronouncement he was about to offer up. She strode forward, giving us her first smile.

"I know for a fact the amount of magic we threw at these students surpassed anything Wellington has dished out to its monster hunters in probably two decades. So, *bravo*." She turned to Symmes, and I found myself warming toward her, her sophisticated drawl making me wish she would talk to me.

"I understand you want their graduation to proceed without them finishing their final year? I don't see any reason why it shouldn't. We can even skip the ending rituals, no? They're always a mind-numbing bore.

"Ahh..." Symmes began, but Claudia stepped forward.

"No. The final ritual must be completed," she said crisply. "We can't allow hunters to go out without every advantage."

"Oh, really?" the woman retorted. "That's worked out really well for the previous hunters, wouldn't you say?"

"Elaine." It was the older man who spoke, his voice carrying out over the room, low and resonant. "We have no formal standing at the academy anymore. You know that."

"Clearly not," the woman, who I assumed was Elaine, shot back drily. "If we did, Wellington probably wouldn't be in this mess."

"You were the one who chose to leave," Claudia reminded her, and Elaine bristled at the accusation in her voice, although surely the decisions they were referencing had taken place generations ago.

"Because we saw the future, and we chose to work with it, not against it." Elaine countered. "But even we have a need for monster hunters, and this is a fine crop, I would say."

She turned and scanned the five of us with an assessing eye, and I didn't miss how she lingered on Grim. Grim, for his part, was back to looking like he wanted to pound big rocks into gravel, but he said nothing.

"Bottom line, we still have a bit of a mystery, I understand," Elaine continued as her gaze drifted toward me. "An orphaned girl whose mother played a very dangerous game."

There was no doubting the edge to her voice, and I stiffened despite myself. She didn't miss it.

"Don't worry, Nina, we *will* find your family. Someone with as much strength as you should never have been hidden away for as long as you have. Someone will pay for that, rest assured. You're safe with us."

The way she said it, I didn't feel safe at all, but Mr. Symmes stepped forward. "The presentation is at an end. The five of you," he continued, turning to face us with an air almost of surprise in his expression, "acquitted yourself with a strength I have never seen in a presentation. Typically, though this fact is never shared, at least one or two class members fail this particular test. The fact you haven't is a testament to your schooling and strength."

"It's a testament to their collective, you mean," the younger male Hallowell said. Inwardly, I groaned, but these people clearly were well-informed. They'd probably read all the same books that we had, and theirs probably hadn't had the guts cut out of them. "A mixed-gender collective, the first in, what, a hundred years?" He tossed the question to his sister or wife or whoever she was, Elaine, who nodded.

"And oh, not a *sanctioned* collective either. How dangerous of you all," she mocked.

"On the contrary," Mr. Symmes countered with a remarkable amount of pride. "We specifically ensured it would happen."

This, of course, was patent bullshit, but he served it up

with such satisfaction that even Elaine Hallowell looked a little hesitant. Her expression cleared quickly, and she smiled, focusing on me.

"Well then, color me impressed," she drawled, giving me a little nod that, once again, strangely warmed me. "I look forward to seeing what other surprises you have in store for us. But for now, let's dance. I think Nina and her surliest protector, your name is Grim, yes? You should go first."

Without a sound, Grim turned and reached out to me.

I swallowed my sudden anxiety and took his hand.

The music picked up its pace.

24

The floor cleared, but not entirely. Several couples joined Grim and me, and Elaine singled out Liam, who held her in a formal style while trying not to look like he was going to throw up. Claudia Graham paired off with Tyler, and Zach moved to the side, putting his head together with Frost in what was apparently a Very Important Conversation that superseded his need to dance. How he'd managed that, I didn't know, but I couldn't focus on much of anything but the feel of Grim's bulging arms around me, his arm bent and his hand clasping mine as if somewhere along the line, we both had learned how to ballroom dance.

We hadn't, and I squeaked in alarm as Grim lifted me off my feet, pushing me backward as if I was taking the steps naturally before swinging me gently around.

"Let me lead," he said, but a note of exasperated humor had entered his tone, which helped me unwind a notch.

"Did you feel the magic being thrown?" I asked him quietly, our words muted beneath the flow of music. "Because I have to tell you, I totally didn't. As far as I know, we just played a life-size game of Chutes and Ladders, and I still don't know what the point of that was."

"I felt it," he confirmed. "The guys did too—except Liam. He didn't seem as affected. Which, given the givens, he should have been."

Something in his tone tipped me off to his inference, and I colored. "Do I want to know how you figured that out?"

He chuckled, the sound like gravel. "No. But it'll come out soon enough, especially if your connection with him failed to level him up."

"I'm sure it *did* level him up," I insisted, though of course, I had no way of knowing. Still, of all the guys, I really didn't want to fail Liam. He needed it more than the rest of them. "Or at least, I hope it did," I added a little lamely.

Grim regarded me coolly with his pale-gold eyes, turning me around with a catlike grace, and I suddenly remembered that he, also, was a member of the monster hunting collective, and so, arguably...

His lips thinned, and though I knew he couldn't read my mind the way Zach did, I still felt the flush crawl up my cheeks. "Um, so...have you ever seen these Hallowell people before? Because they kind of—"

"It's time," Grim grunted, cutting me off as he turned and, once again with a grace that surprised me, handed me off to Liam. In turn, he and Elaine were left staring at each other, but both seemed to reach the same conclusion. They turned and stalked off in opposite directions.

"Was it something I said?" Liam offered, *sotto voce*, and I grinned at him with genuine pleasure, relieved to sink into the familiar static of our connection. I hadn't realized how stressed it had made me to touch Grim—and I got the feeling he'd been equally put off. Well, with any luck, we'd never be stuck in close quarters together again, so he'd be safe from my cooties.

Liam turned me around easily, and once again, I was struck by the ability of pretty much anyone in the room other than me to dance. "Is Dancing 101 something you guys learned during your sophomore year or something? Because it wasn't on my schedule," I groused a little bitterly.

"Well, for Tyler and me, it's something we were forced to do when we were really young. Zach picked it up after he moved here. Not a lot of dancing in the churches in southern Georgia, to the surprise of no one. And Grim—I don't know. I don't think I've ever seen the guy dance, at least not when he wasn't in the middle of trying to kill something."

"It kind of felt like that, not gonna lie," I quipped, though that wasn't necessarily true. Liam laughed as he turned me again, then his gaze dropped to the line of pearls around my neck. He frowned. "Did you get those from my mom?"

I bit my lip, startled at the dismay in his voice. "Is that okay? She thought I didn't look quite finished and that the pearls would help."

"Oh, she thought the pearls would help, all right, but probably not because she was worried about what you look like. I wonder..."

He angled me across the room, the arc of our turning dance steps taking us closer to the edge of the ballroom floor. Tyler was there, having shaken off his Claudia detail. He and Liam exchanged a glance, one that apparently meant *head over this way*, because Tyler rolled his shoulders and strolled in our direction.

Liam slipped his hand under my left arm as Tyler came up on my right and took that elbow. I blinked, the dual contact with both guys sending a stream of shivers skittering through me. We still hadn't figured out if Liam had upgraded his skillset, but I was definitely picking up on something.

"So here's the deal. I'm not the only Graham who likes his toys," Liam said quietly. "But I don't know if Mom attempted to augment your skills or dampen them. More to the point, I don't know why."

"Seriously?" Tyler asked, glancing at me sharply, his gaze immediately dropping to my neck. "The pearls. How are we going to be able to tell? And why would she do that?"

"Knowing my mom, because she wanted to control the outcome of this little event. My gut says she wanted to augment Nina's abilities, to hold off whatever magic was going to be thrown at us during our little walk-through. But she doesn't know how strong Nina is, which means she doesn't know if her attempt to jack things up might have sent Nina spiraling out of control. That's not something she would typically overlook."

"But the other doesn't make any sense either," Tyler countered. "If she tried to blunt Nina's powers, whatever they may be, that would have left Nina unprotected. I can't see your mom doing anything that would keep you from graduating, my man."

"Agreed," Liam sighed.

"How do we know it's not anything but a strand of pearls?" I asked. "Maybe she literally didn't want me to look silly, nothing more."

It was a testament to how much these two agreed about the nature of Liam's mother that both of them snorted with equal parts derision and doubt.

"Not likely," Liam said. "But there *is* a way we can test it..."

He lifted one shoulder, but for once, his pack wasn't on his back, and he blinked down in apparent surprise as nothing slid into easy access of his hand. "I knew when Frost told me I wasn't able to wear my pack that I was going to regret it," he grumbled. "I friggin' hate being poorly equipped."

"Or maybe it's not as difficult as all that," Tyler said. "Maybe we just need to overload the necklace's circuits a little bit, see what the reaction is?"

"Overload its circuits how?" I asked warily. "We could just take it off me."

But Liam was now studying me with an interested gleam in his eye. "We could, but I've been kind of wondering about this, actually."

He slid his gaze toward Tyler. "You thinking what I'm thinking?"

"I sure hope so." Tyler grinned. At this point in the conversation, we'd moved all the way through the crowd and now stepped out into the hallway behind the ballroom chamber. It was dark here, and no staff hovered at the doorway, the music instantly damping as we moved farther into the shadows. Heavy, ornate paintings hung on either side of the corridor, so it clearly went somewhere, but just not anywhere anyone needed to be, apparently, except us.

"So," Tyler said, turning toward me. "You want to kiss Liam or me?"

I squinted at him. "How is that a choice? What are you guys up to?"

"Liam and I have been talking about the nature of your connection with the other members of the collective. You can link to Zach at will now, turning him on and shutting him off whenever you want access to his mind or to allow him to access yours, am I right?"

I glanced around, half expecting Zach to pop out of the shadows as well. "Yeah...."

"But Liam and I, we're best friends, and we have been for most of our lives. So maybe there's a connection to be had between us as well, even if we're not mind readers."

"Maybe," I allowed, turning back to Liam. "But how does that help us figure out whether your mom's necklace is a power enhancer or a jammer? I don't get it."

"Honestly? It doesn't," Liam admitted. "That doesn't mean I still don't want to try this out."

Without any further warning, he leaned forward and brushed his lips against mine. The usual zing of electricity was there, and I temporarily lost all sense of where I was, eagerly leaning forward to kiss him more deeply. Then Tyler moved, leaning down and kissing the delicate skin beneath my ear, right above the edge of Claudia's strand of pearls.

Sandwiched as I was between the two guys, I had nowhere to go, but I barely suppressed a yelp against Liam's mouth as my body jackknifed, Tyler's arms going around me to keep me from banging into the wall. The dual shock of kisses from the two guys had created a level of spontaneous combustion both inside and outside my body, as the pictures rattled against the walls, and at the far end of the hallway, a stone globe rolled off a table and bounced along the marble floor with a resounding boom.

"What in the..." We sprang apart as a man poked his head out of the ballroom, looking hard our way. Liam and Tyler pressed me back against the wall, Tyler murmuring something long and complicated sounding in Latin. The man squinted, then shook his head. He ducked back into the ballroom.

"What the hell was *that*?" I asked tightly, and Liam chuckled.

"That was, believe it or not, a subdued reaction. Agreed?" he asked Tyler.

Tyler nodded, his assessing gaze now fixed on my necklace. "Totally subdued. Which is a testament to both of you, because you still managed to cause a jolt to the world around you, just nowhere near what it should have been. It was like there was a stranglehold on the energy pouring off you, which was probably a good thing, because otherwise, we would've been set on fire. We're going to need to test all this out a little bit more, I suspect—with your permission, of course."

"What?" I protested as Liam nodded.

"I'm so onboard with that," he said, the two of them grinning with such schoolboy delight that I didn't know whether to take them seriously or not.

"Still," Tyler said, focusing on my necklace with a more somber expression. "Why would your mom want to subdue Nina's abilities? That doesn't make any sense."

"Or maybe it does, if you're playing both ends against the middle. If mom was so confident that Nina would overcome the magic being thrown her way even with the barrier, then it argues that she didn't want to tip our hand to anyone else. In other words—"

"In other words, she's trying to hide Nina in plain sight."

As this conversation continued however, I felt an unexpected scratchiness at my throat, not inside like a cough threatening to burst free, but an actual burning sensation around my neck, following the line of the pearls.

"Um, guys?"

"Holy shit, she's smoking," Liam barked, reaching up to pull the strand of pearls free from my neck with a practiced tug. The pearls glistened in his hand, still steaming slightly, and he traced his finger along them. "We may have over-loaded the suckers after all," he said.

"LOOKS LIKE IT," Tyler agreed. "Let's head back to..." We turned to the ballroom, only now Grim stood at the door. He looked absolutely furious.

"What are you guys doing?" he demanded in a low, urgent voice.

"Hey, man," Liam said. He held up the pearls. "Just divesting Nina of some of my mom's trick pearls. Don't let Claudia dance with you, or she may try to trick you out with a pair of earrings to dampen your power."

Grim's gaze shot from me to the necklace and back to Liam.

"Good. I'm glad you got it off her," he said, then disappeared back into the room. We all exchanged an uneasy glance.

"Is it just me, or does he get weirder every day?" I asked, and Tyler chuckled.

"With Grim, it's impossible to know."

We entered the room and glanced around for the big guy, but he wasn't anywhere to be seen. Then Tyler cursed beneath his breath. "That's not right," he muttered.

"What the..." Liam said at the same time. I looked up to see Grim at the far end of the ballroom, deep in conversation with Frost.

"How in the world did he..." I began.

"He didn't," Liam said tightly. "That guy in the doorway wasn't Gri—"

Before he could finish, every window in the room exploded, and a gale-force wind blasted across the floor.

25

_____

It was a testament to the superior breeding of the first families of Wellington Academy that nobody screamed. I didn't even scream, though I really felt like it. A swarm of six-foot-tall, winged creatures, like hornets with long, spindly human legs and arms, antennae flapping furiously as their multiple appendages shot out in all directions, attacked the first families. The abdomens of the hornets curled between their obscene-looking legs, dripping poison from a large, long barb.

This also should have been scream-worthy, but it was nothing compared to the reaction when the closest hornet attacked an elderly woman with hair so frosted, it appeared almost blue beneath the lights. It buried the dagger-barb deep into her abdomen, and she definitely screamed then.

"Is this real?" I cried, and it felt like a fair question given the chaos all around us. Across the room, Grim and Frost were punching their way through a swarm of insects that had cornered half a dozen people, their cries for help finally surpassing their need for decorum.

"Sure looks real to me," Tyler shouted. "Liam?"

"Need to get my friggin' pack," Liam gasped, and he grabbed my hand, the two of us going electric with energy as we arrowed our way through the swarm toward the main door of the ballroom. Meanwhile, Tyler took off in the other direction, shouting a long, complicated stream of Latin that set the nearest bugs on fire. All the while, I got the sense that we were being watched, assessed. I didn't like it.

"Is this some new kind of test?" I hazarded, desperately trying to come up with any explanation that didn't end with "we're all going to die," but Liam shook his head.

"Not the kind of test that Symmes and his cronies are behind, I can guarantee you that. This whole building means too much to them. They're not about to screw it up."

As if to punctuate his words, another window shattered as we ran past it, new shouts coming from the front of the building.

We cleared a knot of insects only to plunge directly into the next, this one with an all-too-familiar face at its center, her arms spread-eagled in her gorgeous, glittering dress as two separate hornets tried to haul her off in different directions.

"*Mom*," Liam shouted, and something in his voice shifted through the room, dropping the nearest insects into heaps of scales. Not just his voice, I realized. He had brought his hands around, activating the fire chutes in his palm, apparently oblivious to the pain as he raked the streams of fire back and forth in short, quick bursts. The insects screeched and released Claudia, who crumpled to the ground. I raced forward, rolling her over, but as soon as she registered who I was, her gaze dropped to my neck.

"The pearls, damn it! I knew it." She struggled to her feet as Liam caught up to us.

"The enemy was here the whole time," she said. "I tried

to keep you safe. *Goddammit,* how could I have been so foolish?"

All this sounded a little too much like her slamming Liam, but he seemed to take it in stride. His hands still smoking, he ripped an arc of fire in a wide circle around his mother, keeping the insects at bay.

"Keep them contained," he shouted at her, then grabbed my hand, making me yelp with pain as the heat from his palms seared mine. The shock was instantaneous, but gone just as quickly, and I dashed with him through the door and down the hallway.

We leapt over the body of one of the tuxedoed staffers, who hopefully was still breathing, but we didn't have time to check.

"They got the pack, they got the pack, they got the pack," Liam muttered, but when we burst into a small antechamber halfway down the corridor, clearly some sort of coat closet on steroids, his concerns were proven at least partially false. A trio of flapping hornets had his backpack, all right, but they weren't able to lift it, it appeared. They strained to pull it up off the floor, but it wouldn't budge. The moment we entered the room, the farthest hornet spun toward the wall and screeched at us with an ear-shattering cry. A door opened in the wall where no door had been, and the first hornet rushed through it, leaving its fellows behind buzzing menacingly around the bag. Liam tried his fire palms again, his face contorting in pain as the mechanism failed to work, but our momentum still carried us forward.

"What else you got?" I shouted, but no answer was forthcoming, leaving me to lean down and grab for my iron knife, which of course was *not* attached to my ankle. Instead, I had a pair of gleaming pumps, which would do nobody any good. I ripped them off my feet anyway and came up swinging.

My first roundhouse punch caught one of the hornets somewhere shy of its head but just before the main portion of its body, the motion enough to knock it into its fellow. The two of them were far lighter than I expected, but then again, these things were intended to fly. Having a dense central body probably wasn't a good idea.

Either way, they screeched back upright, their wings pumping as they attacked me, and I darted to the side and then back again, trying to distract them as Liam finally collapsed on his bag. The left hornet was much more aggressive with his abdominal barb, and I screeched in real pain as it connected with my arm.

"I thought these were *illusions*," I protested, and Liam jerked his head up, pulling something from his pack and throwing it my way. Beads, I realized. A net bag of the shiny metal beads Grim had collected from the demonology department for me. I didn't know how well those would work against the murder hornets, but I caught the bag, then turned and chucked it at the pair of insects—who exploded into bug parts.

"It would appear that we are dealing with an illusionist who can also commandeer monsters," Liam said grimly. "One who really has a thing for bugs."

"You got that right," I muttered, leaning over and blowing out a heavy breath. We could still hear the sounds of fighting behind us, but both of us turned toward the door that had been cut into the wall.

Liam shouldered his pack and strode over to the hole, peering down.

"This totally connects to the subterranean passages. It has to. There probably was an actual door in this wall at one point that got covered over with all this paneling. Which means..."

I was getting the hang of things now, so I finished for him. "Which means our illusionist bug wrangler knows Wellington Academy. He or she's gotta be someone from the founding families. It narrows down the pool of possibilities a lot, yeah?"

"Kind of stupid, though," Liam countered. "Why expose yourself? Why put yourself at risk?"

"Because you got what you needed? Your work is done here?"

We looked at each other, a sudden chill striking us both.

"You're probably right, but that's not good. We need to get that bastard and find out what he knows—and what's coming." He leaned over again, trying to peer through the gloom. "I don't know what's down there."

At that moment, a stream of insects burst from the hallway and into the coat closet, screeching toward us with flapping wings outstretched and barbs dripping poison.

"I don't care—let's *go*." I pushed Liam through the hole and followed immediately after.

The fall was a bit farther than I had planned. Liam hit first with a noticeable *oof* and scrambled over onto his back, his arms going up to protect himself against my much less graceful tumble. His body ended up absorbing most of my weight, and we lay there, dazed for a second, breathing heavily and watching the angry buzzing swarm far above us. The insects apparently had not been given permission to follow us into the tunnel, which, frankly, was okay by me.

"So now what?" I asked as we shakily brought ourselves to our feet. Liam clipped a light to the handle of his pack, cutting through the gloom.

"You got jabbed by the things, right?" he asked.

I nodded and held out my arms. The welts bubbling on my skin were visible in the dim glow of his pack lamp. "I don't think that helps us, though. I mean, it was definitely a monster, not an illusion, but it wasn't the illusionist himself."

"Maybe yes, maybe no, maybe something," Liam muttered, pulling out a cloth from his bag and pressing it down on my skin. I hissed in pain, but when he lifted the cloth, the welts had decreased markedly and the towel bore a deep purple stain.

"That's a manufactured poison," he said. "A manufactured poison injected into a monster that likes to jab things. Pretty cool, pretty slick. Someone's been dicking with monster parts. That's all kinds of screwed up." Once again, he was muttering, locked in some plane of analysis I couldn't follow, but I let him ramble.

"We've got to move," I said when he finally stopped muttering.

"Yup, we do," he said, apparently having come to some conclusion. "I've got trackers that can help us with that."

He slid his pack forward and rummaged through it, coming up with a small key-fob-size device, much like the compass that had taken us back to Fowlers Hall.

"The most basic tracker of all," he confirmed. "It just picks up on magic. Hold my hand."

He didn't have to ask me twice.

WITH LIAM AND ME LINKED, the tracker didn't target us, but pointed to the shadowy passage ahead. We took off at a fast clip. The corridor ran without any turnoffs for a good fifty feet, then teed off to the right and left. Liam tried turning right, but the tracker insisted that he go the other way, so we did.

"I'm thinking, and this is just a guess, that these passageways aren't as familiar to the illusionist as he'd like them to be. I'm down here all the time, and I'm tracking all the time. There's generally nothing down here but me. So if he took off in a blind rush, he's going on old information and not expecting to find anything in his way."

I slanted him a glance. "What kinds of things might be in his way?"

Liam shrugged. "I've laid so many booby traps down here, it'd make your head spin. I didn't count on a bad guy who could fly, though. That cuts down on a lot of my toys, but maybe—"

Far down the tunnel, someone cursed with sharp, staccato rage.

Liam turned to me and grinned. "Bingo."

We pushed ahead in a hurry, but within only about fifty feet, I noticed that something else had gone wrong. Liam was grunting, trying to move forward but being dragged back. The corridor opened to our right, the new pathway veeing off in two directions, and the compass guided us up and to the right. But as Liam struggled forward, it was as if he was slogging through molasses.

"What the hell," he muttered, sounding disgusted as he pulled his pack around to glare at it. "Someone's been messing with my shit."

"Your pack?"

"Yeah. Which means the bastard got ahold of it before his bug posse was left to stand guard. He could have stuck anything in here. *Fuck.*"

"Here let me grab it," I said. I pulled it off him, and it was surprisingly light in my hands. "It doesn't seem to be bothering me."

Liam perked up, straightening his shoulders. "Oh, *excellent*. You can follow, then?"

"Absolutely."

He pulled a few things out of the pack as I held it, then he grinned at me. "I'll be right in front of you. I just want to lay some perimeter traps. If that asshole is where I think he is, we're going to need them."

"Go. I'll be right behind you."

He nodded. "Give me maybe twenty seconds, then start coming after, but walk at a normal pace, okay?"

He took off without needing me to confirm, and I counted out the seconds, then stepped forward—

And didn't move.

My eyes widened, and I opened my mouth to shout Liam's name, but no sound came from my throat. The bag lurched backward, jerking in my hands, and suddenly weighed about a metric ton. I dropped it, and it detonated in a burst of light and sound around me, hemming me in, lashing me tight.

I threw up my hands and cowered back.

I was trapped.

26

My sight blacked out, then rushed back again, and I realized I'd fallen to the ground. I scrambled upright, but the light streaming from Liam's pack still surrounded me in a pulsing stream. I reached out tentatively, breaking the flow with my hand, then ripped my arm back with a strangled yelp. It was like putting my hand on a live wire while being doused in acid. Not the way I planned on dying.

I turned, then turned again, trying to get the bearings of my trap. Dimly, I could hear the sound of shouts in the distance, but I couldn't help Liam. I couldn't even help myself. Despite all my great and powerful monster hunting abilities, and even greater skills as monster bait, I didn't have magic. I had energy, I supposed, I had a flair for Akkadian, and I could channel Zach and his mind-melding skills somewhat. None of that helped me right now.

I couldn't remember enough spells to know if I could channel Tyler's most superior skill, and as for Liam...how could you channel somebody's ability to be resourceful? I mean, the guy was awesome. He could do anything, create anything, build anything. He could find and store the coolest stuff...

Speaking of stuff, I slanted a glance down at the back-pack. Why had it turned on me? What had I ever done to it?

The truth hit me like a load of bricks.

Or, well, like a sack of magical gadgets.

"You've been with him a long time, haven't you?" I asked aloud, focusing on the pack. It seemed a little odd talking to a nylon-reinforced sack, but then again, no odder than being attacked by flying insects, spiders, and every other creepy-crawly that had crawled out of the woodwork this week. At this point, talking to inanimate objects was par for the course.

The bag didn't react to my anthropomorphizing opening salvo, but I pushed on. My attention was split between the pack, its swirling force field that currently trapped me in place, and Liam's far-off distress, as he sounded like he was fighting his way through a jungle. I had no idea what all was down here in these subterranean catacombs. It could be a jungle, it could be a crypt. I deeply hoped it wasn't the latter. I refocused on the bag.

"Why would you want to keep me from going to him? I'm not going to hurt him. You have to know that."

The backpack seemed to shudder in response, and a wave of sadness snaked through me, almost a sense of regret. That couldn't be a coincidence. There had to be a reason why the bag was fighting me, and I didn't think it was because it had been booby-trapped by the illusionist. Liam was a master of wards, and his backpack was his most prized possession. He wouldn't do anything that would leave it unprotected. Not something he cared about so much.

A new thought occurred to me.

"He does care about you, doesn't he?" I asked. "I can't believe you're the original pack, but there's some element of you that has carried on through all the iterations, isn't that right?"

As I spoke, I tentatively lifted a hand toward the light field, which dimmed, but only slightly. I might be making some headway, but not fast enough. "What is it?" I pressed on. "What is it you need me to know? I promise, I can take it."

That seemed to get me somewhere, as the color changed and became more urgent, more melancholy.

"You think I'll hurt him?" The colors dropped away from me, muting slightly. I wasn't up a hundred percent on my backpack speak, but to me that felt like a no. Okay...

"Are you afraid I'll hurt you? Are you afraid?" Another change, this one almost playful, the energy practically dancing. Clearly, this nylon bag wasn't afraid of me. I didn't know exactly how to feel about that, but I pushed on. There was really only one option left.

"Do you think Liam's going to hurt me?" The pack's glow turned warmer, but I didn't see how Liam harming me could be possible. As if drawn by my attention, Liam's sharp cry rang out down the corridor, and a stab of fear knifed through me. I didn't have time to play nursemaid to a backpack, for freak's sake. I had to step up my game.

"Okay, let me see if I've got this straight," I said more urgently. "The guy who made you his number one possession, who carries you everywhere he goes and would move heaven and earth to make sure you're safe? That's the guy we're talking about here, and I know that deep down, he wants to keep me safe too. No matter what, I know he's always doing the best he can with what he's got to work with. Because that's what he does. And he cares about me—

maybe not as much as he cares about you, but a lot. I really believe that. He'd never hurt me intentionally. I *won't* hold him accountable for anything he does. I promise."

More than anything else I'd tried so far, those final words made the backpack shake, the lights dancing almost in confusion. I didn't wait for a better opportunity. Rather than simply sticking out an exploratory hand, I leapt over the bag, straight through the veil of light. A burst of white-hot flame broke around me, scorching my exposed skin, and then I was through. I plowed ahead a few steps, then circled back, swooping down to drag the bag forward. This time, it came easily, and I slung it over my shoulder, its message apparently at an end and not a moment too soon. As I bolted down the passageway, I skidded past an opening, suddenly unsure about which direction to take.

Liam helped me out, in a way, by choosing that moment to scream bloody murder.

"*No!*" he howled, and I changed direction, running up a new passageway and around a corner, finally catching sight of a room far in the distance, lit by what looked to be flickering torchlight. I slowed, lungs heaving, and barely avoided crashing headlong into the space. I stiffened as Liam's long, slow moan reached me.

"No," he gasped. "No, don't hurt her. *Please.*"

I frowned, glancing down at the shoulder strap of the nylon bag for any sort of clarification, but apparently, my Nina-to-backpack connection had been exhausted for the day. I didn't know who Liam was talking to or about, but I crept forward, holding my breath as he moaned again in obvious pain.

As I finally breached the entryway to the room, I stopped and stared, my eyes going wide.

I'd stumbled into a torture chamber.

Liam hung upside down from the ceiling, his body encased in something that looked straight out of a four-teenth-century dungeon, all leather straps and brutal hooks, sharp barbs, and twisting chains. Twisting being the opera-tive word as Liam hung and slowly swung like a side of beef, his head extended toward the ground, his mouth caught in a rictus of pain, his eyes wide. I wanted to say his name, but once again, words failed me. This time, not because of any magic spell, but my own frozen shock.

Liam stared over at what looked like a raised labyrinth. Black liquid glistened on its surfaces, running down passageways and over and around. In the center of the maze sat a stack of pages. At first, I wondered if it was my letter, but there were far too many pages for it to be that. So what were...

Liam's low groan caught me again as he continued turn-ing. Now he was staring at something at the far end of the wall that I couldn't quite make out from where I stood. I edged forward, my hands coming up to secure the bag more firmly against me, sliding it over both shoulders. I didn't want to run the risk of upsetting the damn thing, but more to the point, this was Liam's prized possession. Maybe there would be something in it that could help. With that small hope, I peeked around the corner to see what it was Liam was staring at with such dismay.

I drew in a strangled breath.

It was me.

Similar to the suspended net of pain that currently had Liam trapped, another apparatus hung on the wall, a cross of sorts, with stakes and daggers bolted into it. A person hung there—no, an illusion. It had to be an illusion, right? Because I was standing *here*, and yet the apparition that was hanging on two of the rods looked so much like me that I jerked in pain as a bolt of electricity danced from one rod to the next, visibly going through my body. Not *my* body, I reminded myself; the illusion's body. But it still made me wince.

"*Tell her,*" a voice sounded from another part of the room. I froze, then turned my head slowly, so slowly that I felt like I was moving through concrete. When I finally swept the rest of the room with my gaze, though, there was nothing there. The voice was as ephemeral as the illusion, but I had heard it. I know I'd heard it. It was low, haunting, maybe feminine? I couldn't tell, and it didn't repeat itself. It didn't need to, because with that one phrase, the words bounced from wall to wall to wall, circling round and round as the electricity danced and the apparition's hair started smoking.

"Stop," Liam begged, but the echoing command of "*Tell her*" continued. He sagged in his leather-and-metal harness as I dared to inch forward again. Nothing stopped; no one seemed to notice me. Even the apparition on the wall stared out with nothing but vacant pain in her eyes. Liam focused only on her—on me—as I very quietly and carefully dropped to my knees. I'd just begun crawling forward when he started talking.

"I was going to tell you everything, everything that I found. I just wanted to know it all first," he gritted out, and I froze again. "I know that wasn't fair of me. I don't ask you to understand, but I've been hurt by information I didn't understand before. I didn't want you to be hurt. No, no, that's not true. I'm sorry!"

Liam's voice lifted with an agonized fervency as a new round of electricity rattled through my poor effigy on the wall. That was totally going to leave a mark, but my attention was split now between my own image and the words spilling out of Liam, more quickly now.

"I didn't want you hurt, but I didn't care about that as much as I cared about learning the shit I needed to know. The Apocrypha held the truth, it held the answers, I knew it had to. Page after page of how the harbinger would blow the doors off everything, that you were the missing link. You were what we were waiting for, and we'd better hold on to you with everything we had. Because if we didn't, we were fucked. Better that we kill you the moment we saw you than let that happen. It was all right there, and I should have told you, but I couldn't. I needed to know. I had to *know* if you would finally set me free from the trap I was living in, the trap of not being enough. Not ever being enough. And you were. You so were. And I'm—no! Take me—stop that. *Stop.*"

But whatever was torturing Liam didn't stop, maybe couldn't stop, and a new wave of electrical sparks jittered along my now-smoking body on the wall, making Liam struggle more desperately in his snare. I had no idea how he'd managed to get himself into that thing, but as distracted as he was by the operation on the wall, I suspected it hadn't been a fun process. I inched forward, sliding the bag off my shoulders and bringing it around, squinting up to try to understand how the harness was attached to the ceiling. There was no way I was going to be able to extricate him from that. I only had one shot, and that was...

I rooted around in the backpack, my fingers brushing across all manner of strange items, some fuzzy, some slick, some weirdly gooey. When I finally struck pay dirt, I pulled out the blinking box that Liam had used to shatter illusions before. I didn't have his magic or his technical know-how, but that thing on the wall was an illusion, and this should stop it. I pressed the button...

My effigy burst into flames.

"*No!*" Liam screamed.

Whoops.

27

I leapt up, racing around Liam's harness thing, and, without thinking about it too hard, because my brain would explode if I did, reached up to wrench my fake body off the wall. It was surprisingly solid, and also legitimately on fire.

I flung it away from me, toward the strange, raised labyrinth in the corner of the room. The moment the body crashed into it, I realized the glistening liquid I'd noticed in the labyrinth was oil, and with the addition of a big stuffed burning dummy, it went up like a funeral pyre. Perhaps not the best image for the already-traumatized Liam to be seeing, but fortunately, he was staring at me now, the real me, as opposed to the rag-doll-of-fire me.

"I'm here, Liam, I'm here," I said as his tormented gaze fixed on me, his horrified eyes peeled open wide. "I don't know what you thought you were seeing, but it wasn't me. Look at me. I'm not on fire. I'm not hurt. I'm okay. You're in a bad way, and I don't even know what that is you're hanging from, but I'm good, okay? Are you with me?"

He shook his head, his mouth working, but it took a second before words came out. "I don't..."

"Focus, sweetheart. I'm right here. Are you with me?"

"Yeah..." He shuddered. "Yeah. I just..."

His eyes cleared, and he looked over at me, then beyond me to the burning pyre.

"Oh my God," he breathed. "The book."

I winced. "Sorry about that. But it was either that or watching you spaz out in your little harness of agony. I did what I had to do." I peered at him more intently. "What is that thing, anyway? And why are you inside it?"

Liam wasn't willing to completely get with the information-sharing program, unfortunately, but I decided to cut him some slack. After all, he was going to have to do the lion's share of getting himself out of whatever the hell it was he was in.

He didn't say anything more for a second, so I pushed on. "Sorry I was a little late to the party. Your pack sort of got snagged up in some magic and it took me a minute to unsnag it."

He blinked, his eyes clearing. "Really?" The mention of his backpack made him frown. "It's never done that before."

"Yeah, well, don't give it a hard time. We're all just trying to do the best we can." He looked at me a little oddly, but then again, he was the one in the harness.

I gestured to it. "You want to explain to me how this is a thing?"

He grimaced, swiveling a little, then did some move with his arms that seemed to give him a bit more breathing space.

"I have this setup as sort of an exercise room," he finally admitted. I glanced around at the harness, the rack on the wall, the still-burning oil-slicked maze.

"You ever think about just joining a gym?"

He chuckled, made another small adjustment, and one of his feet emerged from the top of the harness. "When I came in here, I saw you hanging on the wall. I didn't stop to think that that was impossible, it just seemed so real. I heard a voice tell me it was a new test, that my confusion was simply part of the test, and that I needed to escape the tourniquet if I wanted you to be freed."

"Tourniquet. That's what you're calling that thing you're in?"

"Yeah. It's an old magician's trick from a hundred years ago that no one was ever able to replicate safely enough for public appearances."

"Uh-huh. So of course you thought the thing to do would be to put it in a cave where you were guaranteed *not* to have an audience of, oh, I don't know, first responders."

He laughed again, a little grimly. "Something like that. Anyhow..." He grunted again, and one of his arms slipped free of the binds. With a quick flip of his wrist, the second arm was freed as well. I finally allowed myself to breathe.

"Anyway, I got into the tourniquet, only things got worse from there. I found myself being asked questions I didn't want to admit the answers to." He turned slightly, pausing in his escape routine and grimaced at me. "You heard that part. I'm sorry."

"Keep getting yourself free. We'll talk about all that in a minute." I shut down any further attempts at conversation until he'd loosed the final bond and hung there in open space, clearly gathering his strength to drop to the floor. I couldn't hold anything in any longer.

"What happened to the illusionist?" I blurted. "Was that who was asking the questions?"

"I mean, it's gotta be, don't you think? Even though I never saw him. As soon as he had me strung up, he split. I don't know where his voice was coming from, but dude didn't stick around."

"But where would he go?" I asked. "Up to your room?"

"I don't think so." Liam shook his head. "Those wards are pretty good, and getting out of Fowlers Hall is no easy feat. Plus, that level of magic would be tracked. I think he was probably distracted by one of the other rooms, maybe."

He sighed. "I've stashed a lot of books down here when I don't want anyone to see me reading them, even in my own room."

"Yeah?" I looked around. "What kind of books?"

"Oh, arcanum, mostly from the Library of Alexandria."

I rounded him. "The what? I thought that burned to the ground like two thousand years ago."

"Yeah, well, there's this magician who lives out in Vegas, and he swiped a ton of its books back in the day without anyone noticing. He sends them to me from time to time." By now, Liam had loosened the final bond, and with an act of impressive grace, he exited the harness completely, performing a slow assisted somersault in the air, to land lightly on his feet.

Any thoughts of Liam and his arcane books fled my mind. "That was a heck of a dismount, but dude. You're bleeding from a dozen different places."

"Hazard of the job," he said. He reached down for his bag, and I wasn't surprised to see the thing lean toward him, so subtly that Liam didn't notice.

"Where did you get that backpack anyway?" I asked. "It's kind of...sentient, if you don't mind my saying so."

"I don't. It has way more magic than I do, and I love it for it." He laughed, giving it an affectionate pat. "I've had it a long time. Tyler gave it to me originally, and when the first one wore out, I took some of its threads and wove it into the next one, and the next one after that. It's seen me through quite a lot." As he spoke, Liam liberated a small vial of salve from his pack. When I gestured for it, he gave it to me with an expression of surprise. That expression only intensified as I applied the salve everywhere it looked like he'd been gouged by the hooks embedded into his tourniquet of death.

"It goes a lot quicker with you doing it," he commented, and I was relieved to see the wounds healing almost as quickly as I applied the ointment.

"This is pretty good stuff," I commented, a little drily. "You should probably put a patent on that."

Liam's smile held a wince. "Nina, I...I'm really sorry."

He didn't need to wave at the Apocrypha burning on the pyre for me to know what he was talking about. "You cut those pages out of the book, didn't you? It was you all along?"

"Yeah," he said. "That first night after the Run, when Frost mentioned the work, I went looking for it. To be fair, there'd been plenty of pages that'd already been excised, but I figured that wasn't a bad idea, and it would allow me to review the pages in secret. I should have told you, and I didn't."

"That's all right. It saves me the trouble of reading them. Did you find anything useful? Other than what you already said?"

He shrugged. "I told you the part about you ushering in a new dawn of monster hunting prowess?"

"Yeah, I caught that part."

"And about the need for us to make sure you stayed on the side of angels instead of monsters so we didn't have to kill you?"

"Yup, I picked up on that too. I'm thinking you're probably good on that score."

"Then you're pretty much up to speed—oh, except for the part about us needing to have sex as often as possible to ensure your safety."

I snorted. "Really? You hadn't gotten to that bit before I caught myself on fire."

Liam winced. "You're taking this a lot better than I probably would have."

"Well, when you start out your life as monster bait, pretty much everything from there is up." I looked from him to the remaining embers of the burning Apocrypha. "So now what? Should we look for the illusionist? Assume he's gone and get back to Guild Hall? I'm not sure how we do that, though, other than going around to the front of the building."

"Yeah." Liam blew out a long breath. "Honestly? I wouldn't mind just sitting here for a second. If the illusionist comes back, we're going to have a fight on our hands, and if he's really gone, we've got a bit of a trek to get to Lowell Library. I'm a little tired."

I looked at him with new concern. Liam's sandy-brown hair had fallen over his brow, and his eyes had slipped nearly closed as he slumped against the wall. As familiar as I was with the sight of him bouncing with energy, cracking off quips and jokes and sharp-edged observations, raring to go...seeing him so weary made my heart twist. For once, his long, lean body had gone still, his breathing had become slow and almost labored, and his hands lay at rest on his legs. He looked like someone who hadn't exhaled in so long that now that he had, there was no more energy to draw breath back in. I held myself tightly in check, not wanting to unwittingly prod him back into action, but desperate to help him at the same time. "Hey. Are you okay?"

"Oh yeah," he sighed. "I just...need to take a bit of a break."

He sagged back a little farther, and I tilted my head, lifting my hand to brush a long lock of hair from his brow.

"How long do you usually hang in that crazy harness thing?" I asked.

He chuckled softly. "I recently hit a new record. Six minutes and forty-four seconds, which is a long time to be hanging upside down, in case you were wondering."

"With sharp jabby things poking into you, yeah. I would think so."

He smiled a little, and something about that smile arrowed through me, so it was the most natural thing in the world for me to lean closer to him and brush my lips across his. The kiss was intended to be familiar, almost friendly, but the spark of desire that erupted within me couldn't be denied. The fear and worry and horror of the last few minutes came crashing back to me all at once, and I pulled Liam to me roughly, holding him close, horrified to hear that I was sobbing against him.

"You *have* to take better care of yourself," I whispered. "You treat yourself like you can be thrown away, and you *can't* be thrown away. I don't know what I'd do if I never got to see you again, and I've only just met you. You have to take better care."

"Hey, hey, it's okay," Liam tried, but he hugged me back just as tightly, and then we were kissing in earnest, my hands in his hair, his pulling up the skirt of my dress, pressing against my skin, the warm, vital truth of him and me together crackling with furious delight.

We made short work of our clothes and even shorter

work of virtually crawling inside each other's bodies, the rush of our connection lighting up the room all over again. That fire was restorative, the energy building upon the base we'd already formed, forging new lines of power between us. I could feel the strength of that connection and knew it was even stronger than it had been before. It built and built and built—and then exploded, my eyes temporarily blinded by the burst of electricity that shot out into the room in all directions.

"Liam," I said a little shakily what seemed like half an hour later, and he sighed against me, our shared convulsions ebbing away.

"Yeah," he whispered. "Magic. That's the gift you've given me, Nina, the gift no one else ever could."

The words had barely died away when a harsh, mocking laugh sounded over us.

"God save me from the fools of Boston's first families, but I do appreciate the show. It was...most instructive," it mocked. "If your own family isn't going to tell you the truth, Liam Graham, allow me to do so. You were *not* born the runt of the family. If your mother didn't know it, your father definitely did. Those tuning rods you've got stuck inside you aren't supposed to help you *borrow* more magic...they're meant to keep you down. The harbinger just helped you override them."

We stiffened, and Liam stared at me. I flapped my hands, less freaked out by the bodiless voice than by what it was saying.

Liam had no such issues. He rocked to his feet, his long, lean body turning, and he bounded over to one corner of the room, then the other. Finally, he liberated a portable speaker from behind the raised labyrinth.

"I can figure out who you are just from this," he yelled into it as the unit started to smoke. "You know that."

"I *do* know that," the voice taunted. "Fortunately, I'll be long gone before you get that chance. But do me a favor and at least own your birthright, will you? Your mother is an arrogant fool. She should know how badly she was duped. And *you* should know how much you've been made to suffer for your family's misbegotten fear. Fools, every last one of you. But fools are easily led. That part won't change, and I thank you for it in advance."

The speaker poofed into fragments in Liam's hands, turning to ash.

28

_____

We dressed quickly and reclaimed Liam's pack, making sure the fire over the oiled labyrinth was out. Then we headed for his rooms. As soon as we got high enough in the subterranean passageways to have cell service, Liam contacted Frost. The response was immediate, demanding our presence in Lowell Library as soon as we could make it there, promising a full update on the aftermath of the attack in the ballroom.

We made our way out of the caverns and back through Liam's bedroom. Liam was too keyed up to change, but I insisted we needed to detour to my room long enough for me to switch out of my ridiculous dress and into a tank top, jeans, and tennis shoes—and I strapped on my iron knife again for good measure. Then we exited Fowlers Hall and headed for the library, Liam texting the entire time with Frost. The more he worked his phone, though, the glummer he got.

"I don't like any of this," he muttered as we hustled through the shadows. "He says dampening rods aren't unprecedented among the families of Wellington. There's such a need to not be embarrassed that any rogue magic outside the lines of expectations for a family's given station gets suppressed."

I eyed him, aghast on his behalf. "How does anybody think that's normal?"

He lifted one shoulder, dropped it. "I don't know what to tell you. If the illusionist, whoever the fuck he is, is to be believed, my mom didn't know. My dad died when I was a kid, but I do remember him being an asshole. He just wasn't there one day, and I was too young to really understand it. But he'd left very specific instructions that I'm sure my mother followed to the letter. I think he probably would have left her destitute if she hadn't. That's just the way my family rolls."

I shook my head. "That's so horrible."

He sighed. "You're not wrong. I know you think you had a rough upbringing, and let's face it, you did, but your mother at least seemed to love you, to do what she could to keep you safe."

"Maybe," I allowed. "Or maybe she was part of the whole screwed-up group you have here. I can't say I would have blamed her for wanting to escape the Hallowells if that really was her family, or honestly, anyone we saw in that ballroom tonight. They all sucked."

Liam laughed. "They all had their issues, that's for sure."

By the time we reached Lowell Library, it was nearing midnight. From what Frost had told Liam, the Wellington first-family aristocracy had managed to quell the hornet uprising once we'd left the building. The entire group of illusions had winked out with the departure of the master illusionist who had been their ringleader. That was still a major point of confusion, though, because nobody had ever left the room—no one was missing but Liam and me.

Frost himself had conducted a census of the entire guest list, Liam said, and according to his data, the same number of people remained after the fight that had been there before it—apparently, the giant hornets had all been brought in for the night's entertainment. But we knew that wasn't the case, because *somebody* who hadn't been a monster had gone into the subterranean passages, leading Liam and me on our merry chase. The illusionist had to have been one of the guests...but who? And how had he left without anyone noticing? We argued that point back and forth as well, but came up with nothing useful.

"I mean, think about it. Somebody made themselves look like Grim, and we believed it was Grim. How hard could it be for them to create the illusion that they were there until they were able to return and take up their position again. Answer? Pretty damn easy," Liam finally said. "They beat us at every turn."

"Yeah," I sighed, because he was right. As much as I hated to admit it, whoever was behind these coordinated monster attacks on Wellington's campus, they knew what they were doing. Not only in this particular case where they'd hired a magician of no small ability, but they also had monsters at their beck and call. Who did that? Monsters, by their very nature, weren't easily controlled. Even the ones on campus, who were held in the monster quad, to the eternal dismay of Merry and her friends, were not domesticated. They may have been a little old and tired, but they were still monsters.

And monsters weren't meant to be controlled. I believed that in my heart of hearts.

Frost was waiting for us in the war room, along with Zach and Tyler.

He lifted a hand as we entered. "Before you ask, I don't

know where Grim is. We've put the alert out for him, but he's in the wind. I think he got cut up in the attack, and that never sits well with him."

"He'll be okay," Tyler said staunchly. "He was a little banged up, like Frost said, but he's tough, and he's pissed. I think he wants to work through all that on his own time."

"Nothing wrong with that," Liam agreed, and I felt another surge of pride for my team. They were all willing to accept Grim for who he was, even if he didn't behave in a way that was traditionally acceptable. These were good guys, and I was glad to be on their team.

"So where are we netting out?" Liam asked.

Frost eyed him. "Honestly, my biggest concern is with the issue you raised in your text. Liam, you're one of the biggest assets that the team has, and we've always stood with you. The idea that you could have been kept from understanding and accessing your true strength is abhorrent to me, regardless of the reason. We need to get to the bottom of that right now."

Liam nodded. "How?"

Tyler stepped forward. "The easiest way is an X-ray device, to identify the tuners you have in you and remove one of them for analysis. That's kind of like major surgery, though, so not something we want to enter into lightly. Plus we don't have time for it, which leaves us nowhere. Then again..."

Liam turned to him. "Then again, what?" he asked, a flare of excitement in his voice. "I know that 'then again.' I'm a big fan of that 'then again.' What are you thinking?"

Tyler blew out a long breath. "Well, Frost was telling me there's this spell of, I guess you would call it revelation. It wouldn't take the tuners out of you on its own, but it might show their true nature. And if we found them, we could maybe get them out on our own. It's pretty arcane stuff—"

"But we're a pretty arcane group," Liam ended for him. "I'm in."

"All right, then." Tyler grinned. "I think we should stay in here. You guys maybe stand back a little bit. Commander Frost over there, Zach at the door just in case any spiders or hornets or other asshole insects show up, and Nina…"

I reached for Liam's hand. "I want to stand with him," I said.

"You don't need to do that," Liam began quickly, but I shook my head.

"I've always known that there was more magic in you than you gave yourself credit for. This just lets me be the first person to get to see that I was right."

I didn't look at Liam as he glanced toward me, but the flow of electricity through our linked hands was enough for me to know how my words touched him. I hadn't needed the bodiless voice of the illusionist to call Liam out on the horrible acts of his family. I knew in my bones that this was the truth. Now he would know it too.

Without further preamble, Tyler pulled a thick, heavy tome toward him across the table, and opened it to a marked page.

"This passage is way too long even for me to memorize, and I pray to God I'm not going to have to memorize it for repeated use. But here we go."

He nodded to Zach, who killed the lights in the room, dropping us all into shadow. Then he began speaking, his voice measured and resolute, weaving the pattern of the spell layer upon layer. I felt the push of magic against Liam, against myself too, forceful enough to lift me onto my toes. It didn't hurt, at least not me, but Liam hissed out a long breath, a telling sign for someone who had as high a tolerance for pain as he did.

I felt a biting pain in my side, then wondered if that was the faintest echo of what Liam was feeling, transferred over to me much as I'd been able to share in Zach's pain. Either way, I stood with my hand locked around Liam's, both of us bracing and leaning slightly forward, as if being buffeted by an unseen wind. A light built around us, and I whooshed out an unsteady breath as Tyler's voice faltered a little.

"My God," Zach said from behind us, and I turned to look at Liam. His hand still remained in mine, but his other hand now spread wide, his chin lifted, his face tilted toward the ceiling. His eyes were unfocused and his breathing had gone shallow. And his body was lit with an unholy fire.

In that fire, we saw the truth. And the truth was flat-out horrifying.

Liam was plugged so full of insertables, he practically vibrated off the floor under the influence of Tyler's spell. In addition to the devices that lined his collarbone, half a dozen other metal shards made their presence known, glowing incandescently at his waist, his thighs, his forearms, his ankles. And as to their nature, they coated his body in an inky wave of pressure.

"Suppression," Commander Frost said, and Tyler nodded, even while lifting his hands to forestall any other commentary.

"Liam?" he murmured.

"Can you get them out?" Liam asked tightly. His body quivered with pent-up energy, making the tuners shimmer beneath his skin.

Tyler stiffened, and Zach stepped forward, but it was Frost's turn to lift a quelling hand. "This isn't the time for that," he said.

"But we *can* do it," Tyler protested. "That's the very next spell, and we just need someone to keep Liam from stroking out."

There was a sudden movement at the door, and I turned to see Grim standing at the threshold, his brows drawn together in a furious scowl.

"What is this?" he asked sharply, sounding genuinely alarmed.

Tyler lifted his hands again. "Looks like Liam's parents were assholes. They've been suppressing his magic this whole time."

"Then we free him." Grim announced. He strode forward. "What do you need?"

"I need you to back up Nina," Tyler said. "I'm going to make cuts over each tuner, and they should come out on their own. But they'll be fiery hot, so brace yourself to go all barbecue tongs if you need to."

Grim grunted, but I was glad he was here. It felt right for him to be with us in solidarity, especially as Liam began to tremble in earnest. I was shaking too. The stitch in my side throbbed insistently, only an echo of what Liam was no doubt feeling that took my breath away. What must Liam be enduring, if I felt this bad?

Tyler began the spell. He wove the Latin around Liam with a haunting melody that made me lean into it, reveling in its beauty and grace. Then he stepped toward Liam, and with a speed I could barely follow, he lifted a knife and sliced along Liam's collarbone. The tuners shot out with an angry hiss, and Liam convulsed, crying out in pain.

Zach put his hands on either side of Liam's temples, his own body going rigid as he attempted to take on some of Liam's pain. I gripped Liam's hand tight, but beside me, Grim pulled his own dagger free as more tuners glowed beneath Liam's skin. He whirled toward Liam, slicing deep against his rib cage.

Liam staggered to the side, blood gushing as new tuners spilled out, and I watched in horror as lights flared at other points in his body. Enough holes had been rent into his skin that these hideous machines could make their way out on their own, and they sought those paths eagerly.

Electricity crackled around the room as more devices spilled out of Liam, making everyone shout—and Liam flat-out scream. Frost surged forward, Zach clamped his hands on Liam's temples, and Tyler bent into his makeshift surgery, his blade flying.

In the cacophony, a fiery pain exploded at my waist, and I jerked away from Liam and slapped my left hand down, feeling the thick ridge of scar tissue—the scars I couldn't remember receiving. Beside me, Grim hissed, his face unreadable, and as he lifted his blade toward Liam one more time, he instead turned and thrust it toward me in a cruel, slashing arc.

I watched in horror as the blade sliced down, cutting through my tank top, laying open my skin, and then the small silvery curve of a strange device spit out of the wound and clattered onto the table.

"What the *hell*?" I gasped as Grim scooped up the device and shoved it toward me, closing my hand around it. The entire operation had taken less than three seconds, and with Tyler, Frost, and Zach converging on Liam, no one had even noticed what Grim and I were doing.

"Liam's parents weren't the only ones who were assholes," Grim grunted, his pale-gold eyes drilling into mine. "Tell no one."

29

————

Chaos surged around us. Liam's hands went wide as he tried to brace himself against the table and nearly collapsed. Tyler stopped shouting in Latin, and Frost and Zach shifted to Liam's side to hold him up, while Grim pulled me away and braced me.

"I didn't realize I had that many inside me," Liam finally managed, while I squeezed my own tuner tightly, never mind that it was still covered in my own blood. The idea was sickening, but not because of the ick factor. More because I'd never known something had been inside me. I felt the heavy weight of the device, one side sharp and pointy, the other jagged. How could I not have known this thing had been inside me? And more to the point, how could my mother have never told me? She had to have known, right?

Granted, the device had been buried beneath the absolute worst of the scars I couldn't remember receiving. Even now, I pressed my hands tight to my side, surprised to feel the skin had already merged back together, the wound closing up now that it had revealed its secret. Hell, Grim's slash to liberate me from the device had been so pinpoint accurate, the rip in my shirt barely showed. Breathing out a careful sigh and making sure no one was paying any attention to me, I slid the half-circle tuner deep into my jeans pocket. I'd have time to figure out its crazy later.

"How are you feeling?" Tyler asked, patting Liam on the shoulder as we all stared at the pile of tuners on the table. "Besides about five pounds lighter?"

Liam laughed. "You know, I feel pretty good. I don't feel like I've just been mortally wounded, I'll tell you that much. I feel good."

"Your energy is seriously strong," Zach said, his hands still lifted. "When those things came out of you, the overriding emotion I felt from you was relief. Apparently, the burden of trying to keep your own energy down was taking its toll on you, and you weren't going to put up with it anymore."

"You got that right." Liam looked at me with a grin. "You leveled me up *despite* those friggin' tuners. Imagine what I'm capable of now. Or what we could do together next."

The fire in his eyes kindled something deep inside me, as it always seemed to. Even having had these devices ripped from him, the evidence of his family's betrayal laid out for all to see, Liam was already on to the next adventure. I wondered if he'd ever stop long enough to truly consider the danger he put himself in, to process all the lessons he seemed to learn at a breakneck speed.

Then I thought about the harness that hung from the wall far beneath Fowlers Hall, intended to trap him in place until he had the ingenuity to break himself free. Those few minutes, trapped and in peril, when nobody knew where he was and nobody could save him if they wanted to, were probably the equivalent of days' worth of contemplation for an ordinary person. Liam would never be ordinary. And we were bonded, an answering fire in my own blood stirring as his gaze intensified.

"What was your mom thinking?" Tyler muttered, leaning over the table. "These are top-of-the-line. I've never even seen technology like this."

"Neither have I," Zach agreed from the other side.

"I don't think it was Mom, actually." Liam glanced over to me, and I nodded.

"I don't think so either. I think it was your dad. Still, there had to be a reason why they wanted you suppressed."

Frost grunted in disgust. "There is a reason. I told you that already. It's shameful, but it's part of the dark history of Wellington Academy—of all those magicians who first gathered in these hills. The Grahams have always been known as magicians of great renown, but they're not the highest echelon of the first families. They've been allowed their position in the hierarchy of Boston's magical society because they've known their place and haven't sought to rise above it."

Liam shook his head. "Yeah, you said that, but I still call bullshit. Why wouldn't we try to be the best we could be? We've had some of the most extraordinary magicians in the city in my family—those guys didn't exactly try to hide their light under a barrel."

Frost nodded. "And again, the Grahams have performed well within the parameters you were allowed. Even your Great-Uncle Spencer channeled his magic for the amusement and entertainment of ordinary Bostonians and the other magical families. Imagine if, instead, he'd tried to make real magic? Imagine if *you* did, free as you are now from suppression. That would make the Grahams a threat to those families who sought to remain at the top of the magical hierarchy."

"But it would make our family awesome," Liam protested.

"No, it would make *you* awesome."

To my surprise, it was Grim who spoke. His voice was low and menacing as he scowled at Liam, though who he was mad at, I wasn't quite sure. "You, not the Grahams. The Grahams as a family would have been put at risk. Your father needed to protect his people, just as all the generations before him had. It doesn't make him right, but it makes him understandable. Your parents should have told you. In the past, parents probably did."

It was Liam's turn to laugh darkly. "Yeah, well, that wouldn't have worked in my case. I never would have accepted it. If I'd known they were suppressing my magic, I would have ripped those friggin' tuners out the moment I'd gotten the chance."

He sighed again, eyeing the devices. "I really don't think my mom knew what these really were. Do you?"

"I don't," Frost said. "Or at least not on any sort of conscious level. I don't think she would have allowed it. From what I know of Claudia Graham, she would have wanted to celebrate your strength, not suppress it."

Liam coughed a laugh. "You've got that right. So now what?"

As if the library had been waiting for its chance, a hollow, keening note sounded deep within the building, almost as if it were coming from several floors beneath us.

Tyler shot a sharp glance to Frost. "What the hell is *that*?"

"And where is it coming from?" Zach added.

Frost had already turned, uttering a sharp command I'd never heard him use before.

Instantly, all the screens surrounding the room flared to

life. They were showing the views of the surveillance cameras throughout Lowell Library, I realized immediately, and they revealed absolutely nothing of interest. Room after room of books, shelves, and tables, oversized furniture stacked up neatly, heavily framed works of art lined up against the wall and covered partially with tarps. But no monsters making keening noises that sounded almost familiar, for all that I couldn't place them.

I didn't have to wait long.

"Oh my God, are those caralons?" Tyler demanded, half turning toward Liam as he jabbed his finger at one of the screens, just as something slipped past, too quickly for me to identify. "Is that possible?"

"The way our luck's been going, yeah. It's possible," Liam sighed. He flashed me a sharp look. "You remember the caralons? From the Run?"

I made a face, searching the screens for another glimpse of the creatures. "Like low-level succubi?"

"Exactly like that. They're nothing to screw around with, though, and they've been on my nuts since I started training as a monster hunter. I have no idea why."

"Of course you do. Now, anyway," Frost said, while Tyler nodded vigorously.

"No friggin' kidding, of *course*." He turned to Liam. "Caralons, like succubi, need power. All they want is power. You had power. They didn't care if it was being suppressed within an inch of its life, they knew it was inside you and they wanted to get it out. No wonder they've been all over you every chance they get."

"And they're coming back now?" Zach demanded. "How in the hell are they even on campus? Are our wards failing that much?"

"Different kind of monster," Grim said. "The wards were

238

set for the monsters that would have the most impact for the most people, but there are ways to get around that. There's always a way to get around a ward. You just have to know where to look, and have been living long enough to know the ancient ways."

He sounded particularly grumpy about that explanation, even for him, but my attention was immediately distracted by another haunting wail that sounded far below.

"It didn't take them long to realize that your magic has amped up, did it?" Tyler groused. "You might as well have rung the dinner bell."

"Friggin' great," Liam muttered as Frost barked out a shout.

"Look there. If they're caralons, they won't need an elevator to get around. They can dissolve right through ceilings and floors." He pointed to a screen in the middle of the wall. I caught the movement as it flashed by, then new creatures appeared, female in appearance, easily a dozen of them, their lower halves lost in roiling smoke. Their faces were dominated by enormous gaping mouths, eyes sealed shut, hair a wild entangled mess. Whoever had dreamt up images of nymphlike beauties and applied them to the succubus myth had clearly never seen this variant.

"There was something in the frame before them," Zach said urgently. "Someone else is here."

"The illusionist," Tyler said. "Has to be."

"Agreed," Liam said, as the guys spread out, obviously bracing themselves for an attack that could literally come from anywhere. "Maybe he's the one leading them this way. He definitely knew the lay of the land already, given his spider attack."

"And what's up with the whole insect invasion, anyway?" I asked. They all turned to look at me, and I flapped my hands. "I mean, we've had spiders here and hornets in Guild Hall, and Liam and I ran into an entire nest of flying rodents —which were monsters but definitely screwed-up, buggy-looking monsters. You're not picking up a theme here?"

"I..." Frost blinked at me, but before he could say anything more a dozen screaming creatures burst through the war room's floors and walls, heading for Liam. The guys and I leapt into action. I yanked my iron knife from its sheath and turned as Grim shouted. I pivoted and lifted my hand to capture the small mesh bag he hefted my way. I knew what was inside it—another round of silver beads, the touch of metal cool through the loose weave. I welcomed them now as I swung the full bag at the nearest creature.

It screamed and dissolved into a shower of smoke and sparks, and I turned to greet the next caralon. Out of the corner of my eye, I realized that Liam wasn't taking on the caralon that found him first. Instead, he let them come, his face a mask of focus.

"Liam, what are you doing?" Tyler shouted, and Liam barely reacted before the first caralon reached him. He turned his hands outward, a burst of flame no longer shooting directly from his palm, but seeming to come from all the way up by his elbows. It incinerated the creature at three feet, and the one following behind as well.

A blast of heat ripped through the room, and Zach yelped as the caralon he'd tackled disintegrated beneath him.

"Tamp it down," Frost yelled out, sounding genuinely pissed, which seemed unfair because Liam was being awesome, but Liam dropped his hands anyway, and we continued the fight using more conventional levels of magic. I thought this odd until high, screeching laughter echoed through the great hall of the library, beyond the war room.

"What, you would repress him? You would step away from the strongest magic you've ever experienced? This is why you're weak, you and your whole academy. This is why you're destined to fail. This is why the management of monsters should never have fallen to anyone like you."

The cry was high and piercing, and remarkably feminine. This was no monster. It had to be the illusionist.

Tyler had the same idea.

"Liam," he shouted, and the two of them headed for the door, Frost barely getting out in front of them, his hands held wide. For the first time, I realized that magic fire crackled from Frost's fingertips, and I felt a wave of energy spread out as our group passed through the door and into the larger chamber. Some sort of force field, had to be.

And judging from the enormous fiery dragonfly now hovering in the center of the library chamber, we needed all the protection we could get.

A second later the bug's body disappeared and a stunningly regal woman stood in its place, still flanked by iridescent wings. She was tall and slender, with fair, flawless skin and dark hair flowing wildly around her face, obscuring her features but somehow not diminishing her beauty. She radiated power from the tips of her fingers to the billowing wings that flowed out around her, breathtaking in their span.

"Holy shit," Liam breathed, the only words he could get out before the creature roared in pure, unfettered joy, and with her arms and diaphanous wings spreading wide...

She unleashed her power on us.

30

A fireball lit up the room, catching everything in a white-hot, shimmering blaze, and out of that fire sprang a half dozen fiery swarms of flying chaos.

Another thing about this dragonfly of destruction, she was the real deal. Before when I'd encountered monsters, I understood what I was facing. They were creatures of flesh, bone, and brains that I could get a knife into, that I could take down. I'd never once doubted myself, at least not since I'd gotten up my strength and speed to where I didn't feel vulnerable.

But this wasn't a monster, this was a human overlaying a giant bug, a magician, an enemy unlike any other I'd ever faced. Tyler started shouting Latin spells, while Liam stood next to him, practically levitating with power as he laid down ropes of his own internal fire to hem in the cloud of thrashing, slashing insect destruction. Zach kept up a litany of information about the magician's thoughts and emotions. Every point around the room where she turned her mind and directed her swarm, he followed and reported on, until she finally snarled something and flung her hand toward him, arrows of light piercing Commander Frost's force field, one of them breaking through to drive Zach backward. He sprawled into a bookshelf, his commentary cut off with a strangled scream.

Frost shouted a curse, and I recognized that something important had happened. The swarms winked out, but the illusionist expanded to almost double her size. There was plenty of room in the library chamber, with its soaring ceilings and wide open center space, but it was still alarming to see how much more mass she occupied. Her magic pressed against us in waves, and as she forced it forward, she shifted as well. First becoming the enormous multilegged spider, then the buzzing rat moths from the Beacon Hill Prep Academy, then a gloriously beautiful succubus, not a caralon, her face a vision of beauty, her hair black and wild and flying in the riot of light and wind.

"Frost?" Tyler shouted. I shot a glance over to him, surprised to see Grim by his side, momentarily as flummoxed by all the magic as I was. I hefted my bag of silver beads. The movement caught Grim's attention, and he turned to me and shook his head in a hard no. There was something remarkable in his face that I couldn't quite understand, an expression that almost pleaded for me not to show my hand. A second later, it was gone.

"We can't hold her," Liam called out. "Not the way we're doing it. You've got to…"

"*No,*" Frost shouted, and it was clear to me he was also telling Liam not to betray his hand. What the hell was going on? This was a magician in our midst, a monster by any other name. We needed to take her *out*.

Not two seconds later, a loud chorus of shouts sounded from beyond the illusionist, easily a dozen voices, men and women alike, commingled in fury and excitement. Then

Symmes and the board surged into the room, with Claudia Graham and Theodore Perkins at their head. Claudia's hands were alight, and Perkins held up a gleaming sword that seemed to go brighter as Claudia cried out words I couldn't understand.

Anderson Reid and, to my shock, Meredith Choate came around on the other side, also chanting something in an entirely different language. Behind them, more people filed in, academy board members I'd never seen before, but apparently strong enough that they'd passed Spell Craft 101. The illusionist turned, her beautiful face transfixed with anger, and then she was surrounded by a net of sparkling lights, which shot outward and then constricted just as quickly, trapping her diaphanous wings against her, binding her tight. She howled in fury, then twisted and twisted again, becoming ever smaller with each rotation. Then finally, Claudia stepped forward, and holding out a velvet sack that she'd apparently brought with her for the occasion of bagging her own dragonfly.

Liam stepped forward. "Use this instead," he instructed. He whipped his pack off his shoulder, dumped its contents summarily on the floor, then threw the bag to his mother. With a final flourish, she stuffed the illusionist in the pack and zipped it up. All the rioting light in the room vanished.

We all stared, and Claudia straightened, staring at her son.

"Liam?" she asked a little breathlessly. "Are you okay?" It was a testament to a mother's intuition that she knew something had changed, even if she couldn't quite figure out what.

Liam didn't have to see Frost's hard look to smooth it over.

"I'm great—and wow, Mom. That was pretty awesome,"

he said. I was startled to see Claudia's cheeks redden at the unexpected praise.

"Well," she sniffed delicately. "It's been a long time since we've been called on to work together. It's good to know we still can."

She turned to Tyler's father and handed him the pack. "We'll need to figure this one out sooner rather than later," she said, and he smiled—the first genuine smile I'd seen the man ever crack.

He slung the pack over his shoulder as if he were no older than Liam and nodded to her. "We've got just the place set up for that kind of interrogation. We'll learn what we need to know, count on it. This bastard tried to embarrass my family, and that will not stand. The politics of Wellington Academy aside, we need to work together, not apart."

Claudia nodded, and several of the men and women surrounding us did as well. "We'll learn what we need," she agreed.

They left, and the six of us stood looking at each other, the fatigue of the last several days seeming to catch up to all of us at once.

Frost blew out a long breath. "Thank you, Liam, for your discretion. This was the academy's battle to fight, not ours alone. In some ways, they needed the win perhaps more than we did, and more to the point, they needed to remember the magic we have baked into the walls of the academy, not only what's locked up in the very able forms of you all. They'll determine the identity of the illusionist, and we'll go from there. Meanwhile, you all need to get some sleep."

"What? What are you talking about?" Tyler demanded, turning on him. "We should be there helping them. My magic and spell-casting ability alone probably outstrips half of theirs, and we don't even know what Liam's capable of at this point."

He gestured to Liam. "I *also* noticed him going all inferno there for a second, in case you missed it."

"Oh, I noticed," Frost said. "And what I'd ask is that we have the opportunity to explore his newfound strength on our own terms, not under the scrutiny of the board. We've lost so much of the Apocrypha, there's no way of knowing what we're really looking at here."

"You don't think that's the end of it, then?" Tyler asked. "If the illusionist is behind the Boston Brahmin attacks, and now we've got her—or him—locked down, is the academy in danger anymore?"

"It's in danger," Grim said. He sounded resolute, and Frost nodded as well.

"I'm forced to agree with Grim. The issues we face haven't stopped while the illusionist played her hand. There are new, legitimate monster sightings coming through by the hour, especially now that we've worked out the glitches of the notification system. And there's still the question of the other monster hunters, the previous graduates who are now quite inconveniently dead. Don't think that hasn't figured into the thinking of the administration to expedite your graduation process. The presentation brought out all the families, and it's already paid dividends. Even the Hallowells are renewing their engagement with the academy. That can only go well for us."

He folded his arms over his chest. "For now, though, you all need to get some rest. There's much that will be coming and we'd better be prepared for it."

"I still think we should be there to interrogate the illusionist," Zach groused.

"Oh, we'll be there," Liam put in. We all turned to look at him, and he sat with one hip propped on a table, his manner not one of bravado but simple confidence, the confidence of a guy who no longer had to prove anything.

He gestured to the stack of stuff that'd spilled out of his pack, that he'd been reassembling as we'd talked.

"I may not have *completely* unpacked my bag prior to tossing it over to Mom," he said with a grin. "There *may* have been a tracker involved, with audio. Video, I don't think I managed to turn on in time, but at least we should be able to hear what goes on. That has to count for something."

"You're kidding me," Frost groaned, but he couldn't help the grin.

"I try," Liam said with a wink, and he tossed another device Frost's way. "Once they unzip that bag again, it's go time."

"And I'll look forward to that," Frost said, eyeing the small speaker. He waved it at us. "Again, get some rest. Report tomorrow when I notify you. I doubt quite seriously they'll begin the interrogation process until after they've had a chance to shore up their magical reserves and possibly recruit some new hands to the fight, but when they do, you'll be the second to know."

His phone buzzed, and he pulled it out to look at it. A smile crept across his face.

"Well, well, well," he said. "If it isn't Dean Robbins asking for an update. Apparently, word has gotten out that there was some excitement here at Lowell Library."

"What will you tell him?" I asked.

Frost gave me a conspiratorial wink. "Exactly what he wants to hear. That the board was able to take care of it, no monster hunters required." He glanced around. "Get out of here. Tomorrow is going to be a busy day."

31

Nobody seemed quite willing to turn in yet, and we argued about what family might have spawned the illusionist all the way to the edge of campus and into the White Crane bar. Apparently, such arguments were better over beer.

The bar was hopping more than usual tonight, and I wondered briefly if the outskirts of campus had picked up on the energy flowing through the academy, or if Wellington really was a city unto itself. Tyler went to the front of the bar where the bartender leaned against the counter, laughing with a few guys I'd come to think of as locals. They'd been in the place practically every time I'd been, no matter what hour of day. Didn't they have jobs?

Either way, Tyler came over a few minutes later with two beers in his hands, the bartender following close behind with a tray carrying three more and a bowl of chips. My stomach growled as she laid the food down on the table.

"Kitchen's closed," she said, her voice low and graveled, like she'd spent the day smoking cigarettes and pounding whisky. She nodded to me as I looked her way, and I didn't miss the dark shadows under her eyes, the more pronounced lines at the corners of her eyes. I'd only been here a few days ago, but it may as well have been a year, as tired as she looked. "You guys need food, you can order it in."

"We're good," Tyler assured her, but as she turned to walk away, I blurted, "Hey...are you okay?"

She stopped and pivoted back to me, and I realized that the weird half-light in the bar had played tricks on me a bit. She looked...better, I decided. Still exhausted, but not quite so gray. "Oh, sure. Long day," she said, and when she smiled, more of her fatigue cleared away. She was probably used to putting on a good face for customers.

She looked like she was going to say something else, then seemed to decide against it. Instead, she nodded to us. "You all take care. Let me know if you need anything else."

We assured her we'd be fine, and she seemed to accept that, though her sharp gaze swept over us again, and I got the feeling she probably didn't miss the fact that our energy was keyed up and we were stressed to the max. Once she moved off, Liam leaned forward. "We're going to have to be prepared for the illusionist to be a member of the first families. Probably someone that no one expects."

Grim leaned back in his chair and grunted in disgust. "The families," he muttered. "You all have so many secrets, how can you trust anyone?"

"That's not a bad question, actually," Tyler said, tilting his head. "It comes down to the old agreements struck, the alliances, yeah?" He looked at Liam. "And you know, a lot of the monster hunters from years past came from those first families. Not all of them, like Zach here, though I bet if we searched long enough we'd find a distant link. But still, a lot."

"And now those monster hunters have gone missing... and are maybe even dead," Zach said thoughtfully. "That's gotta make for some unhappy families. You think they're striking back?"

"Could be. There's definitely a lot more attention being paid to the minor, right?" Tyler mused. "Maybe they think we will pay more attention to their missing sons and daughters if they stir up threats?"

"But why the cloak and dagger?" I protested. "Why didn't they just contact Frost or Dean Robbins and demand they start a search?"

"Robbins," Liam said, and it was his turn to sound disgusted. "I still can't get over him and that Mr. Bellows at your apartment. That's some shady shit right there. We can't trust them not to be working for both the academy and whoever this illusionist is."

"Agreed," Tyler sighed. "The illusionist has been ahead of us at every turn. First he—or she, I guess, if it's actually a woman—carved up that grave marker to dick with us, then she showed up as Grim at Guild Hall."

Grim sat up sharply. "She what?" he asked.

Liam shook his head. "Sorry, my man, totally forgot about that part. But Tyler's right. When we were trying to overload one of my mom's gadgets right after the presentation, you showed up in the doorway. Only, it wasn't you, which we realized less than a minute later. It had to have been the work of the illusionist. She's really fucking good."

Grim grunted something that sounded like a curse, though I wasn't sure of the language, and he didn't look happy. "Did she take the form of anyone else?"

"No, but I've been thinking about that," Liam said,

leaning back in his chair and casting his gaze toward the shadowed ceiling, gesturing vaguely at me. "The bug thing, you know? You said something about it, and you're right. From the rat moths to the spiders to the dragonfly to those murder hornets. What's the big bug deal?"

Zach blew out a breath. "Well...insects are everywhere, they're strong, they've been around since ancient times, and they seem impossible to kill. I guess that makes for a good theme."

"They're also massively adaptable," Liam agreed. "They can survive some shit. And I mean—that poison they were spitting out in Guild Hall? Somebody put it in those monsters, and it *worked*. That...is kind of friggin' scary."

"They also incite fear," Grim put in. "Among all the creatures, there is something unnerving about insects as attackers that terrorizes people at a base level. That's why the illusionist chose it. She wants to cause terror."

His words hung over the table with frigid finality, and Liam took a long, slow pull of his beer. "Man," he sighed. "When it comes to enemies, we sure do know how to pick 'em."

"Speaking of enemies..." Zach lifted his own beer, and gestured to us. "What's up with those elf guys—or the Laram, I guess it is? Are they in league with the illusionist too, or..."

"No way," Liam said, but Tyler immediately countered, and the debate was on...a debate that had no conclusion, of course. We simply didn't have enough information about the shadowy watchers—other than they'd tried to turn Zach and me into pincushions. But was that part of a conspiracy, or simply monsters being monsters?

Two beers later, we were still arguing, but the debate had gotten decidedly louder and...less focused. By the time we finally stumbled back to Fowlers Hall, we were all dead on our feet—so tired that we instinctively headed to our own rooms. Even Grim, I suspected, though I had no idea where his rooms actually were in the enormous building.

I got lost only a couple of times, then finally made it to my room, stepping into the enormous chamber with a sigh before carefully shutting the door. There was enough moonlight streaming in through the tall windows that I could see easily, so I didn't bother hitting the lights.

I was halfway to the bed when I realized I wasn't alone. I froze, then turned slowly to the side. "You realize I've killed monsters for less."

Liam sat in one of the wing backed chairs that flanked the honest-to-God fireplace in my room, a fireplace that was not currently lit, but had suspiciously new-looking logs piled up.

"Are you surprised? You gotta be surprised right? Come on, tell me you were surprised," he said, leaning forward and grinning as he rested his elbows on his knees. "I didn't mean to scare you, but, I mean, I haven't been rattling around this mausoleum of a residence hall for all these years without figuring out how to get around, you know?"

I shook my head, but couldn't help but laugh. "I'm surprised," I assured him. "But I guess I shouldn't have been. How did you get here so quickly?"

Liam waggled his brows. "A magician never reveals his secrets," he said, as he hooked a thumb toward the fireplace. "But going forward, if you're not looking for unexpected guests, I recommend lighting a fire. It would take someone with a lot of grit to get through the way I just did, if a fire was going strong."

He cocked his wrist with a sharp gesture. A thin stream of fire zipped across the room, landing in the grate and catching the logs ablaze. The fire swept up quickly, making me wonder again just how fresh those logs were, but I didn't really mind. Having Liam in my room, cozied up for a fire-side chat, felt more right in this moment than anything else I could imagine. As I moved toward him, he stood and hefted a pile of blankets and pillows, which he tumbled in front of his chair and spread out on the thick rug that covered the hardwood floor.

"Did you have any of this set up before tonight?" I demanded, but he just laughed.

"Nah, the idea came to me as we were walking back from the White Crane—and I guess I was motivated."

"I'll say." I felt absurdly happy as I flopped down on the pillows, leaning one elbow onto the seat of the wingback chair. Liam did the same, the two of us facing each other in front of a roaring fire.

"I guess it just felt like we've never really had a normal date," he explained without me asking the question, because of course he did. He looked off toward the fire, as if slightly embarrassed by the revelation. "And I wanted that with you, you know? I want everything with you. From our first fight, to our first round of makeup sex, to our first day on the job as fully graduated monster hunters, to our first fight in another city, another country. It doesn't matter what, really. I want an entire lifetime of firsts with you."

His words were quiet and a little rueful, and my heart tugged as I drew my fingers along his arm, an arm I'd seen bloodied and scorched not all that long ago.

"Just the firsts?" I asked, as his head came around, his gaze once more meeting mine. "What about the lasts, too? What if I want you to be the last guy I see as I close my eyes at night, the last voice I hear whispering that everything is going to be okay? The last guy I kiss in front of a roaring fire on a warm May night?"

"I have it on good authority that all those things can be yours." Liam's words were harder, almost gruff as leaned forward to brush his lips against mine. Then he pulled back to look at me, his expression fiercer than I'd ever seen it. "I love you, Nina. And everything is *going* to be okay, because no matter where you go, no matter who you fight, no matter what monsters you find waiting for you in the dark, I'm gonna be there, too. I'm going find you when you're lost. I'm going to bring you home the moment you say the word. And I'm never going to let you go."

He gripped my arms, then, pulling me close, his whispered words coming fast as his heart beat frantically against mine. "*You're* my family. You're everything. You're the first person whoever believed in me just by looking at me... without me having to prove a damn thing. I'll never stop loving you."

"Oh, Liam," I managed, but there wasn't any more need for words after that. Liam and I collapsed into each other like two starving people presented with a feast, the electricity of our symbiotic magic leaping and arcing as we kissed, touched, and devoured each other. With every stroke of his finger along my skin I came alive, with every kiss and taste of him, I felt him gasp and shudder, the surge between us undeniable.

I didn't know whose clothes came off first, but it felt as if they had been burned away. Liam drew me up to my knees to straddle him as he laid flat, letting me sink over him. He stared up at me, his eyes filled with more magic than I had ever seen, and I couldn't stop the burst of emotion that welled up within me, half a laugh, half a sob, and wholly, completely Liam.

I shivered with happiness as we began moving together in perfect time to the crackling, leaping fire. The shadows danced along the walls to their own soundless melody, and for just this moment in time, everything was perfect. Everything was right. "What am I going to do with you?" I sighed.

"Well that's easy," Liam smiled, sliding his arms around me and anchoring me tight. "Whatever you want."

32

I t wasn't until two o'clock the next afternoon that my phone blared, with Frost summoning us all to the library—and I was still in bed at the time. It took me a second to fully comprehend where I was, alone in an enormous canopied bed, Merry's beautiful dress draped over the nearest chair, and me boneless in the sheets. I stared around, trying to get my bearings, when my phone buzzed again. It was Liam, with Tyler and Zach right behind. Even if I'd wanted to keep sleeping, I wouldn't have been able to, so I got up and hurriedly dressed.

Within a few minutes, we met at the front of Fowlers Hall—most of us anyway. Zach, Liam, Tyler, and me. As usual, Grim was off somewhere else.

"Did Frost tell you anything at all?" Tyler asked Liam as I trotted down the steps. Liam shook his head.

"Not nearly enough. He said it was worse than he thought and that we needed to get over there, which is basically a whole lot of nothing, but I guess we'll find out."

"Something's definitely going on," Zach said, his head tilted slightly, one hand raised as if to get a feel of the very air. "They've got a perimeter established around Guild Hall. That's gotta be where they're doing the interrogation, which is kind of curious, don't you think?"

"Really?" Tyler said. "I wonder if that building has more built-in protection than we thought. Makes sense given all the magic they were trying to throw at us during the presentation. So who were they really trying to protect? I'm betting there were a whole bunch of cross-currents going on there that we didn't realize."

"I suspect you're probably right," Liam said. "What I would do for a do-over now that I can pick up a little bit more on that sort of thing."

Tyler laughed. "I have a feeling you'll get your chance, my man."

We made it to Lowell Library a few minutes later, the only one not making an appearance being, of course, Grim. That guy would probably be late to his own funeral.

Frost nodded to us as we filed into the war room. "Don't get comfortable," he said. "They began transmitting about two hours ago, not making much headway at first. Then there was a lot of commotion and a lot of arguing. The Hallowells' name was mentioned repeatedly."

I perked up at this. "Really? They're bringing them in?"

"Unclear. Most of the commentary centered around the idea that they were going to be extremely angry about the outcome of the interrogation. Then there was a lot more static, screaming, feminine in nature, a loud slam, then a lot of quiet rumbling. Symmes started talking at that point, sounding remarkably satisfied. And it's been quiet for some time now."

We gathered around the speaker, exchanging glances. Just as I was about to ask how long we should expect to wait, a new voice broke in. Dean Robbins.

"Our fearless leader," Tyler commented drily as Robbins began apparently to protest the treatment of the illusionist. Liam spluttered, but Frost lifted a hand and Robbins's voice came across clearly.

"There's no reason for us to continue this outrage," he insisted. "This is a Hallowell problem, and one they can fix far more easily than we can."

"It's a Wellington problem now," Symmes retorted, speaking sternly. "And one that's been going on apparently for some time. We'll deliver that problem back to the Hallowells, but we'll also hold them accountable for solving it."

"Oh, aren't you brave?" a rasping voice sounded, muffled and furious. No longer a strictly female voice, it was nevertheless impossible to identify. It sounded vaguely familiar to me, but I couldn't quite place it. A voice I'd heard recently—maybe in the tunnels below Fowlers Hall? It had to be.

"Commander Frost and his team should be here," Symmes said abruptly. We all perked up at that, even as Frost gave us the round-up gesture for us to head out.

"Absolutely not," Robbins retorted. "I'll have you know that I have received strict instructions from the academy's administration to keep them as far away from this situation as possible. They're untrained, unvetted. They're also the last monster hunters the academy has. Do you really want to risk them for a photo op?"

We all exchanged glances, though by this time, we were moving quickly through the main chamber of the library, heading for the front doors.

Claudia Graham spoke next. "I can't speak for my son anymore, but I can tell you he would not stand down from this fight."

Liam gave a thumbs-up as Robbins chimed in again.

"Oh?" Robbins sneered. "Even if it meant the closing of the minor? No students, no minor. And that *would* be a shame, wouldn't it?"

Dean Robbins's callous suggestion seemed to put a pall on the group gathered in Guild Hall for a moment, and we quickened our pace. But it was Theodore Perkins who spoke next.

"The monster hunter minor is the most important thing in my son's life, but I can tell you right now, he would sacrifice anything for the greater good of Wellington Academy and his fellow hunters. I know that for a stone-cold fact. So you can keep your politics under your hat for another day, Dean Robbins. We need to summon the team."

The arguments on the floor continued, and by the time the formal summons came through, we were almost at Guild Hall. We hurried up the front stairs, and the door opened to reveal another completely impassive attendant, who expressed zero interest in the monumental events taking place in the ballroom. He escorted us back to the same room we'd been the night before, though I noticed the coatroom had been locked up tight.

"Holy smokes," Liam said as we walked down the long hallway. "Are you guys feeling this? The force fields they've set in place here are epic. They've got a criss-cross weave over all the doors, additional reinforcement at the windows. The floor is completely impenetrable. You can bet that nothing is going to be coming up from below this time."

Zach nodded. "We've got a lot of minds at work here too," he said quietly. "Both inside the building and surrounding it—concentric rings of effort. This is a big deal."

Tyler grinned excitedly. "I'm not gonna lie, I like having all this advance intel," he said. "Imagine the damage we could cause if we could enter a place that's been infested by monsters, already knowing where all the players are? This is *excellent*."

"We *don't* know where all the players are," Liam pointed out. "Where's Grim? He should be here."

"He will be," Frost said. "He's doing a perimeter check around the entire academy, testing the wards. He'll be here presently. His gifts aren't all that helpful against straight-up magicians, but he'll be here."

I snorted. I felt for the guy. I wasn't all that impressive against straight-up magicians either. No matter how well I could wield a knife or hurl a bag of magic pellets, I wasn't awesome against magic thrown by another human. Something to focus on in my postgraduate study it appeared, since from the sound of things, we weren't going to be finishing out our senior year like normal students. Hell, we were barely getting through our junior year.

We breached the door to the ballroom of Guild Hall.

"Gentlemen, Ms. Cross," Mr. Symmes called out as we stepped into the room, making everyone turn our way— never mind the sparkling pyre of energy in the center of the room. His gaze went to Commander Frost. "Mr. Lockton?" he asked.

"On his way," Frost informed him staunchly. "There's no need to delay for him. What do we have?"

Mr. Symmes nodded. "We're looking at an infiltration of our defenses that comes from within, but more than that, we're looking at a flagrant violation of everything that Wellington Academy holds sacred."

"Oh for God's sake," Dean Robbins scoffed. "You're not giving an election speech, Symmes. There's no need for the dramatics."

"And may I remind you that you are here at our behest,

Dean Robbins, not the other way around," Symmes lashed back at him. "This breach of our wards is happening on *your* watch. Don't think you won't be held to account for it."

Robbins rolled his eyes, but Symmes didn't back down. He pinned us all with a sweeping glance.

"These many years, we've been laboring under the assumption that monster outbreaks have been diminishing. There was a reason for our confidence in that assessment. It was given to us by the Hallowells as part of their agreement with the academy arranged a century ago. They became our first line of defense against our enemies, and our most important avenue of monster management. In return, they had greater latitude in exercising magic within the private sector than any other family wanted to explore. We took the decline of the monster population in stride and made adjustments accordingly, reducing the number of resources allocated to the monster hunter minor. We accepted new students as they arrived, but we didn't do anything to grow the minor itself. It seemed the most prudent course."

"It was the most prudent course," Robbins put in. Nobody paid any attention to him.

As Symmes continued, there was a slight rustle of movement at the doorway, and I saw Grim enter the room. I sighed out a breath I hadn't realized I was holding. It made me happy that he was here, part of the team. It hadn't felt right without him.

Symmes soldiered on. "Our most sensitive information regarding the state of monsters among us for the past thirty years has come to us from perhaps the strongest member of the Hallowell clan, Elaine Hallowell. She was the unofficial spokesperson for the family and proved to be their most consistent liaison. We have been gratified to work with her over the years, which makes this newest development particularly troubling."

Without any further fanfare, Symmes turned to Claudia Graham, who lifted her hands and made an expansive cutting gesture. The lit-up pyre in the middle of the room flashed white—and then the light winked out, and there in the center of the room stood Elaine Hallowell, bound with magic, her face shifting every three seconds to a new image —spider, wasp, succubus, Elaine, and a dozen more in between. Every monster I'd ever encountered, and quite a few I hadn't.

When the image settled on her own beautiful face with its icy-gray eyes, she stared daggers at Symmes and Claudia, while I could only gape.

"Based on her own confession, Elaine Hallowell is the magician behind the attacks of the Boston Brahmin, behind the unusual vigor of the demon assault on Wellington Academy, and she herself was the illusionist with such strong magic that she was able to dismantle the finest wards this academy could mount. However, despite every apparent effort, she was not able to dismantle the academy itself," Symmes said.

"The Hallowells would *never*—" Robbins began, but Symmes merely waved a hand to shut him up.

"The Hallowells didn't," he confirmed. "We have been in contact with them, and they are every bit as horrified as we are at this turn of events. Their daughter has gone rogue, and this is not the first time. She's the most powerful magician in the Hallowell clan, but behaved herself well enough until a little-known distant family relation entered the net around Wellington Academy some twenty-five years ago. Elaine took issue with that relative, and turned on her with murderous intent."

He drew in a heavy breath, and my heart almost stopped. A chill raced along my arms as Symmes turned to me. "Elaine, we now realize, tried to get this young woman killed. She didn't succeed, and the family hushed it up. However, Elaine did manage to tip her hand enough to Rose McKinley—a local teacher and botanist who'd stumbled on her potential connection with Hallowells and then found herself unduly harassed—that the young woman left town when she realized she was pregnant. She later gave birth to a baby girl, a girl who also managed to find her way back to Wellington Academy after her mother died more than twenty years later."

"Rose should never have been born," Elaine said now, her voice low and dangerous. Her eyes bored through me. "Better for you that you'd never been either."

I stared at her. *Rose McKinley?* I'd never heard the name. Could this possibly be who my mother was? "So what now?" I heard myself ask.

"Now we need to return Elaine Hallowell to her family and begin to unravel what she has wrought," Symmes said heavily. "They've asked to see Nina as well."

"But they can't go by themselves," Theodore Perkins declared. "I don't care how advanced the Hallowell magic is. We can't trust them."

"We'll all go," Tyler chimed in.

"*No.*" Symmes and, surprisingly, Grim barked this response at the same time, startling me.

Grim looked mutinous as Symmes continued. "There's work to be done here, to contain the monster outbreak we believe has nearly reached our walls without us even realizing it, that even now hovers, waiting to break loose. Elaine Hallowell has been contained within a dead zone, but as a result of the strength of that ward, anyone with innate magic needs to steer clear. That means everyone but Grim, whose skills don't rest in his abilities to wrangle magic. He is the strongest nonmagical hunter we have. He goes."

Grim nodded as Symmes turned to me. "Nina, whether you go is up to you. The Hallowells now believe they're your family through this McKinley relative. They would like to meet you. And, I understand, you have the letter of your mother's to share."

"I burned your stupid letter," Elaine sneered. "Your mother knew enough to make it so that once it was destroyed, it couldn't be recreated.

"*Au contraire,*" Liam piped up. He tapped his temple. "I'm here to inform you that I memorized the first ten pages— and I've already transcribed them, thank you very much. More to the point, we also have the last two pages that you conveniently missed. We'll be able to recreate the letter completely for the Hallowells, if Nina wants that."

Elaine cast a malevolent glare at him, and he offered her a cheeky grin. I kept my gaze on Symmes.

"I'll go," I said. Grim would protect me, I knew, but more to the point—I needed to do this, once and for all. I needed to meet my mother's family, to understand who she truly was. Who I was, too.

"We won't be long behind you," Tyler said. "And if you need us, we'll be right there."

He stepped toward me, and the other guys shifted too, drawing closer. I could feel the strength of their solidarity in that subtle movement—Tyler's charisma as our leader; Zach's psychic reassurance; Liam's quivering, electric energy; Grim's solid power. "I know," I said, trying to keep my voice steady. Because they would be there, without a shadow of a doubt. Forget who my mother's family was. This team was my family.

I turned to Elaine Hallowell, who glared at me and all the guys with hatred in her cool gray eyes. I stared right back, unflinching. So this was the truth of things, the real enemy my mother had tried to protect me from. Not the monster hunters of Wellington Academy...but the monsters within the school's most storied family.

But I didn't need my mother's protection any longer. It was well past time for me to meet my fate.

"I'll go," I said again.

33

I sat alone in my beautiful dorm at Fowlers Hall for a few minutes longer than I technically should have, delaying the moment when I would leave with Grim and Elaine Hallowell to drive to New York. Frost had told me we'd be going by limo. Probably a good thing, since I wasn't sure Grim could drive.

Despite my anxiety, I knew I'd be in safe hands. I could vaguely sense Zach's mental touch, waiting patiently for me to access it more fully. Beyond that, I could feel a faint flare of electricity from Liam, the two of us remaining connected no matter how far away we were from each other physically, at least while we remained on campus.

I didn't think that connection would last across the miles, but Liam had given me options for that situation as well. I smiled down at the small pouch I held in my hand. My Protector Zoo of tiny animals was now outfitted with a new addition, one that looked distressingly like a tiny cuttlefish with legs. Nothing said love like my very own miniature Tarken land worm.

Liam had also given me a flash drive with a digital copy

of my letter, which now lay tucked into a pouch that hung beneath my shirt. A second paper copy of the letter was in my pack. Liam had me covered. Because of course he did.

Tyler hadn't been without his offer of protection either, giving me a bracelet that had been inscribed with a long line of Latin, the words so tiny that I didn't even try to read them, let alone decipher them.

The spell that bracelet contained only needed to touch my skin for a short while before the words were inscribed into my flesh, Tyler had told me. A few hours, no more, would be all that was needed. Grim would keep me more than safe until then. Still, I didn't want to leave quite yet. I especially didn't want to leave this room. I'd only been here when I was distracted or exhausted, and now, with the sun streaming through the large windows, I felt strangely melancholy to be abandoning the beautiful canopied bedstead, the ornate framed pictures on the wall, the rich carpeting, the majestic fireplace. Like everything else in Fowlers Hall, it was like something out of a fairy tale, and I wanted to be its princess for just a little while—

My phone blared, an insistent text coming from Frost. *We have everything set up, waiting for you out front. Take your time.*

I snorted. He might as well have ordered me to report on the double, but I understood his urgency. Elaine Hallowell might be in a portable dead zone of magic, but that didn't mean she wasn't dangerous. I needed to get this over with.

When I reached the front steps of Fowlers Hall, I was surprised to see the guys there. They stood at the ready, pride and genuine affection flowing out from them like its own magical force field.

"Guys, it's not like I'm going off to war," I said, and Liam grinned.

"We're not allowed to touch you, per Frost's express command," he confided. "Apparently, we've got eyes on us, and we should get used to that, at least until we get through the graduation protocol. But we couldn't just not *see* you."

I looked beyond them to the limo that now sat in front of Fowlers Hall, its motor idling quietly.

"I don't suppose it's too much to ask if Elaine's in a box in the trunk?"

Tyler snorted. "That certainly was discussed, but no dice. She's wrapped in a cloak of invisibility, sitting in the main cabin of the limo, but she's tranqued on top of being in a magical dead zone. It's only a few hours to New York, though. She shouldn't bother you."

I nodded and stepped forward, not trusting myself to look back at any of them. Frost stood at the door of the limo, and as I approached, he opened it wide. The door to Fowlers Hall opened at the same time, and I watched as a middle-aged woman I'd never seen before trotted out of the building with a case, which she carried toward the back of the limo.

"What...?" I began, and Frost harrumphed.

"I had her get your things—everything you had in your room that wasn't a weapon," he said. "Just in case you want to change clothes overnight. I figured you wouldn't think to do that."

"Oh." I frowned. I hadn't thought about staying the night, but Frost continued.

"The car is bugged, and so is Grim. You'll be fine. We'll be watching you the whole way, and we've got friends of the academy who live in New York who are also connected with the Hallowells. Everyone is well aware how important this meeting is. We're following all the protocols to the letter."

"Protocols I know nothing about," I pointed out, and

Frost's mouth kicked up in the corner.

"Probably the most important protocol is that Grim has never lost a fight he didn't want to lose," he said. "I'd put my money on him."

I grinned back at him, even managing a soft laugh. Then, with nothing more to say, I ducked into the car.

The first person I saw was Grim, mainly because there was nobody else immediately present. I looked around the spacious interior of the limo, then met his pale-gold eyes.

"Where is she?" I asked, and he pointed at the back bench seat.

"The dead zone enacted by the board makes her invisible to us. An illusionist is most successful if she can distract you. If you can't see her, you can't be distracted."

I nodded. Well, that at least made sense. The limo set off, and I glanced toward the front. "Who's driving?"

At this, Grim tightened his jaw. It was good to know he was still playing the hard guy. "There are two drivers. One commissioned by the Hallowells, one by the academy. Practically every member of the board wanted to ride shotgun. Their excitement is good, though. It's right. They need to be prepared for war on every front."

I thought I heard a hissing breath, almost a laugh, emanate from the back bench seat of the limo. Could Elaine hear us? What was the purpose of a dead zone if people could sneer at you from the other side of the veil?

I shot a glance to Grim, and he shrugged, still looking stern. He didn't like Elaine Hallowell either, I knew instinctively. Then again, he didn't like most people.

The car rumbled on, and I watched the tree-lined streets of Boston give way to the suburbs of industry and middle-class America. I wasn't familiar with the main thoroughfares into New York, but I got the sense we were driving vaguely west, which was where we should be going, heading into the setting sun. It was only when we turned onto a major highway that I allowed myself to relax a little, settling back into the cushioned leather seats. I blew out a long sigh, finally ready to focus on what awaited me in New York and what my new family had in store.

A low, breathy laugh was my first indication of trouble.

"Are you going to tell her," Elaine's voice floated through the cabin, "or should I? Oh please, let me."

I pressed back into my seat in alarm as Elaine Hallowell flickered into full and resplendent reality, fully at her ease on the back bench seat of the limo.

Instead of her formal gown from the night of the presentation or her full regalia as the mad illusionist, she was dressed in a crisply pressed black suit buttoned over a blood-red silk shell, a jet-black stone hanging at her neck. Her hair was swept back from her coldly elegant features, and her gray eyes assessed me with gleaming interest.

My heart beginning to hammer, I shot a worried glance at Grim. He stared directly back at me.

"So I'm not really sure how this dead zone thing goes," I began uneasily. "But it seems to me if the bad guy's supposed to be invisible and she's not, that's maybe not a good first sign."

"It's not," Elaine confirmed. "And since Grim is gracious enough to allow me to continue, I'm delighted to share that I'm no longer *in* a dead zone. Of course neither are you, but I don't think that's going to be a problem. Furthermore, there are *two* limos diverging in the wood right now, and one is taking a road, shall we say, less traveled by, and that will make all the difference. The vehicle containing a gorgeous Grim-like brute, an insipid little girl, and a rather unprepossessing strong box will head into the family stronghold in upstate New York, carefully monitored by your well-meaning team. We, however, are going somewhere else quite different. You really should have stayed lost, Nina Cross."

I turned to Grim again, adrenaline jacking through me. "What is she talking about? What's going on here?"

"Oh, I wouldn't waste your time turning to him for protection," Elaine answered for him. "He's been working for our family for quite a long time. In fact, you could say you were his number one assignment. You have been for many, many years."

Elaine glanced at Grim. "I have to hand it to you, when you failed in your mission, what was that now, nineteen years ago? When you came back without Rose's head on a plate, telling us you'd never found her, we believed you. We still believe you. You see, good help is hard to find, particularly the kind of help a monster can bring you. Happily, you did finally snag a better target in the end."

I widened my eyes, fixing Grim with a horrified stare as Elaine studied us both.

"Oh, come now. You had no idea? I guess bait never does in the end. Such a shame that all the power you supposedly have was wasted on a fool." Elaine settled back in her own seat, clearly delighted to continue her story. "Your mother was right to hide you from us. But pride always gets you in the end, doesn't it? Rose McKinley was a pitiful wreck of a woman. She believed, much like some members of your precious academy, that monsters could be reasoned with—befriended. Even loved. Idiot. Monsters have only a few uses. Properly motivated, however, they are quite effective."

She leaned forward. "What happened to her in the end, Nina? What made you come to Boston? She'd done her job so well, secreting you away. The letter she never sent was never *supposed* to be sent now, was it? Yet here you are. It's rather an odd thing, isn't it?"

"I don't have anything to say to you," I offered stiffly, surprised I could even get the words past my throat.

"Oh no, well, you certainly don't," Elaine agreed. "In fact, there isn't very much you could say that would matter at this point. Your mother tried her level best to raise you for the role to which you were uniquely born, but she, as usual, wanted to reach a little too high above her station. There's a reason why we stamped out harbingers anytime they came along, and that's because they weren't good for the family business. Fortunately, it seems you do have some skills we could leverage, or at least that's what Grim here thinks, and we have valued his opinions for long enough that we're willing to at least entertain them. After all, we're about to witness the end of Wellington Academy. It seems like it's only fitting we give it a proper send-off, no?"

I blinked and turned toward Grim, but he stared past me with flat disinterest in his eyes, the pale-gold orbs flicking back to me only briefly.

"I told you that when you finally understood what you were, it wouldn't go well for either of us," he said coldly. "We all have our place and our role in this world. Your mother was right to try to hide you."

"Yes," Elaine said with evident enjoyment. "She managed to hide you so well that even the best tracker money could buy couldn't find her. And we couldn't find her either, which was another reason why we believed him. But now I begin to wonder just how much our hired tracker knew about *you*, Nina, both when you were a sweet young thing of five years old and now. That should be fun to determine, don't you think?"

There was something undeniably dark in her tone, and I

barely suppressed a shiver. "What do you want from me?"

"Well, that should be obvious," she said. "First, I want every last shred of whatever power you have. If we can't bend it to our will, we will destroy it. And then I want you dead. As dead as your mother before you, God rest her miserable soul."

Her callousness cut me to the quick. "What did she ever do to you?" I protested, though I immediately regretted my outburst.

Elaine, however, merely shrugged. "She beat me," she said simply. "At least for a little while, she believed she'd won. I don't know how well you know the magical first families of Boston, but I can tell you this. A slight like that can never stand, and so now, I'm afraid, you will pay—and pay, and pay, if I have anything to do with it, with Grim here to make sure we won't be interrupted."

She settled back in her luxurious leather seat, then gave me a radiant smile. "And if I haven't said it already—*welcome* to the family, Nina."

THANK you for reading THE HUNTER'S SNARE—I appreciate you joining Nina on her adventure. If you enjoyed the book and would care to leave a review on BookBub, Goodreads or Amazon, I thank you for that as well! For a sneak peek of the final book in the Monster Hunter Academy series, read on! Grim is more than ready to share his perspective on things!

THE HUNTER'S VOW
Monster Hunter Academy, Book 4

Prologue: Grim

KILL HER.

The orders were clear, direct. They always were. I was to find and kill the woman who'd defied possibility. Who'd escaped the most powerful magicians in two realms, vanishing into the night without a trace, never to return. Five years after her disappearance, every other magical means of tracking her having failed, it was my turn at the hunt. I was supposed to unearth the bitch from her squalid hole, murder her in the night, then bring back the evidence of my kill and toss it before my masters like the prized beast I was.

They owned me, after all.

They believed they'd created me.

That all their years of imprisonment and torture had finally honed me into the perfect killing machine, ruthless and obedient, filled with hatred for anything but ripping creatures apart.

They weren't entirely wrong. Fulfilling a vow so old, I'd long ago forgotten its details, I'd walked for generations in their filth, mired in the stink of their ambition and pride. I'd pushed aside what it was to feel the open sky above me, the warmth of a sun not proscribed by their magic or their rules.

By the time they sent me on the hunt for the woman who'd defied them, I already carried a dozen unhealable scars. Other scars, they couldn't see. My mother and father, skinned before my eyes, trophies from their first wave of terror. My people, gutted and scattered before we'd learned to fight back, reawakening old alliances and unearthing ancient lore.

I didn't hunt with my people, though. I was the sacrifice

on bended knee, bowing beneath the magicians' rod and flame. And I had vowed to accept any charge of my masters, obey any order, until the time was right for us to strike these dark invading bastards dead. Every last one of them.

So at my masters' command, I went into the forests and picked up a five-year-old trail laced with magic and unexpected wards—wards I knew at once that no magician could break.

I could break them, though.

And I did. I found the woman who had so betrayed my keepers. An ordinary woman, with the barest flare of magic within her, for all that she carried protections from far beyond the bounds of her simple world. I didn't care. I was proud. Relieved. Ready for the kill.

Driven and tormented by the twisting spells that bound me, I leapt at the chance to cement my position with my enemies, to bring us that much closer to the final war. I tracked the wretched creature, following her mysterious wards and the trailing perfume of the plants she carried with her that had no place in her forested idyll. I raced faster and faster, and finally, her scent in my nose and mouth and the fever of death in my eyes, I broke through the canopy of trees to take her—

Only...she wasn't there.

Instead, a fierce and furious child stood in that clearing, waiting for me. A little girl of five years old, her dull iron knife held high, her eyes blazing with a pure and desperate power that unleashed a torrent of emotion in me so intense, I froze in place. This girl was magic. She was *fire*. She was every treasured memory ever made and every hope for a future yet to be born. She was the harbinger we were waiting for. The promise of the ancient oracles.

She also wasted no time.

She attacked.

We came together in a jolt of magic that ripped open our flesh to the bone, scored our skin, and mixed our blood, a fury of slashing knife and claws and teeth. With every cut, she tore through me. With every strike, I claimed her. I could not, would not kill her. But I would mark her, through and through. Mark her so deeply that she would never be anything other than mine.

Then I left her. Bleeding, battered, delirious. Close to death. But she wouldn't die, I knew. She was the harbinger. She would fulfill the prophecy.

So I watched. I waited. Lying to my masters, feeding them lies and possibilities, eventually convincing them to let me set foot upon the hallowed grounds of Wellington Academy. I gained the trust of young magicians I had sworn to destroy. I learned their ways, their dreams. And when I felt the keening cry of the girl whose blood ran through my own veins, mourning the death of her beloved mother, I knew it was time. I pushed her, just a little, to come to this city of dark magicians and lies.

After that, the plan was simple. I would betray the now grown-up harbinger. Bend her to my century-old plan to free my people once and for all. With her as a lever, a weapon of perfect and powerful force, I would fulfill my vow. I would use her, kill her, if necessary. I would make the final sacrifice, no matter what it took.

But then I fell in love with her.

CONTINUE the adventure with THE HUNTER'S VOW, and please visit me on Facebook to say hello!

Most of all, thanks again for reading THE HUNTER'S SNARE!

ABOUT D.D. CHANCE

D.D. Chance is the pen name of Jenn Stark, an award-winning author of paranormal romance, urban fantasy and contemporary romance. Whether she's writing as Jenn or D.D., she loves writing, magic and unconditional love. Thank you for taking this adventure with her.

www.ddchance.com

Made in the USA
Middletown, DE
30 March 2021

36563113R00159